FIGHT OF EAGLES

Eagle's hands closed around Chris Colt's throat and he panicked. He had never been gripped so tightly. Chris's right fist shot up and punched the behemoth with all his strength. It had no effect, and he felt himself going out as the blood was shut off to his brain. Desperately he jabbed forward with his fingers poking the big man in both eyes. Eagle grabbed his eyes, and Colt scrambled to his feet.

Eagle faced him and said, "The eagle tears his prey apart with his talons and beak. He shreds its miserable flesh."

"My name is Wamble Uncha," Colt said. "It is Lakotah for One Eagle. I am the One Eagle around here."

Eagle said, "You are a worthy enemy. I will soon eat your heart and be much stronger. Then I will kill your wife. Then I will destroy your children."

Chris Colt stared at the giant and said, "You aren't gonna do nothing but die, Big Man."

Saying it was one thing, but doing it was another—and Eagle was not like anything Colt had ever fought before. . . .

COYOTE RUN
BY DON BENDELL

On one side stood the legendary Chief of Scouts, Chris Colt, with his hair-trigger tempered, half brother Joshua, and the proud young Indian brave, Man Killer. On the other side was a mining company that would do anything and kill anyone to take over Coyote Run, the ranch that the Colts had carved out of the Sangre Cristo Mountains, with their sweat and their blood. Their battle would flame amid the thunder of a cattle drive, the tumult of a dramatic courtroom trial, the howling of a lynch mob, and a struggle for an entire town. And as the savagery mounted, the stakes rose higher and higher, and every weapon from gun and knife to a brave lawyer's eloquent tongue and the strength and spirit of two beautiful women came into powerful play.

from SIGNET

Prices slightly higher in Canada.   (0-451-18143-3—$4.50)

EAGLE

Don Bendell

A SIGNET BOOK

SIGNET
Published by the Penguin Group
Penguin Books USA Inc., 375 Hudson Street,
New York, New York 10014, U.S.A.
Penguin Books Ltd, 27 Wrights Lane,
London W8 5TZ, England
Penguin Books Australia Ltd, Ringwood,
Victoria, Australia
Penguin Books Canada Ltd, 10 Alcorn Avenue,
Toronto, Ontario, Canada M4V 3B2
Penguin Books (N.Z.) Ltd, 182–190 Wairau Road,
Auckland 10, New Zealand

Penguin Books Ltd, Registered Offices:
Harmondsworth, Middlesex, England

First published by Signet, an imprint of Dutton Signet,
a division of Penguin Books USA Inc.

First Printing, May, 1996
10 9 8 7 6 5 4 3 2 1

ACKNOWLEDGMENTS

I began writing this Western historical novel on January 1, 1995, the twenty-sixth anniversary of my sobriety as a recovering alcoholic. This book was made with the help of a very close longtime friend. One who has been honest with me when I needed it. One who has helped me sort out and toss away demons from a war long ago, and from a destructive and self-centered lifestyle born of low self-esteem and a very powerful mind-altering drug, alcohol. A very knowledgeable psychologist and administrator, she is executive director of Rocky Mountain Behavioral Health, Inc., and she helped me a great deal with research on this book, providing me with information about sociopaths and serial killers. But more important, she has been a very special and close friend to both my wife and me. She has helped thousands affected in some way by the effects of chemical abuse, the taproot of most of the violence and insanity in our country and our world. Thank you so much, Louise Jose, and God bless you for your help and friendship.

DEDICATION

I have seen women working among the lodges, tanning hides, cooking, gathering wood for the cooking fires, and sewing. Their work is very important, but I respect most those few women who have taken up weapons and fought side-by-side with warriors in battle. Some of these women have even led braves into great fights, challenging the men to greatness. It happens more than some braves like to tell, but I do not mind telling, because I can count at least one of them as my friend. Warrior women such as these have been named Walking Blanket Woman, Buffalo Calf Road Woman, and Joan of Arc. They have counted many coups and even taunted their enemies, waving blankets at them and darting their ponies in and out between bullets and arrows.

One warrior woman, Louise Jose, has fought a good fight against mental illness in others. She has not fought the long battle by making weapons or sewing hides. She has chosen to take up the lance and bow and has stood out in front of all the tribes, men and women, and has raised her hand, signaling, "Follow me." She is truly a strongheart, this woman, this warrior woman. With love and gratitude and respect, I dedicate this book to you, my good friend, Louise Jose.

—Don Bendell

To My Wife, Shirley, on Our 14th Winter

And so, our winter count has grown so long,
But still, my heart is very young, as is yours.
Our winters together, now cannot be even
Counted on the fingers of both hands.

Yet with each day-passing, I look,
I see the woman of my youth, the girl
Who makes me want to breathe hard still,
The one who makes my heart leap like the cougar.

She is the warrior woman with the courage of the
    bear,
The voice of the singing breeze in the trees,
The softness of the fur of the baby hare,
The woman who makes me want to count coups.

Fourteen winters past, on this day, we walked.
We walked together into the white lodge,
And that day, we entered each other's souls.
We are now, and always, one and two, the same.

You have the strength of the greatest warrior,
But the beauty of the fairest maiden,
You are my fellow warrior, who will stand
And fight at my side against my enemies.

Sometimes, I fight myself and you the very same;
But each year, I collect more eagle feathers,
More ponies, and more wisdom; and each year,
My love for you has grown into a giant mountain.

I love you, Shirley!

—Don Bendell
from *Songs of the Warrior*

No great genius is without
an admixture of madness.
—ARISTOTLE

CHAPTER 1
One Eagle

The sun had been blistering hot and the riding had been hard for the tall man and his big horse. Although there was often snow up at timberline in southern Colorado's Sangre de Cristo mountain range, this day had simply been blistering both down low and up high.

These glasslike mirrors of wetness shining so brightly in the late summer sun were aptly named Lakes of the Clouds. Not too many people were able to drink from the crystal-clear water or eat one of the many rainbow or cutthroat trout filling their depths. An occasional miner, trapper, wayward cowboy, or serious Indian hunter would sometimes come by their shores, but they were so high up and so far from civilization that, for most, their beauty and pristine qualities could only be appreciated by imaginings. The man had removed his clothing and weapons, after stripping the saddle from the black and white paint horse and rubbing him down with dry tundra grass, and had slipped into the glacier-fed water. It was cold, ice-drip cold, but that was what he wanted. He ducked under and sipped in mouthfuls of water.

One needn't ask a thing about the man. Standing now in his nakedness at his saddlebags searching for a small bar of soap, his tanned and sinewy body painted a living portrait of his past. Through the right thigh was a bullet-hole scar that entered the back and exited the front of the large thigh muscles. A more grotesque pair of entry/ exit scars was found on the left shoulder near the collarbone. The bullet had entered the front and made but a small hole, but mushroomed as it exited the back and tore a large jagged hole there. There were two scars above the nipples on his massive pectoral muscles, where a shaman had pierced the flesh with eagle's talons and stuck two wooden pegs through. Leather thongs had been attached to the pegs while the man performed the sundance ceremony and pulled back with the thongs against the heavy buffalo skulls weighing them down after they had been passed over a pole in the ceiling of the sundance lodge. The man had danced forward and back, staring up at the sun through the hole in the center of the lodge. He did this with the flesh on his chest being pulled out grotesquely, until the flesh finally tore away and the man, falling in a faint, experienced a vision.

On the right side of his abdomen, low down, was a knife scar, and the little finger of one hand had been cut off with a knife. There were three long claw marks, apparently from a bear or mountain lion, on his very large right bicep. There was also a minute, almost imperceptible scar on one cheek from a razor-sharp arrow, only visible when the man smiled—which was often. His hazel-colored, intelligent eyes, in fact, always seemed to be slightly smiling, as if he knew a secret that nobody else knew. His face was chiseled and ruggedly handsome, and he could have been in his late twenties or early thirties, but nobody really knew his age. His dark brown hair wasn't too long, and it pretty much traveled where it wanted and added to the man's appearance.

He was tall, maybe six foot four, and his body showed he was used to years of hard work. His muscles were large and firm and his body was well balanced.

He looked over at his big paint, a gift to him from Crazy Horse, his blood brother.

The horse still wore an eagle feather in his mane and one in his tail in tribute to his former owner. The horse, War Bonnet, cropped grass peacefully, and beyond him marmots whistled to one another and grazed among the tundra grasses and mountain flowers above timberline. Unwrapping the little bar of soap from its oilskin pouch, the man returned to the water. He whistled an unidentified tune while he scrubbed and lathered himself all over with soap. This accomplished, he set the bar on a rock and dived underwater doing a whale roll and swimming through the clear liquid. He turned and swam back, breaking the surface where he started. Grabbing the bar, he carefully and methodically shampooed his hair with it, working it into a great lather.

His ranch was less than ten miles away, down below in the Wet Mountain Valley, and he had a beautiful wife and a cute little girl and boy waiting to see him. He had been out on the trail for over a week, and he wanted to ride home smelling and looking good and clean. He also wanted to give his horse a little break to catch his wind and replace some of the weight he had lost riding hard for the past ten days or so. It was difficult for the horse, riding at altitudes of more than twelve thousand feet.

The man appreciated the solitude of the "high lonesome," as he called it. He always headed up into the high country to sort things out in his mind, and he had had a very rough journey and a tough week.

The man went under water to rinse off the lather in his hair. He swam away from the shore and rubbed his hair with his hand, coming up for air and diving back under right away. When he felt all the soap was rinsed out, he finally surfaced and burst up into the fresh crisp air and gasped for breath. The air was so thin, the least exertion caused heavy breathing, so holding his breath and swimming underwater took its toll.

"You shore are a purty swimmer, mister," a voice said dryly, "I thought ya was a dad-burned catfish the way ya was swimmin' 'round under thar fer so long. Wasn't you impressed, Lem?"

The man swam toward the shore and stood up when the water was chest deep.

Two men stood on the bank of the high mountain lake and one was holding the reins to the big paint's bridle, leading the horse behind. The other had already strapped on the big man's twin Colt Peacemaker .45s. The barrels and cylinders were hand-carved silver; on the butts were hand-engraved mother-of-pearl eagles perched on rattlesnakes.

The two men, both very large, were grungy looking and appeared to be down-on-their-luck miners. The one called Lem drew one of the Peacemakers and admired the balance.

He said, "Newt, I git the guns."

Newt said, "Ya holt onta yer horses, there, Lem. I'll tell ya what ya take an' what I take."

Lem spun the pistol and cocked it, pointing it at the big man, saying, "Ya want I should plug 'im, Newt?"

The leader of the pair held up his hand and said, "Naw, hold on. We don't need ta do thet, maybe. We're jest stealin' his outfit."

He looked at the big man and pointed the man's own Colt revolving shotgun at him.

He said, "Mister, we're takin' yer horse, guns, an' possibles. Now, we can plug ya, or I'll take yer word, ef'n ya give it, thet ya won't try comin' after us ef'n I let ya live. Do ya give yer word?"

The man said, "No, I can't. That horse is my pard, and I like my outfit. I don't give my word and then break it, so I guess you'll have to shoot me."

Newt rubbed his whiskers a minute and stared up at the main peak of Spread Eagle Peaks in front of him. Large wisps of snow blew off the uppermost reaches and glistened in the sunshine.

The robber said, "Wal, I guess we'll have ta shoot ya, then, ef'n ya ain't gonna give yer word, but I shore like ya, mister. Ef'n ya kin come up with a different plan, I won't pop ya. Got any idees?"

The tall man walked out of the cold water, letting the sun dry his tanned skin.

He said, "I can give you my word that I'll give you a one-hour head start, then I'll hunt you both down. I can also promise you that you'll both get to stand up in front of a judge and jury before you're hung for horse stealing—that is, unless you try to fight me when I hunt you down. If you do, I'll have to kill you. I can promise you all that, and that I'll forget it if you both let everything lay and leave now."

"Man, you shore do have spunk, I'll give ya thet, pilgrim," Newt said, "Tell ya what Ah'm gonna do. Walk over here."

The big man walked forward while Newt motioned with the gun. The thieves tied his hands behind his back and tied his ankles together. Then the two men saddled the big paint and Newt mounted him, after he tied the naked man over the saddle of his worn-out bay horse. They led him and headed up one of the long ridgelines covered with snow.

He felt himself freezing as they made their way up a bighorn sheep trail. He looked up ahead of him and saw the two men putting their slickers on to ward off the freezing cold wind blowing across the fourteen-thousand-foot peak. He knew he couldn't last long if he didn't get out of his predicament soon.

In thirty minutes they halted the horses and he felt himself being cut off the saddle and toppled into the snow. He slid down an embankment and saw a giant snow- and ice-covered avalanche chute below him. It was a sheer drop of a thousand feet, with boulders sticking out of the snow at intervals. Shivering uncontrollably, he looked back at the two outlaws, and they both pointed his own weapons at him.

Grinning sadistically, Lem said, "We gonna kill 'im now?"

Newt said, "Nope, we're gonna shoot both kneecaps and leave 'im. If'n he can live through thet, more power to 'im. He won't be a runnin' after us, will he?"

Lem laughed and said, "Not as fer as Mexico nohows."

Newt shot Lem an angry glance and said, "Idjit! Ya tole him where we was headed. Now we gotta kill 'im!"

The big man took the few seconds that the killers took to argue to take his chance. He dived headfirst over the lip and down the avalanche chute. Shots rang out and the angry crack of bullets echoed in his ears, but nothing hit him. With his hands still tied behind his back he slid down the ice and snow of the almost vertical chute as cliffs and rocks seemed to whiz up past his face on both sides at a dizzying speed. The friction from the sliding tore at his bare skin and burned like a hot poker, but he blocked the pain out of his mind and looked below, trying to figure out some kind of plan.

The tall cowboy hit a soft patch, and he tumbled over, sliding on his arms and rear. Up the mountain, he got a glimpse of the would-be killers running the horses down the ridgeline trail, apparently figuring he would soon be dead. He shoved down with one foot and flipped back over, burning his stomach, genitalia, and thighs, but he had to see where he was headed. It looked as if the ground leveled out a little about two hundred feet below, and he saw a precipice lip to his left front. He figured that if he chanced going over the lip of the precipice, he might land in soft snow on the more level area. The man dug his left foot into the slide, and headed to his left. He was falling so fast that it was only a matter of seconds before he felt himself flying out into space, spinning over in midair and closing his eyes and waiting for the impact. He hit into soft snow that cushioned the fall that had thrown him fifty feet down and thirty feet forward. He rolled over but the snow quickly ended the fall. It was totally black and the man knew he had to act very quickly—he was inside a pocket of snow and didn't know how deep he was buried.

He spit and felt the spittle come down on his forehead, so he knew now that he was lying on his back and headed slightly downhill. He also felt that his hands were free, and he rubbed his wrists. The piggin string that had bound them apparently snapped from the tremendous pressures during the fast slide down the mountain. The naked man didn't even bother with his ankles yet. He reached back with both hands and extended his body, pulling down with both arms while kicking with his feet. Almost as if he were swimming a backstroke, he continued this maneuver; he saw the snow above his head get lighter and lighter, until his hands, then his head, finally broke free and out into the bright sunlight.

He was near the bottom of the slide, and the timberline was only about one hundred feet below. He swam and struggled but finally made it to his feet. He bent over and quickly untied the bonds on his ankles, but kept the small rope, wrapping it over one shoulder. He ran and tumbled down the rest of the slide, his breaths coming out in pants, but he knew the exertion would keep his blood flowing and might save his life. He made it into the trees and kept heading downhill, walking at a quick pace, his feet bleeding and aches and pains beginning all over his body.

The man would not allow himself to stop until he was a good thousand feet below the snowline, where he finally halted in the afternoon sun in the midst of a high mountain meadow. He lay down in the grass and the mountain flowers and soaked in the warmth of the sun. He slept for an hour, then stood and surveyed his wounds. He had no frostbite, but he had burns and bruises from his fall down the avalanche chute. He didn't believe any bones were broken.

The man carefully picked his way down the mountain, knowing exactly where he was headed. There was a game trail around ten thousand feet that went north and south across the eastern face of the Sangre de Cristos, and he knew he could travel quickly along it. The outlaws had made the mistake of letting him know they were headed south. He figured that they wouldn't know about this trail, as they probably were not from the area. That was an easy deduction, because they never would have picked him to rob if they were from this part of the West. He was Deputy U.S. Marshal Chris Colt, the famous gunfighter and former chief of scouts for the U.S. cavalry. Whenever men gathered together in saloons and spoke about the most deadly men in the West, some names always came up: John Wesley Hardin, Wyatt Earp, Bat Masterson, Wild Bill Hickok, and Chris Colt.

This man had been blood brother with Crazy Horse; had scouted on campaigns against Victorio, Cochise, and Geronimo; and had been with Chief Joseph when the great orator and leader led the Nez Perce on their famous seventeen-hundred-mile fighting retreat from the U.S. cavalry. He had been blinded, tortured, and wounded; he had gone through many hells in the past. But he was still a living legend. And these two thieves would not bring his career to an end, either, Colt decided.

They had his horse, his clothes, his guns, even his knives, while he had only the burned and bruised and battered flesh on his body. But more importantly, he had his brains, his knowledge, and the heart of a true American hero. The name Colt meant much. Justis Colt, a Texas Ranger, was building his own reputation to equal his older cousin's. Down in the valley below him, Chris Colt could see the lands that comprised his ranch, the Coyote Run. It was run by his half-brother, Joshua Colt, the bastard son of Chris's father and a black slave from Ohio. Some years older, the image of Chris with a brown complexion, Joshua was a true cattleman and leader of men, a real hero in his own right. Also down below was Chris's beautiful auburn-haired, green-eyed wife, Shirley, herself a pioneer woman of courage and determination, and their two little children, Joseph and Brenna. Living in the valley also was another young man who owned a small piece of Colt's ranch and was a very wealthy rancher himself, for his new bride, Jennifer Banta, had inherited millions. The young man's name was Man Killer. He had been Chris Colt's sidekick since boyhood and had grown into a man of two worlds. Extremely intelligent, Man Killer was a very proud Nez Perce warrior from the band of Chief Joseph, but he had learned how to live and succeed in the white man's world, too. A former scout with Colt, he now worked with Chris as a deputy. Man Killer, too, on many occasions, had proven himself a hero, especially when he purposely got himself shanghaied on a ship to Australia to locate and rescue his kidnapped then-fiancée, Jennifer.

Colt's challenge now, though, was to find and defeat the thieves alone, without help from his brother or friends. They didn't know where he was, so he could build a fire and send up a smoke signal, and they would come to his aid immediately. But that was not Chris's way. What separated Chris Colt from other men were some of the tough decisions he made. An ordinary man might head straight down the mountainside for his home and family, or signal them to come up and rescue him. But Colt was not that way. He had been caught off guard and outwitted by a pair of outlaws, and he did not want any stories getting around about how two men did that to him and got away with it. There were already enough men, fancying themselves gunfighters, who wanted to pursue him and his rep. And although most of them ended up in Boot Hill, Chris did not want that memory to remain with him. Self-respect was another important part of the makeup of U.S. Marshal Chris Colt.

He ignored his home and friends far below and trotted along the face of the mountain, employing a slow, steady run used constantly by the Apache. Using another of their tricks, he stopped momentarily to pick up a small white pebble. He spit on it and rubbed it clean with his fingers while he ran. Satisfied that he had rid it of much of the dirt that had been caked on for years, he placed the pebble in his mouth where it moved from one hiding place to the next. This movement kept his salivary glands activated in the semiarid climate and prevented "cottonmouth."

He trotted along the game trail for a full three hours before he felt he should stop for a short rest. Colt looked behind him and out across the valley. He could still see his ranch house and outbuildings. To his left front were the bustling little towns of Westcliffe, then Silver Cliff, and, a short distance to the east, Rosita. Wagons, buggies, and horses were going back and forth along the Texas Creek Road, one after the other. The road wound along uphill from the Arkansas River canyon, closely paralleling the course of the glacier-fed stream. Colt could see wagons backed up at Copper Gulch Road and Reed Gulch Road waiting to pull out onto the busy thoroughfare leading into the bustling mining centers. It was odd to him that he could see so much activity, and even see his home where his wife and son and daughter anxiously waited his return— yet he was naked and close to death in the wilderness.

The mountains on the other side of the valley were nothing like these mountains. In the distance, he could see the upper half of the more than fourteen-thousand-foot Pikes Peak. Before that, though, were the Greenhorns, which were named for the only peak in the chain of any real size, just over twelve thousand feet. The Sangre de Cristos, on the other hand, where Chris Colt now was, were mainly thirteen- and fourteen-thousand-footers, one after the other. They started near the Collegiate Range near Salida and ran south all the way into and through New Mexico. The valley between the two ranges was called the Wet Mountain Valley, although that name could be misleading, for much of the foothills and mountains running along the Front Range from north of Canon City and Pueblo down into New Mexico were really part of a semiarid climate, with little rain or snowfall each year.

Many world travelers to this area remarked that the Sangre de Cristos were the most beautiful range of mountains in the world. Colt and his wife never tired of their view of the mountains' pristine beauty, which they could watch from horizon to horizon. But he also knew that these beautiful sentinels of rock, lumber, and ice were also killers if they were not respected. A midsummer snow or ice storm could suddenly come in on a hot summer day. A raging thunderstorm could suddenly appear over a peak at any time and cause flash floods anywhere along the range. Lightning bolts would strike everywhere during these giant storms, which could also trigger rock slides or avalanches. And there was always the chance of a forest fire sweeping up the tree-covered, wind-swept slopes.

Colt sat on a log and looked at his bruised and bleeding feet. He had aches and pains all over his body. The skin had been burned and scraped off of his groin, his stomach, and the front of his thighs. His shoulders were both injured and one finger was broken, but Chris Colt was the man who had made jokes while a ruthless torturer had sawed his little finger off with a knife. He could withstand pain when he had to, as he'd proven over and over again, and this was one of those times that he had to. He had a score to settle and settle it he would, in spades.

Newt Clinton grew up in St. Augustine, Florida but left the orange and lemon groves, the continual sunshine, and the warm ocean breezes for colder climes after three girls around there had been found molested and murdered within a one-year period. He spent several years in New Orleans but left there quickly after being questioned about the rape and murder of a young prostitute.

After that, he drifted west and tried one honest job in a mine but found the hard work distasteful. He got a job backshooting a banker for an angry and jealous wife who wanted to collect the man's holdings before one of his mistresses did. After that, he wandered around and tried a little bit of everything outside the law.

Newt was tired from the day's work and couldn't wait to have a nip from the bottle he hid in his pack and catch some shuteye. He pictured the look in the eye of the man he had tried to kill, and he shivered slightly.

It was an old Indian trick that plains boys used on badgers, so Colt decided to try it. He had gone up higher toward the timberline, after identifying the night location of the bushwhackers. On the way, he found what he had been looking for all afternoon—a sharp rock shaped like a spearhead. He chipped more flint away on the edges to make it extremely sharp, and he kept going uphill until he thought his lungs would burst. At the edge of an alpine meadow, he spotted what he wanted—marmots. They were eating the rich grasses that mainly stayed under snow and ice most of the year. He stepped out into the meadow and immediately a dozen marmots scattered for their holes all over the meadow.

Chris crept up to the nearest hole and sat down slightly uphill above it, waiting without moving. After five minutes, he got into a half crouch and remained still. Within five minutes, he saw two marmots come out of their bunkers. It would be soon. The marmot poked his head and looked around. Colt was above and behind him. The little animal came all the way out of the bunker and stood on its hindlegs looking downhill. Colt jumped up in the air and raised his feet together. The other two whistled and the little mammal dropped to all fours, but it was too late. Chris Colt came down with both feet on the animal's back and head. The marmot died instantly.

Colt looked skyward, shivering.

"Thank you, God," he said.

He grabbed the limp body and started downhill as quickly as he could, for he was freezing cold in his nudity. On the way, he quickly worked with his knife to remove the hide from the marmot's body.

Lem Boricker had been dropped off a wagon seat by his mother as an infant and had landed on his head. Up until then, he had been the favorite baby of all the women on the wagon train. But after laying unconscious for three full days before coming around, he never again became the smiling, happy toddler he had been. The accident changed his life dramatically. Feeling guilt over dropping him, his mother constantly babied and pampered him and bailed him out of trouble all through his childhood.

Lem hated her because of that, and because of all the teasing he took from other children over it. So one night when he was fifteen, he repaid his mother's kindness by taking a shovel to her head. That night was replayed in his mind every time he slept— each night he lay down and stirred before finally falling into a fitful sleep.

From that night on he was always outside the law, but he always followed others' lead. He did not have the intelligence or common sense to make his own decisions.

Chris Colt was scared and cold, and upset over what had happened to him as he looked at the changing colors of the late-afternoon sky. He had cried earlier out of relief over killing the marmot and out of rage and frustration. Although Colt did his crying, and his best thinking, up here in the "high lonesome," it was usually by choice, when he felt he had to get away and ponder things. He didn't cry around people, but tried to control the situation and then get off by himself. And though he believed in God and prayed regularly, he preferred to do his most important praying up high where he felt closer to the Almighty. But right now, he knew he had to concentrate on the task at hand and push fear and pain out of his mind. It would soon be dark and the temperature would drop drastically.

Colt sat in the lee side of a pile of boulders and worked on the marmot's bloody hide. He could use the fur to make quick, simple moccasins to protect his bloody and bruised feet, but instead he chose to make a breechcloth to cover and protect his crotch. Maybe it was the way he was raised, he thought, but he would rather be barefoot than totally naked. For some reason, with his groin area exposed, he felt much more vulnerable in a fight. The men had made camp early, and he could see the smoke from their fire curling up through the aspen grove they had stopped in down below and a half mile to the south.

Colt had intended to wait until they slept, but was now considering going in right after dark, so he wouldn't have to worry about getting too cold. It was then that he remembered the cinch ring on the trail. A half mile back he had spotted a rusted cinch ring that some hunter or prospector had lost. Someone had hung it on the little stump of a small branch growing out of a fir tree along the trail.

* * *

Colt had to hurry before darkness fell. He dropped down the hill and trotted on sore feet back the way he had come. Minutes later, he spotted the tree and then the ring. He grabbed it and looked skyward, mouthing another "Thank you," and headed back south toward the outlaws. He made camp a short distance from theirs but far enough so that they would not see or smell the smoke from his own fire. With the flint-knife blade and steel cinch ring, he was able to strike sparks into an old, dry chickadee nest and get his fire going. Using smaller branches, Colt built his fire even bigger than normal. He warmed himself to the bone, then let the fire die down a little.

In the meantime, he cut strips of leather from the edge of the hide to make thongs for his weapon, and he used a wild grapevine for a belt to hold on his breechcloth. Hungry, Colt decided to use a little energy to search for food and comforts. He found some wild turnips and some sassafras, then pulled sheets of bark from a white birch tree and fashioned a bowl out of them. Next, he got water from one of the many streams cascading down the Sangre de Cristo mountainsides. He added sassafras shavings to the water, placed the bowl over the fire, and waited for the liquid to come to a boil. He knew that the birch bark would not catch fire below the waterline, so his bowl would be useful for at least one meal.

After eating, Colt lay down and curled up close to the fire and allowed himself to sleep for several hours. He would awaken around midnight; his self-discipline and experience were all he needed for an alarm clock.

Although Chris Colt slept soundly, he began to feel a presence. Not that he heard or smelled or saw anything—he just felt it. It was a sense of knowing that many warriors have developed to a keen sixth sense. He felt as though someone were standing over him while he lay curled up in front of the dying embers. Colt felt a chill running up and down his spine and, suddenly, a strong urge to urinate. He tried to keep from shaking.

Slowly, his mind went through a mental checklist. Where were his weapons? He had none, except for a spear. What did he have to take this person out? Could he slightly open his eyes and squint at the person? Could he keep his head and not panic?

Colt opened his eyes slowly and thought, at first, that a giant grizzly was standing directly over him. But when he opened his eyes all the way he almost screamed. There was a behemoth of a long-haired, bearded man, dressed in furs, monstrous in size. He held a long Bowie knife in one hand, ready to plunge into the muscular torso of Chris Colt. Stifling a scream, heart pounding, Colt sat up and breathed heavily as he saw the shadowy figure was gone. It had been a nightmare.

He stood and relieved his bladder against an aspen trunk, his shoulders and head shaking with a sudden chill. He felt unnerved; the nightmare had seemed so real. Colt's heart still pounded and he tried to slow his breathing and relax his neck and back muscles. He had learned long before that he could relax and calm himself by concentrating on slackening those muscles. He had to have his senses and body in top condition very shortly, so he had to put the nightmare behind him.

It was about one in the morning when the shadowy figure of Chris Colt walked slowly up to the dying embers of Lem and Newt's fire. Colt's eyes looked almost satanic in the firelight as he added more wood to their fire and the flames licked skyward. Both men seemed to awake at once and Lem screamed as he looked at the war-painted face of Chris Colt, dark from the many symbols painted on it. The men looked at the breechcloth he had made with the fur turned in and the fleshed-out marmot hide turned out.

Lem reached for Colt's revolving shotgun leaning against a nearby log, but Colt's powerfully thrown spear went right through the man's forearm and pinned his arm to the log. Lem screamed but Colt didn't wait. He knew that Newt would immediately reach for his nearest gun, thinking he would have chance against the now-unarmed attacker. But Colt's right foot lashed out and hit the edge of the campfire, sending burning sticks and brands at the outlaw leader just as he had started to draw one of Colt's Peacemakers. Newt screamed as several sticks landed on him; he brushed at them quickly. As his shirt caught on fire, Colt jumped across and caught the man with an upper-cut right on the point of his chin. Newt went up on the balls of both feet and down in a heap, his shirt still on fire.

Colt reached down quickly and grabbed the Peacemaker and rolled with a somersault into the darkness, a millisecond before the Colt revolving shotgun boomed and behind him leaves and bark tore from trees. He came up off the ground and put three shots into the body of Lem in the space of a second and the man flew backward over the log. The shotgun fired and blew a small branch of a tree directly above Lem and the branch fell on the man's face, the leaves hiding it.

Newt sat up and rubbed his jaw, shaking his head from side to side.

He looked at Colt blankly and shook his head once more to clear the cobwebs.

He said, "Who the hell are you, a white man or an Injun?"

Colt grinned and said, "The Lakotah call me Wamble Uncha, One Eagle. You can call me Marshal Colt, Chris colt. You're under arrest."

The man's mouth dropped open, and he said, "Yer Colt? *The* Colt?"

Chris smiled. "I don't know about that. I'm just a man, but the wrong one to steal from, partner. Grab some clouds."

Newt raised his hands and shook his head slowly. He couldn't believe he and his idiot partner had tried to tangle with the famous Chris Colt.

CHAPTER 2

The Animal

The Circle T was a sprawling spread east of Parker. In the distance, you could see the magnificent mountains due west of Denver, and you could see the Rampart Range that ran down to Colorado Springs. The ranch ran good grass and water and was situated on a series of rolling hills. Some of them were lightly wooded but most of the ranch was grass.

Tommy Steed had been a hand on the Circle T for thirty a month and food. He was a good hand and could probably make more on some other spreads, but he liked the Wilson clan and liked how they treated their hired help.

Beside that, Tommy enjoyed the Sunday afternoon poker games in the bunkhouse with his riding partners. The Wilsons insisted that their ranch hands do as little work as possible on the Sabbath and Steed appreciated their Christian attitudes on the matter.

On the Sunday that Chris Colt rode down toward Westcliffe, leading Newt, tied backward in the saddle, and the body of his late friend Lem, tied across his saddle, Tommy Steed was engrossed in a good game in the bunkhouse almost two hundred miles away.

Tommy looked across the rough board table at Old Bub Waller. The aging hand had a poker face but had just raised four bits. For Bub, that was a serious bump. The man never bluffed and four bits was a heavyweight wager.

Steed looked at Turkey Neck John Crewes. The tall, flabby man shifted uneasily in his seat. Sweat ran down his windburned cheeks in rivulets that went into the creases of his heavy jowls. Turkey Neck John matched the wager of Old Bub's and bumped it another four bits.

Tommy got upset as he felt the gastric pain starting again. He had gone to town the night before and couldn't remember what he had drunk but had awakened that morning in the back of the Circle T supply wagon. Since arising he had already made four trips to the two-holer outhouse back behind the bunkhouse.

* * *

The mind of the predator was already preparing for the redheaded cowboy to make another return trip to the outhouse. But this time it would take its prey, like it had easily done with humans so many times in the past. During Tommy's previous trips to the outhouse, the predator only watched from the tree-covered hillock overlooking the ranch buildings.

Now, he watched the cowboy through the window as he came down the hill through the high grass. There was no noise except the wind. He would make several steps forward through the grass, his eyes peering between the tops of the blades. Every few seconds, the predator would stop; his nose would work hard, his nostrils flaring in and out as he tested the wind. He would listen carefully, then look all around to insure that no other predator was sneaking up on him.

He moved on and down into the gully that led up to the back of the outhouse. Two of the horses in the corral smelled him when the wind shifted, and the odor was putrid. He had been feeding for a week on the carcass of a horse he had killed. The body had been decaying and the predator even slept against the carcass several times, not wanting buzzards or coyotes to come near his kill.

Another half hour brought him to the door of the outhouse, which came open easily. He slithered into the darkness. If another of the men came out to this building he would take him, but his eyes had been on the red-haired one.

Tommy Steed called and waited to see what Old Bub would do. He bumped another dollar and Turkey Neck John raised another dollar. Tommy looked down at his cards again. They were playing draw, and he had asked for three cards. "Dagum sucker hand," he thought, as he looked at the trip sevens he held. He had kept a pair of sevens when he asked for cards and drew another seven along with a king and a nine. The hand was just good enough to make him stay in the game, but he was afraid that at least one of the other two would have a straight, a flush, or even a full house. It was part of the challenge of the game.

Tommy called and so did Bub.

Turkey Neck John laid down his cards, and Tommy got excited. John held three fours, a ten, and an ace kicker. Tommy's heart skipped a beat, and he felt it pounding in the sides of his neck. Bub laid down his cards then, and Steed's heart sank. Old Bub had an eight, nine, ten, jack, and queen—a straight. He won the pot.

The predator watched the human creature with the red hair. He could sense the redhead was upset, that there was anger. He could also sense pain coming from him.

Inside, Tommy felt that pain again in his intestines and that dull throbbing headache that just wouldn't go away. He would have to run out to the outhouse again. Tommy Steed did not ante for the next hand. He grabbed the old catalog he had used for reasons other than reading and headed out the door.

The predator moved quickly and silently into his hiding position. He could hear the footsteps of the redhead when Tommy rounded the corner of the bunkhouse and headed toward the outbuilding. Light streaked in through the door, making a half-moon shape on the seats, but the predator could not be seen anywhere among the shadows. He could tell the approaching man was the redhead just by the sound of his footsteps.

The door opened and Tommy Steed stepped into the outhouse. He pulled down his homespun trousers and long johns and sat on the wooden bench. Down below, the predator looked up through the opening above him, the light blocked now from the other hole. It was wet and hard to move and the smell was very strong from human waste. He breathed very hard, though, because he was about to make another kill. It was more fun to kill humans than other animals. They were more challenging.

The predator would wait until the human passed his waste then move over into position. So many flies buzzed around him that he blinked his eyes continuously. But his smell was so horrible that he was constantly covered with flies anyway.

Tommy Steed couldn't wait to get back to the game, but the hangover he was suffering was horrible. The cramps hit him in waves, and the headache pounded behind his eyes like a silver miner swinging a double jack. He could not believe the horrible stench in the little building and made a mental note to tell the foreman that some quick lime was needed.

Tommy grabbed the magazine that sat on the edge of the old wooden plank that the two holes were in. Something sent chills down his spine—a feeling, just a feeling. He looked down between his legs and saw a pair of eyes staring up at him from the darkness below. Something shot up out of the black and grabbed his groin. He felt the flesh tearing and he screamed. He was grabbed in the back also and was suddenly yanked down into the dark stench. The wood around the hole splintered as he crashed through.

Down there in the dark, Tommy heard a growling sound and felt excruciating pain. He instantly remembered every nightmare of his childhood. Teeth tore into his windpipe, cutting off his scream; he panicked even more as he felt himself being plunged down under the level of putrid, liquid waste. Something burst in his chest and the pain was unbearable. Everything stopped.

Later, the predator looked back from the tree-covered hilltop overlooking the ranch buildings. Finally, the other human animals emerged from the bunkhouse and went to the little building where Tommy Steed had been staying too long. The predator turned and walked into the trees.

Chris Colt rode alongside his half-brother Joshua heading toward the town of Westcliffe. There was so much wagon and buggy traffic along the Texas Creek Road that the pair actually rode their two big horses off to the west side of the roadway.

Joshua was meeting a cattle buyer who was supposed to ride up from Pueblo, due east but three thousand feet lower than Westcliffe, and Chris Colt had to check on his prisoner Newt, who was being kept in the Custer County jail, courtesy of Sheriff Schoolfield. Lem had been buried in a cemetery to the north of the towns of Westcliffe, Silver Cliff, and Rosita. Some nights, for as long as people in the Wet Mountain valley could remember, mysterious lights had occasionally appeared in that cemetery, and it was rumored that it was actually an old Ute burial ground. Because of that fact, poor old Lem had no visitors and no flowers on his grave. In fact, very few occupants of Boot Hill outside Westcliffe were visited by family or friends. For most, it was much easier and more convenient to keep their distance and think of their passed loved one with fond memories.

The two brothers rode into the bustling mountain mining town and headed toward the nearest saloon. The day was hot and the beer was iced, with fresh replacement ice brought each day from the glacial caps high up on Hermit Peak.

Chris and his older brother sat at a table

in the corner, where Chris Colt always placed himself out of habit. He had to have his back to the corner, his eyes watching the doors and windows. It may have been a bit much for some, but it had kept Christopher Colt alive for just over thirty years now.

They were in the Horn Silver Billiard Saloon and discussed shooting a round of billiards, but decided instead to just shoot the breeze and relax for a few minutes. This was the saloon where Joshua was to meet his cattle buyer later in the day.

As the two men were discussing their father, Colt noticed a couple of men in the corner who he could tell were troublemakers. Both were tossing back their drinks pretty fast and their glares at the two Colts were becoming more frequent. Chris talked with his sibling but kept an eye and an ear in their direction. One of the men was dressed like a cowpuncher; the other wore a frilly white shirt, black leather vest, black western tie, and gray trousers with black pinstripes. He also wore over-the-trouser shined black boots with tiny brass rowels on the spurs. Joshua recognized the bottom of the man's legs and footwear.

Joshua told Chris, "That Fancy Dan was

one of the Klan members who visited us at the ranch and tried to brace us. I remember the boots, pants and spurs."

Both men stood and hitched their gun-belts simultaneously, sauntering over to Chris and Joshua Colt.

Chris whispered, "Oh, no, can't we even have a beer in peace?"

Fancy Dan said, "Ain't you the famous Chris Colt and ain't you his nigger brother?"

Chris started to speak but Joshua put his hand on his forearm and answered, "Look, you boys apparently didn't learn anything the night you visited our ranch hiding beneath your hoods and robes, so just go away now, or you'll learn a tougher lesson."

The words struck home. The two had been discovered as Klansmen who had also taken part in a want-to-be raid at the Coyote Run Ranch.

That didn't bother them that much, though, because they had been run off and totally humiliated by the Colts and had practiced ever since with their six-guns. Day in and day out, the two men practiced, several hours a day. Contrary to what the popular dime novels printed, shootists don't bang away with bullets all day, because ammo was too expensive, so these two would practice dry firing and quick draw hour after hour. This was all done in secret and with one purpose in mind—to plant the Colt brothers on Boot Hill.

The Fancy Dan said, "Fine. You know what we're about, so I'm here to tell ya'. I don't care how good ya are with a hogleg, Colt. We've practiced for hours ever since ya' made us all take water. You ain't practiced like we done, and its gonna be yer ruination. Sides, yer brother there ain't a gunhand like you nohow."

Joshua said very quietly, "It's a shame you boys practiced so much just to kill us because you two aren't going to kill anybody."

The man said, "Says who?"

Joshua moved so quickly neither man could react. He lunged out of his chair, his powerful right hand closing over the fancy one's gunhand and bringing a scream of pain from the man's lips. His left hand clipped the other on the point of the chin with an uppercut from the hip.

Joshua smashed the fancy one full in the face with a powerful head butt, pulping his lips and knocking several teeth loose. Not letting go, he head-butted him again and held the man up by the arms, then tossed his loose, unconscious body backward out the doors of the saloon, where he tumbled like a ragdoll down the second-floor stairway to the ground below. Joshua then picked up the other and sent him through the door in the same way.

He and Chris grinned at each other and shook their heads, then got up, paid for their drinks, and walked out. With a laughing crowd watching, they picked up the two want-to-be gun slicks over their shoulders and carried them to a Main Street watering trough and dropped them in. Both men came up blubbering and spitting water. Chris and Joshua looked at each other and grinned and each swung a vicious punch at the two troublemakers, hitting them both full in the face and sending them back under water. The two brothers walked away with an amazed crowd of onlookers laughing.

Smiles-At-The-Bear was a southern Ute who lived a little west of Pagosa Springs at the base of Wolf Creek Pass. He had been having an affair with Laughing Crow, the wife of his cousin. She had eyes that promised many secrets, and he could never resist them, no matter how ashamed he felt. His cousin, Barking Crow, had been captured by a hand of Mescalero Apache when young and spent several years with them before returning to his band, after having acquired quite a taste for mescal, which that tribe of Apaches was noted for imbibing. Each night, he fell asleep early—or, more accurately, passed out in a drunken stupor—and his cousin dutifully performed the man's husbandly chores as often as possible. This was normally accomplished by moonlit rendezvous with Laughing Crow under the trees along the banks of the fast-flowing Piedras River.

It was a warm night when the two met next to the river and were soon engaged in a passionate embrace. They were consumed with their lovemaking and did not hear the breathing or smell the putrid smell. If they had only looked across the rapidly flowing watercourse they would have seen the moonlight shining off of the dark brown eyes of the predator. He had eaten part of a rabbit earlier in the day but was now hungry again. The female looked good to him, as her meat would be easier to tear apart and swallow. The male he would just enjoy killing and dominating.

Chris and Joshua Colt went to the Powell House in Silver Cliff and ordered a pair of large steaks and a glass of the house wine. Afterward they went to their respective appointments, agreeing to meet back at the Powell House for dinner. They would ride back to the ranch after dark.

Chris got the court date for his criminal and heard from Sheriff Schoolfield that he suspected that the man would end up dying of a "turrible case of hemp fever."

Joshua left his meeting and decided to stop by the Rosenberg Mercantile Store, mainly so he could look at the Widow Rosenberg. She and her husband had come out from New York City on a wagon train, because he had dreams of discovering the largest gold mine in the west. Unfortunately, Ira had gone up into the Sangre de Cristos and made it all the way above timberline on Crestone Peak, to where he could look back at night from his camp and see the lights of his own house. But a late-summer snowstorm had come in and dumped a foot of snow on his camp, and he did not know how to find dry firewood or tinder or get his fire started. The more he tried, the more he panicked, and eventually hypothermia set in and poor Ira died of exposure. He froze to death while his wife, down at Westcliffe, was complaining to her neighbor about the heat, unaware of her husband's predicament just a short distance away. Ira fell asleep with his back against a large rock; the last thing he saw were the lights of his own home and his neighbors'. Very sleepy, he simply closed his lids and had a dream about finding gold and being warmed by it. He was no longer cold, just very, very tired. He fell asleep there and never awakened.

Heidi Rosenberg was a handsome woman, now over the death of Ira. She was of hardy pioneer stock, much the same as Shirley Colt, and Joshua Colt was secretly in love with her. She accepted him on his own terms and made no judgements about his skin color or the fact that he was the brother of the legendary Chris Colt. There was nothing phony or pretentious about her and she treated Joshua with respect because—although Joshua did not know it—she too was in love with him. Both hesitated to come forward with their feelings because of the difference in their races—a union would have been taboo, even though Joshua was only half black. In everyone's eyes he was black, period.

Joshua walked into the Mercantile and saw Heidi Rosenberg bent over, picking up some seeds that had fallen on the floor, unaware that anyone was in the store. Joshua just had to stare at her for a few seconds before carefully clearing his throat. She jumped up with a start and turned to face him, her hand clutching her bosom and her face beet red.

"Ooh, Mr. Colt," she said, "you gave me a start."

Joshua removed his hat and replied sheepishly, "I'm very sorry, Mrs. Rosenberg. I just thought I'd pop in to buy some cloth for Shirley and pick up some vittles."

Heidi smiled and wiped her hands on her apron, replying, "Of course, Joshua, but please don't call me Mrs. Rosenberg. My name is Heidi."

Joshua looked at the floor and kind of toed a board nervously.

He said, "Ma'am, I believe it would be better if I called you Mrs. Rosenberg."

Her green eyes flashed and she said, "Oh, and why is that, sir?"

He replied, "People, ma'am. I'm a Negro, you know."

"Oh," she said sarcastically, "I hadn't noticed."

They both laughed.

She went on, "To hell with people, Joshua. I was married to a Jewish man for seven years. Do you think I'm unused to upraised eyebrows?"

Joshua said, "Being Jewish and being brown skinned are two different things, ma'am."

She said, "I know, Joshua, but I believe in America. You and I both have the right to do what we want and be who we are."

Joshua grinned and started fingering a new bridle hanging on a peg.

He said, "Ma'am, that sounds wonderful when you are white and you hear it from a well-meaning schoolmarm. The problem is that most well-meaning schoolmarms don't have whip scars on their backs and even worse scars in their hearts."

"In any event," she retorted, "you have never impressed me as the type of man who will let anyone tell him how to behave."

"I'm not," he grinned, and he replied softly, "but on the other hand, I am if you are going to be the one who might bear the brunt of the consequences of my actions, ma'am."

She was at a loss for words and turned away briefly. But then she turned back around. Her bosom heaved and Joshua felt sweaty.

"Nevertheless," she said, after clearing her throat, "I insist that you call me Heidi."

Joshua said softly, "Okay, Heidi."

They stared deep into each other's eyes

for several long seconds, both thinking of forbidden fruit.

Heidi broke the silence by saying, "I just do not understand society."

"I don't either, Heidi, but I learned long ago that there are certain things society will tolerate and certain things they won't."

Again, there was a long silence as they both looked around and fidgeted nervously. Joshua started for the door.

She said, in a panic, "Don't leave! please?"

Joshua turned and stared at her, his hand on the door. Beyond him, out the window, the snow shone brightly off the icy caps of the near-distant Sangre de Cristos, towering high above the town of Westcliffe. Heidi thought briefly of her late husband Ira and a quick flash of guilt went through her mind, but she quickly brushed it aside. Ira had been a nice man, but he had been a fool. Joshua Colt, on the other hand, was a man through and through and Heidi now realized that she could not even breathe properly in his presence. She knew he was black and that society would put a taboo on their relationship, but she could not help herself. She envisioned herself being held in his massive arms and staring close into his dark eyes, and she knew that she would feel protected and wanted if she could but lay for one night with her head on his solid chest. Joshua Colt would never freeze to death in a midsummer snowstorm above timberline. He was the type of man who would survive. This man could only die saving a calf from a grizzly bear or his wife from marauding Indians. He was the type of man she wanted, no matter what.

Joshua walked over to the tins of fruit and vegetables and pretended to not notice her, but all he could think of were those green eyes staring at his back. He heard a wisp of cloth behind him and turned. She was there, facing him, less than two feet away. They looked at each other the way they had so many times before when he made his frequent stops into her mercantile store. In reality, Joshua looked for reasons to travel to Westcliffe just so he could look at her again and wish.

Now she was standing in front of him looking up into his eyes, and he could help himself no longer. Joshua swept the woman into his arms and their lips met, and they kissed each other with all that was in them. He wanted this woman so badly, even though he knew he could not have her. But just this once he would kiss the lips he dreamed about.

The door opened and both of them jumped back with a great start, their chests heaving and their hearts pounding in their ears. Joshua's hand subconsciously went down to his walnut-handled Colt Peacemaker but froze as he heard the simultaneous cocking of his brother's twin mother-of-pearl-handled Peacemakers.

Chris grinned and spun both guns backward into their holsters, while Joshua, embarrassed, laughed at himself. "Well, big brother," Chris said, "guess you haven't had enough bullets shot at you lately. Wanting to stir up some more shooting, huh?"

Heidi interrupted, "Chris, don't blame your brother. It wasn't—"

Chris held up his hand smiling and said, "I'm not blaming anyone for anything, ma'am. If two people love each other, I think that's ten times better than everyone always shooting each other. I was just teasing him, because he already catches hell for his skin color. If this gets out, you both will be on the receiving end of some more trouble."

Joshua said, "So you disapprove?"

Chris replied, "No, I'll be in front of you

with my iron out if you get in trouble, but I just want you both to keep your eyes open."

Heidi walked over to Chris Colt and gave him a quick kiss on the cheek, saying, "Thank you so much, Chris, for being understanding. We just—ah—we just kissed."

Chris Colt said, "Heidi, I've been a tracker most of my adult life, so reading signs is second nature to me. Until my brother popped in here one day to buy Shirley some gingham and laid eyes on you for the first time, he only came to town about once or twice a month. Now he comes to town at least four times a week and always has some reason to stop in here. Now is that a hard sign to read?"

Heidi shuffled nervously and fiddled with the folds of her dress, while Joshua, embarrassed, chuckled.

Joshua said, "Heidi never knew till now how I feel about her, Chris. I didn't even realize it till now. Now, you tell me how you could know it before we even did?"

"I already told you, big brother."

Joshua said, "Why didn't you say something sooner?"

Chris said, " 'Cause I was hoping this might not ever happen."

Joshua doubled his fist and gritted his

teeth together in anger, saying, "What the hell you mean by that, Chris?"

Heidi, also angry, said, "Yes, what do you mean by that, Chris Colt?"

The deputy lifted his black Stetson hat with the beaded headband off his head and ran his fingers through his brown hair.

He replied, "Just what I said. Look, Heidi you are a handsome woman and you've got sand. Any man could be proud to stand beside you, and Joshua, you're my older brother. Our skin and hair look different, but our faces are almost identical and our blood is the same. I love you and would do anything for you, but I meant what I said. I hoped that you two had maybe a passing fancy and that it would do just that—pass with time. Our society has a lot of growing up to do, especially when it comes to people's skin color. Heidi, Joshua has already had to deal with a lot from a lot of people just because of his skin color. Do you have any idea the trouble you're in for if you two become a couple? Do either one of you realize it? And Joshua, do you want to subject her to that trouble? If you two love each other and that's what you want, then I'll stand by you and shoot it out against any army that comes at you two. But I just want you to think things out good first. For your own sakes, not mine."

Heidi and Joshua looked at each other, and he held her hand, giving her a reassuring glance.

Joshua had tears in his own eyes as he looked at her and said, "Heidi, it's true. I do love you, but my brother is right. I cannot subject you to what men would do if you even acted half-friendly toward me. I cannot allow you to go through that. Goodbye."

Joshua turned and hurried out the door.

Heidi, at first, had a shocked look on her face, then burst into tears, throwing herself against Chris's shoulders. He held her and let her cry while he patted the back of her shoulder reassuringly. She stepped back after a few seconds and sniffled into a hanky.

Chris said, "He's right, you know."

Heidi got angry and said, "You and he do not have the right to tell me who I can love or be with. Please leave, Chris."

Joshua was silent all the way home.

Riding down the long driveway to the ranch buildings directly toward the towering fourteen-thousand-foot Spread Eagle Peaks, Chris said, "You know, Joshua, whenever I really have a problem and need to sort things out, I head up there, up in the high lonesome."

When Chris unsaddled in the barn, he noticed Joshua switched his saddle to his big roan Appaloosa.

"I'll be back when you see me, Chris," said Joshua. "Going camping for a bit. May do some fishing up at Lakes of the Clouds."

"Sure," Chris replied, "I'll have Shirley put you up a bag of grub."

He grabbed his Winchester and walked toward the barn door and stopped saying, "You aren't mad at me, are you?"

Joshua gave a little laugh but still tended to his packing and saddling.

He said, "For being a brother? Hell, no. You were right. I appreciate you caring."

That night, the lovely Shirley awakened as she had done so many nights before whenever Brenna or Joseph had a belly-ache or a cold. As she had done on so many other nights, she turned her head to look at the tall, handsome man sleeping beside her. Moonlight streaked through the window and played on Chris's chiseled features, but this night she noticed his eyes were wide open and tears ran down both cheeks.

Shirley threw her arm across his chest and softly stroked his hair.

"Chris," she said, "what in the world is wrong, dear?"

Chris was very embarrassed. He had been crying silently in the shadows and didn't know his spouse was awake. He wiped his tears away as quickly as he could.

Shirley said, "What's wrong?"

Chris said, "I didn't know you were awake."

Shirley said, "I didn't ask that. What's wrong?"

He said, "I'm just worried about my brother. I walked into the Mercantile today and caught him and Heidi kissing. It was love. You can see it in the way they look at each other."

Shirley said, "And you advised them of the dangers of an interracial love affair?"

Colt said, "Yes."

She replied, "And Joshua, the hero like his brother, sucked in his gut and told her it would be too dangerous to be seen with him, didn't he?"

Chris looked over at her and said, "How do you know? You weren't there?"

Shirley laughed and said, "He's a Colt, isn't he?"

Chris said, "So what do you think?"

Shirley replied, "I think you men should

quit trying to do all the thinking for us women and quit thinking that women like Heidi and me are made out of fine china. She's tough and she'll let Joshua know if she wants him or not, and if she does, we'll stand by them through thick and thin."

Chris was flustered now, saying, "Of course we will, Shirl, but why are you mad at me?"

She got up and put on a robe, saying, "Men!"

She headed toward the door and said over her shoulder, "I'm putting on a pot of tea for us."

In the kitchen, she was grinning. She knew she had been manipulative, but starting the little spat with Chris would take his mind off his worry about Joshua.

Shirley Colt had learned several years earlier that she could not worry enough to bring her husband home safely. She would simply trust to God and to Chris to make sure that that would always happen. Chris had a tendency to worry about his family too much and needed to learn that they were all tough, too.

Joshua Colt looked up at the billions of stars in the thin air and was amazed. He had never seen such a sight, and it made his problems seem so small. He was realizing why Chris came up here to solve his problems. Earlier in the day, he had seen a harem of about fifty elk, watched a pair of beavers working on dam improvements on a high mountain pond, and caught glimpses of many mule deer. He had watched rainbow trout jumping on the polished-mirror surface of Lakes of the Clouds near sunset, spooked a wolverine feeding on the carcass of a dead doe, ridden close to a herd of big-horn sheep grazing on a high hillside, and spotted a large grizzly nursing two cubs across a high bowl from him. All of this in one day.

On top of that, Joshua had made his way to the top of the Spread Eagle Peaks and looked out for hundreds of miles in almost every direction. North and south he saw nothing but snow-capped peaks running for miles. To the northeast, he saw Pike's Peak and the Rampart Range. Due east was the Wet Mountain Valley, then the Green-horns, the foothills, and the high prairie stretching out toward Kansas. To the west, he looked at the massive San Luis Valley and beyond that, the San Juans. What was very impressive to Joshua was the cloud bank that stretched out below him in the San Luis Valley. He was actually above the clouds, which were pushed up against the mountain range below him. It was an unusual and awe-inspiring experience to look down at clouds from up above them, as if he were up with the angels for a while.

The high mountain flowers were beautiful, too, and the trees seemed to be more alive and greener. The high grasses seemed to always be blowing in continuous strong breezes that wafted back and forth, directed by various corridors of rock designing their windy paths.

Joshua realized that his brother was right. He needed first to think of Heidi's safety. He didn't know why he had fallen in love with her, but it had happened. It would have been much more practical, reasonable, and safe for him to have fallen in love with a black woman. But he hadn't. He concluded that he had made the right move by saying good-bye and walking out of the mercantile—he had to make a clean break of it and put it behind him. But could he? he wondered. He pictured Heidi's smiling face, her intelligent eyes, her long, shiny hair.

He remembered the time he had walked into the shop and she had been holding her dress up and cooling off at the back door. The bell above the door had broken earlier in the day, and she hadn't heard him enter. She held the bottom of the dress at mid-thigh and Joshua was treated to the sight of the most shapely and beautiful legs he had ever seen. When Heidi felt eyes staring at her, a chill went up and down her spine, and she turned, blushed, smiled coyly, and dropped the dress. She explained about the bell being broken and needing to cool off in the heat of the day. Joshua Colt had smiled through the whole explanation, embarrassing her even more.

Joshua Colt had fought against racism his entire life and had learned to bend some for survival—but only to a certain point. He would not allow himself to bend to the breaking point. First, someone would have a fight on their hands.

Joshua dropped to his knees and folded his hands to pray. Instead, though, he opened his eyes and his hands and spread his arms outward and stared up at the star-studded sky above and all about him. The moon shone brightly on the ice-encrusted peaks, and its reflection gave off an eerie glow. Joshua reasoned that it would be silly to pray with his eyes closed and head bowed when he felt as though he were now so close he could reach out and touch God on the cheek. He would pray with his eyes open and his head up, reveling in what he believed was God's glory at its finest. This was, in Joshua's opinion, a place where the Almighty had dipped a magic paintbrush in shades of dark blue and black and tossed diamond dust into the mix, then swabbed it across the sky from horizon to horizon.

The tall, handsome black cowboy prayed harder than he ever had in his life. Then he replaced his Stetson and started back to his campsite. He had not taken more than two steps when he noticed movement above him in the moonlight. On a cliff not far above him, silhouetted against the full moon, a bald eagle sat sleeping in a large aerie, apparently protecting her brood.

Joshua sat down and watched the eagle and thought about how much that bird meant to his brother. Now he understood why coming up high into the mountains was so important to Chris Colt—who was also called One Eagle—and he was starting to understand why eagles meant so much as well.

Joshua watched the eagle and thought of the story Chris told him; he had learned it from the Indians. A mother eagle, like this one here, had sat on a group of eggs in its aerie high on a mountain cliff. One day while the mother eagle was off searching for food, a great wind blew. One egg was blown out of the nest and it miraculously rolled all the way down the cliff and out into the prairie. It kept rolling, still unbroken, and finally landed right in the middle of the nest of a prairie chicken. Earlier, a fox had come up and had stolen one of the prairie chicken eggs, and the eagle egg landed right in its place. Because prairie chickens have such small brains, the mother didn't notice the size difference when she returned to the nest. She sat on the nest and continued the hatching process.

After the eggs hatched and the little ones came forth, the mother hen still didn't notice that one of her chicks was, in fact, an eaglet.

Six months later found the baby prairie chickens, with their young eagle foster brother, following along in single file behind their father. It hadn't meant a thing to him that the last one in line was already three times his own size. While they walked through the prairie the eaglet looked up overhead and saw his biological father soaring high over the plains, wings outspread on the thermal breezes at the base of the foothills.

The eaglet stopped and pointed skyward,

saying, "Father! Father! Look! Look at that magnificent bird! It is so powerful and graceful. Look at the spread of his wings and the sharpness of his beak. Look at the power in those mighty wings and the clutching, crushing power in those talons! Just look at him! I would love to be a bird like that!"

The father prairie chicken looked up at the eagle and nonchalantly replied, "Well, forget it. You can't ever be like him. He's an eagle and you're just a prairie chicken."

Joshua was now sitting by his campfire drinking coffee as he grinned, remembering the final line of that story. He thought about how Chris told him that eagles would sometimes watch a fierce storm blowing, then dive off the side of the mountain and fly straight into its eye. Using the powerful storm winds, they would struggle mightily, beating their majestic wings and rising higher and higher on the updrafts until they would finally emerge up above the storm clouds. At that point, the eagles would fly around in the bright sunlight while millions of other birds huddled on branches and got soaked, blown off, and sick through the hours of the storm. The mighty birds used the frightening monster storms winds to save themselves, flying right into them and tackling them head-on.

The other thing that Chris always said about eagles was that they did not fly in flocks; they only came one or two at a time.

Joshua realized that he and Chris were eagles—not turkeys, pigeons, or any other bird. He concluded that no matter what he did, most other people would simply consider him an uppity nigger. But, like his brother, he would always keep them off balance, preventing his enemies from getting the upper hand.

He would go down the mountain the next day, ride to Westcliffe, walk into the Rosenberg Mercantile, sweep Heidi into his arms, and profess his love for her. He would then provide for her and protect his love from anyone who disapproved.

With a smile on his face and hope for a love-filled, bright future, Joshua Colt wrapped up in his blanket roll in the warmth of the fire, listening to the nearby sounds of cutthroat trout slapping the water's surface on the Lakes of the Clouds.

What he didn't see was a pair of eyes watching him in the darkness. They were the dark, emotionless eyes of a predator. The predator had been watching this man animal for hours, wondering what the meat would taste like from one with brown skin.

In his bedroll, Joshua was still smiling, but suddenly a chill ran down his spine and his smile vanished. Something was watching him. He hadn't often experienced this feeling but his brother had been saved many times by listening to such gut-wrenching messages from the subconscious. He could actually feel something coming slowly toward his back. Joshua wondered why his horse wasn't whinnying or snorting—he was normally better than a watchdog. Then he spotted the form of the animal, lying dead in the moonlight in a pool of blood.

The wind shifted and blew against Joshua's back. A horrible stench invaded his nostrils and his sinus cavities. He wanted to scream. He wanted to void his bladder. His right hand went to his walnut-handled Colt Peacemaker next to his head. He pulled it out, cocked it, and spun, firing through the blanket. But the giant shadow ducked into the trees a split second before Joshua fired. Colt jumped up and fanned the gun—two, three, four, five, six shots boomed in the darkness. Suddenly, with a roar, the giant form came out of the darkness and rushed at Joshua. Joshua was out of bullets, and he wheeled and fled in panic. Knowing that the only time you had any chance of getting away from a bear was running straight downhill, Joshua did just that, trying to dodge in and out of trees down the mountain. He could smell the beast behind him and could hear the monster's breaths, panting as they ran headlong down the ridge.

Joshua thought back to the most frightening time in his life, when he had run from the plantation as a young man, pursued by a howling pack of black-and-tans and bloodhounds. He'd half-run and half-swum through the swamps, with the dogs close on his heels, wasting time trying to use the water to cover the scent of his feet. What he did not know at the time was that hounds like that did not pick up the man smell off the ground when it was that fresh—instead, they were picking up his scent out of the air.

He'd finally figured that out and headed for deeper water in the swamp. Instead of trying to outrun the dogs and use the water to cover his smell, he decided to submerge himself completely. Joshua simply dived in and swam underwater, barely bringing his nose and mouth out occasionally to take another breath of air. He kept this up and finally lost the dogs, who ran along the solid ground lining the watercourses but couldn't pick up his scent anymore. Finally, in frustration, the canine hunters backtracked the previous scent trail, winding up with the handlers who eventually abandoned the search, assuming that Joshua had drowned.

Now, plunging down the dark, forested mountainside with a growling, frightening giant of a predator close behind him, Joshua Colt knew he had to use his head and think his way out of the situation. What could he possibly do? he wondered. His legs and lungs wouldn't hold out much longer. Whatever was chasing him was slowed a little by the trees because of its massive size, but it was not a grizzly or a black bear because it was running on its hindlegs, not all fours—a bear running on its hindlegs would be like a man running on his hands instead of his feet.

Joshua Colt was frightened to death, but he was also a sensible man. He didn't believe in monsters or ghosts. Something horrible was chasing him and it was real and it meant to kill him—that he knew. But it was not a bear, cougar, or any other large predator he was familiar with.

He thought to himself that grizzlies

couldn't climb trees and black bears could only climb thick trees but not thin ones using branches. The problem was that he was running so fast and the creature was so close, he couldn't even slow to try to climb one. And what if this animal *could* climb one?

Could it swim? He knew that cougars and bobcats didn't like going into water.

Joshua cut to his left and ran straight across a ridgeline and noticed the creature was gaining on him. But he started downhill again and the creature was slightly slowed down. It was very hairy and smelled powerfully, a rancid, horrible smell.

Down below, Joshua saw through some breaks in the firs moonlight ripples on the surface of water—Rainbow Lake. He ran headlong down the hill and dived into it, swimming as far as he could underwater. He broke the surface and gasped for air, while turning to look back. On the shoreline, he saw the creature, his back to him, just before it went into the trees. A shiver ran through Joshua's body.

He turned and swam toward the far shore.

CHAPTER 3

Sasquatch

It was close to daybreak when Kuli came into Chris Colt's bedroom and tugged on his master's sleeve. Kuy was the Nez Perce word for "Go," and was the name that Man Killer gave to the large timberwolf that had been companion to Beaver Banta, the deceased uncle of Man Killer's wife. The wolf had adopted Man Killer and Chris after the death of Beaver, but the canine had gotten very attached to Chris Colt, so Man Killer gave him to his mentor. Joseph and Brenna, Chris's kids, couldn't pronounce Kuy properly, so the name Kuli stuck. The big animal was now Chris Colt's constant companion and treated the Colt family as his pack, but he was very shy around strangers.

This night, Kuli tugged on Chris's arm because wolves don't bark, and it was the best way to warn his master that something was wrong. Chris jumped up and grabbed a Colt revolving shotgun, slinging his double-holster rig over his shoulders. He took his left-hand gun out as an afterthought and dropped it on the bed next to Shirley. He gave her a wink and a smile and followed Kuli out the back door.

In the darkness, Kuli ran out toward the towering mountain range and was soon at the side of a tall man limping in the darkness. Seeing Kuli wagging his tail, Colt sat the shotgun down and ran forward.

"Who is it?" Colt yelled.

Weakly, Joshua said, "It's me."

Knowing he was now safe and sound, Joshua's inner system shut down and his knees buckled. Chris picked him up and a figure appeared next to him. It was Man Killer, who explained, "I rode in earlier, but you and Shirl were asleep. I slept in the bunkhouse."

Man Killer had married Jennifer Banta, who had inherited millions of dollars, and they had her family's ranch further down the valley outside Westcliffe, where Man Killer still raised and bred Appaloosa descended from the herd of his tribe. Some of the herd and several stallions were at Colt's ranch, of which Man Killer owned one fifth, and the rest were at his new ranch. He still chose, though, to be Chris Colt's deputy, and he traveled with Chris whenever he could get away. He'd intended to leave with Colt in the morning to check out the report of a cowpuncher getting severely mauled and partially devoured by a large grizzly near Parker, close to Denver.

The two men picked Joshua up and carried him to the house, his arms over their shoulders. Inside, Shirley already had the coffeepot on the stove and lanterns lit. They took Joshua in and laid him down on Chris and Shirley's bed. He was wearing only denims, with his pistol tucked into his waistband. His feet were bloody and his small toe stuck out to the side. A number of cactus needles stuck out of his shins, calves, and the sides of his feet.

Chris said, "Grit your teeth."

He grabbed the broken toe and pulled it out and up, straightening it back into position. A single tear rolled out of Joshua's left eye and down his cheek and onto the pillow. Shirley handed Chris some bandaging, and he bound the broken toe to the one next to it.

"Broke?" Joshua asked.

Chris said, "Well, when all your other toes are pointing at the moon and this one's pointing at Texas, I'd say that it was broken."

Joshua laughed and accepted a cup of coffee from Shirley. His hands shook as he sipped the hot brew. He winked up at his sister-in-law. Shirley walked toward the kitchen and spoke over her shoulder. "I'm going to make you a big steak and some potatoes and bread, Joshua," she said. "That'll help more than anything."

Joshua looked up at Chris and accepted a cigarette and a light from Man Killer.

Joshua said, "I couldn't tell its size exactly, Chris. Maybe seven—maybe even eight feet tall—hairy, and powerfully built. It wasn't a grizzly. It chased me on its hindlegs for over a mile. It didn't like water, though, and I got away by diving into Rainbow Lake. Smell? It smelled like a winter-killed elk on a hot spring day."

Chris said, "What else can you tell me about it?"

Joshua got a tear in his eye again, saying, "Killed my horse and did it quietly. It growled, even roared when it charged me. It was putting the sneak on me while I was in my bedroll."

Chris lit his own cigarette and blew smoke at the ceiling.

The three men talked for several minutes

and Chris noticed a dread look on Man Killer's face. Shirley brought in a tray full of steak, onions, mushrooms, potatoes, and biscuits, then she brought back the coffee-pot and poured fresh coffee for all four of them. Joshua sat up and ate heartily.

Finally, sensing something amiss, Chris Colt said, "Okay, Man Killer. You're holding back something. What's up, partner?"

Man Killer said, "Sasquatch."

Joshua said, "What?"

Man Killer said, "Sasquatch."

Chris said, "What is that?"

Man Killer's face was grave.

He said, "I have seen one one time, when I was a small boy. In the land I came from, the Wallowa Valley, there was much talk of the Sasquatch. I went one time with Ollikut and Joseph and others toward the Pacific, what we called the big water. We were in the big forest and saw tracks like a man's but much bigger."

All eyes were on Man Killer as he paused to build a smoke. Shirley had a lump in her throat.

He lit the smoke and went on, "Ollikut was the brother of Chief Joseph. He was very large and very brave, but he was also very funny. He always told jokes and played tricks on his friends. Ollikut did not laugh and joke that day. He told us younger ones that the tracks were of the Sasquatch. Its mother is a bear and its father is a man. Many people in my tribe have seen such a creature, but they usually hide in the mountains in the big trees and hunt at night. Sometimes, hunting, they have been seen.

"The day after we saw the tracks we came upon many such tracks going down a deep trail in the forest. We were in a gulch between two ridges. The woods got very quiet and we knew that an enemy was creeping up on us. Daniel, one of our band, screamed out and we looked. A rock as big as a melon had been thrown from the ridge above. It broke his leg. Soon, more rocks came through the trees, and we smelled a very bad smell like bad meat. We heard branches break and brush snap and an animal rolled down the hill and onto the trail. It was a sasquatch. He had very long hair, or fur, and it was dark red. His arms were long and hanged down along his legs. When he walked, he walked like a man—not like the gorilla or chimpanzee we saw in the circus, Colt. He stood two heads taller than the tallest of our men—maybe eight feet."

"My word," said Shirley.

"What did this sasquatch do when he saw all of you?" Chris asked.

Man Killer replied, "He at first looked around, like you do when your horse throws you off and you hit the ground too hard. One warrior drew his bow, but Joseph told us not to shoot. He said to wait, that this might be a spirit animal sent by the Great Mystery to tell us something."

"What happened then?" Joshua asked.

Man Killer said, "He seemed to understand that we were not going to shoot. He turned and walked slowly down the trail swinging his arms in big swings. He would stop and look back, then walk on. He did this twice more before the trail turned, and we saw him no more. No more rocks came down on us, though."

Joshua said, "You know, Chris, something Man Killer just said—about him sensing that they meant him no harm and the rocks stopping. Well, I was pretty unnerved when I smelled this critter sneaking up on me. I turned and fired, and he ducked into the shadows, and I fanned my gun. He didn't charge until I fired up all six bullets from my Peacemaker. Do you suppose he counted my shots?"

Colt said, "I don't know, Joshua. Man Killer and I will head up after first light and recover your camp and gear. We'll see what the sign says."

Man Killer said, "I am sorry about your horse, Joshua."

He looked at the black Colt brother and smiled. Man Killer nodded at Chris, and he looked over, too. Joshua's mouth was open and his eyes were closed, his breaths coming out in a long, slow, steady rhythm. The three of them watched, smiling, as his breathing soon turned into loud snoring. They crept from the room and sat down around the big mahogany dining table. Six chairs, with well-padded leather seats and backs, sat around the table. The legs, backs, and arms of each chair were constructed of cleverly woven, highly polished elk antlers.

It was about six in the morning when Man Killer tossed his saddle across the blanket covering the broad black back of Hawk, his big Appaloosa. Chris Colt did the same with War Bonnet, as the two horses stood, nostrils flaring in their stalls, ears twisting nervously this way and that, anticipating going out into the wilds.

After saddling up the two men went inside so Chris could give his wife and kids hugs and kisses. Little Joseph wore a cowboy hat and a wooden pistol tucked into his waistband. Brenna carried some daisies she had picked before breakfast, a frequent habit of the little lady. The husband and wife kissed and Colt hugged his daughter, but Joseph wanted to follow his dad out to the barn. Joshua was still sleeping and Shirley faced the task of removing cactus needles from his legs and feet when he awoke.

The two marshals mounted up in the barn, and Colt reached down and hoisted his son onto the saddle in front of him. They rode out of the barn and waved at Shirley, Brenna, and their top hands, Tex Westchester and big Muley Hawkins. Little Joseph waved as if he were going on the trip, too, but his father dropped him off at the nearest pasture fence, where he watched Chris and Man Killer as they rode gradually uphill across the pastures, eventually entering the stands of scrub oaks at the base of the big mountains. Joseph turned and ran back through the knee-high alfalfa and turned away to the bunkhouse to visit with Tex and Muley. This surprised but pleased his mother—the little boy wanted to be a man as soon as possible.

At the edge of the scrub oaks Colt and

Man Killer stopped and looked back at the ranch house and buildings.

Man Killer said, "Why do we stop?"

Colt said, "Kuli."

Man Killer grinned and said, "Maybe you should become a scout again. Kuli is ahead of us up that ridge."

Chris grinned and turned his horse around. No sooner had he moved on than he saw the large timberwolf running across a clearing ahead of them up the ridge. They followed him.

Colt said, "Guess I'm getting old."

Man Killer said, "Very old." His comment made him the object of a sidelong glance that could have sizzled a steak.

Several hours later found them leading their mounts around the shoreline of Rainbow Lake. Man Killer found the tracks first, as the two men had split up and gone around separate sides of the lake. The lake was on the south side of the main trail leading up between two mountain peaks and was close to timberline. It was surrounded by tall evergreen trees and very steep ridges on both its north and south sides. The tracks came down from the southern ridge; Colt joined Man Killer and the two investigated them. Colt pulled out two cigars as the men studied the tracks.

The two men lit their cigars and puffed on them while dropping to their hands and knees and carefully studying the tracks, giving each other knowing looks. Joshua's tracks in the mud were clearly defined, though the edges were not totally sharp because they were several hours old. All of the creature's tracks, however, had been smeared. They were deep and large—that was obvious—but they had purposely been smeared out with a rock or large branch so they could not be identified.

Chris and Man Killer checked for an hour around the lake, then backtracked the trail up the ridge and followed it all the way to Joshua's campsite by the Lakes of the Clouds. Joshua had covered a lot more ground than he imagined. They found the horse lying near the lake in the lush grass, torn up, as if it had been done by a grizzly. But Colt found that the horse's throat had been slit and that he had bled to death before being mauled.

Joshua's other weapons were all there, but there was no ammunition, which made Chris and Man Killer very suspicious. The bacon was also gone, along with the coffee and the tobacco.

On top of that, the only tracks from the killer that they could find had been smudged. It was getting close to dark, so they had to decide to stay and risk attack themselves or go home. They decided to spend the night. The men rode to the other side of the lake and put together a campsite.

Curled up in his bedroll, each man slept with his guns close to hand and his senses on full alert. Normally, both men depended on the keen senses of their horses to keep them alerted to the unexpected presence of intruders. But this case was freaky and different and both were unnerved. The fact that the bullets, tobacco, and bacon were missing meant that someone had stolen into the deserted camp, which was entirely possible with all the miners and prospectors in the big range. But it could also mean that the creature was not an animal but a man, which was highly unlikely given the nature of its actions. The third scenario was that the animal was owned or controlled by a man who would have wanted the tobacco, meat, and bullets.

The next morning, they both awakened and ate a hearty breakfast, then set about looking for more clues. The two men left their horses ground reined by the lake and each made a circle, one going left and one going right. They kept going in circles, increasing the size, until they were hundreds of yards from each other. It took them several hours before Colt finally spotted one scuff on a rock and gave Man Killer a hand signal that brought him running up.

They marked the scuff with a kerchief and went on in the direction it headed. One little rock was overturned; it had been dark and moist on the underside and bleached white on the top. It had been kicked or stepped on and was missed by whoever had carefully and expertly covered the trail. The two men marked the overturned stone and went back for the horses.

Walking back, Chris said, "I don't know about the animal, sasquatch, or whatever, but the man who covered this trail is good, probably the best I've been against."

Leaving their horses ground reined near the overturned stone, they continued on higher. At the top of the peak, Man Killer spotted a faint trail and pointed it out. Chris Colt, as keen as his own eyes were, was impressed. In the snow and shadows, going up between two little ridges, in a shallow crevice was a faint trail in the hard-crusted snow. The two men spent another hour climbing up to the trail and discovered that tracks had been made in the snow, but snow had been scooped out and sifted onto the tracks to fill them in. Colt and Man Killer blew on one of the tracks and the powder blew out of the frozen, deep track. It was similar to a man's footprint, but much larger. This lent further credibility to Man Killer's sasquatch theory.

No other trackers could have found the trail these two men had discovered. Whoever had made and covered this trail, Colt concluded, could not have been an animal—there was way too much cunning and intelligence. Colt's mind tried to catalog the native intelligence of various animal species.

The wolverine, although closer in size to a badger, would actually tackle a grizzly bear in a fight, and earn the grizzly's respect in the process. It would follow a trapper's trapline and eat the animals caught in the traps, and Colt had heard of cases where a wolverine had even sprung the traps that were empty. It would then spray the remaining carcass of the partially eaten animals just out of meanness. The spray it emanated was similar to that of a skunk, but, many thought, much more foul smelling.

Bears, after partly devouring a prey, would cover it with dirt and leaves to hide it from other predators. But Colt had never heard of a bear covering its own backtrail. Back East in Ohio as a boy, Chris Colt lay on a wooded hilltop one time and watched his father and uncle hunting for a particular large white-tail buck that favored several cornfields just north of his hometown of Cuyahoga Falls. Colt spotted the buck down below, just as it winded and then spotted Colt's relatives. While Chris watched silently from above, the buck crouched down like a dog in a slight depression that ran parallel to Chris's father's and uncle's trail. The big deer, eighteen long tines on his ankle-thick rack of antlers, like a big dog, silently crawled on his belly right past the unsuspecting hunters who were less than twenty feet away. Unable to remain silent any longer, young Colt jumped up and waved, pointing, but by the time his father and uncle saw the buck, there were only glimpses of a waving big white flag as it disappeared into the woods.

Colt had seen animals do many amazing things to outwit hunters or predators, but he had not seen one with the intelligence to cover his backtrail. What happened next was even more amazing and confusing. The trail ended at the uppermost summit of the peak and the mountain just dropped off for thousands of feet, with the San Luis Valley stretching out far below and for miles in every direction. It was a straight drop and the tracks simply ended there.

Colt and Man Killer looked everywhere for a rope that could have been anchored to climb down, but there was no possible anchor point in the rocks. The cliff not only went straight down for a thousand feet but actually cut in under the summit. Climbing down was out of the question and any rope would have to have been over a thousand feet in length to do any good. The tracks had simply gone to the edge of the cliff and stopped. Whatever it was had to be dead down below.

Any other frontiersmen, wanting to follow out the trail, would have headed north and crossed over Hayden Creek Pass with their horses, but Chris Colt and Man Killer had two exceptional horses with real bottom to them. They also knew that a large harem of elk crossed over from the Wet Mountain Valley side to the San Luis Valley side by following a treacherous pass between Nipple Mountain and Wulsten Baldy. They would do the same.

Man Killer, deferring to his elder, volunteered to return to the horses and came back up to the summit with Chris Colt's Northern Cheyenne bow and quiver of arrows. Colt stuck one in the snow, tying a red kerchief around it at the fletchings, making sure that it would be visible from the valley below with binoculars. Next, he picked out two stands of scrub oak thousands of feet directly below that were separated east and west by a clearing of fifty or a hundred feet in width. Chris attached a piece of ribbon from his quiver just ahead of the fletchings on another arrow. Colt aimed the arrow straight out from the peak and let fly, hoping it would hit the ground near the two stands of scrub oaks. He and Man Killer watched it fall but could only follow it so far until it dropped out of sight. From the fourteen-thousand-plus-foot peak to the valley floor was a drop of seven thousand feet, so looking down, even hundred-foot fir trees looked like arrows sticking in the ground. Seeing a falling arrow all the way down was impossible.

They went down the glacier to the horses and mounted up, heading north toward Wulsten Baldy Peak and the treacherous pass they would attempt. It was close to dark when they reached the crest of the pass and started down the steep San Luis Valley side of the big range. They would make camp near the bottom in the big trees and resume the search in the morning.

Shirley Colt would not be worried about them being gone so long, Chris knew. As his wife, such excursions were an accepted fact. What Colt did not know, however, was that Shirley always worried when he was out like this, accepting the situation and keeping it to herself, but worrying all the same. Chris was a man of the wilderness, at the beck and call of anything presenting danger. Any predicament calling for courage was a magnet to a man of Chris Colt's steel.

All the Colts seemed to be that way, so Shirley now sat in her kitchen mending socks and rocking back and forth, worrying about the eldest Colt, Joshua, who had headed toward Westcliffe, hours earlier, to announce his undying, unbridled love for the widow Heidi Rosenberg. Shirley had no problem with that and would stand by Joshua through thick and thin as she had before. But she was concerned about the actions of some of the more radical citizens of the county who would take exception to a former black slave putting his lips on those of a pretty white woman. She knew that there would be a fury, as many local white men had made advances to the widow and had been politely turned away, one after the other. Heidi's heart had belonged to the tall, dark Colt rancher for a long time now, and since she felt that she had settled for second-best with her first husband, she resolved never do the same again.

When Joshua rode into Westcliffe, his feet were so sore he could hardly put weight in the stirrups, but his spirits were so high he could have floated into town. He could not wait to lift that beautiful woman in his arms and press those big red lips against his own. He couldn't wait to feel the curves and softness of her body against the hardness of his own muscle and sinew.

When he walked into that store, tears flooded her eyes as if she had read his mind. She ran into his arms and was swept up off her feet in a tight but careful embrace. Their lips met, and they kissed long and hard.

With tears streaking down her cheeks and a big smile on her face, Heidi said, "Yes," before Joshua could even utter the question.

They kissed again.

What Joshua Colt did not know, though, was that since entering town he had been followed by two very angry men with a grudge against him. Two men full of hate and rage. Those two men watched from across the street as he and Heidi kissed passionately, which enraged them even more. They rushed to get some friends, some familiar white robes and hoods, and a stout hemp rope. These were the two men who had tempted fate by spouting off to the Colt brothers earlier and had been sent headlong down some very hard stairs.

It was well after dark when Heidi walked Joshua to the door. They stopped and kissed in the doorway and stepped out on the board sidewalk. Leather creaking from a saddle rig caused them both to look, and there in front of them sat five Klansmen pointing a rifle and four pistols at the couple.

Joshua heard one of the hooded men say, "Kill the nigger-loving bitch, too," just as he heard the guns being cocked.

Eyes open wide in horror, Joshua jumped in front of Heidi and took the first bullet in the chest but kept drawing with his right hand while he shoved her into safety in the doorway behind him with his left hand. He started shooting at the hooded Klansmen as he felt another bullet slam into his big body. The first bullet didn't really hurt—it felt more like a hard punch in the chest from Chris. But the second one hit him in the abdomen and slammed him back against the doorjamb. It hurt terribly, and he could barely move with the pain, but his adrenalin was flowing and he went beyond the excruciating pain. Joshua kept earing back the hammer and squeezing the trigger as quickly as possible, pointing at wavy, fading, hooded shadows in front of him. He decided he would take as many as possible with him before he died, and he thought he saw some of the robed figures falling off their horses, but he wasn't sure. Joshua felt the life draining out of him. Heidi was screaming hysterically behind him. He became alert as she rushed for the door, and he shoved her back into the darkness again, taking yet another bullet into his body to protect her.

He saw the forms of men lying in the street and could tell several horses were running off with emptied saddles. The entire scene was surreal to Joshua Colt, and it took every ounce of his strength, determination, and faith to keep from going out fully. But he knew he had to protect Heidi.

He thought he saw four unmoving forms in front of him and some running away, when he knew it was over for him. Joshua started mentally reciting the Lord's Prayer as he felt the Colt Peacemaker slip off his finger, and he saw it hit the floor. He felt very strange, then, as he saw the floor rising up at his face, and he thought of covering his face but his arms wouldn't rise. Joshua felt the hard wood floor slam into his cheekbone and he heard a cracking sound. The sound made him grin; he tried to chuckle but it hurt his belly too much. Suddenly he got very worried about Heidi, and she appeared above him. He could barely make out her face, but he could tell she was crying and he felt her teardrops falling on his cheeks. He heard other footsteps and voices, and then he fell down a long slide into a dark room that got blacker and quieter. Then there was nothing.

Chris and Man Killer had been searching for two days after discovering the arrow buried to its fletchings between the two stands of trees. At first they checked all over the bottom of the cliff face for a body, but there was no evidence of one, or of any predators dragging a body off.

After checking the cliff bottom area fully, they checked the entire base area in case of wind gusts that could have pulled the body off to one side or the other.

Chris Colt and Man Killer had been

tracking and trailing for years, but this time they were totally puzzled. They wondered if the man or creature—or whatever it was—could have climbed down a rope, then climbed back up and made off, hiding his trail. But that idea was discounted by their diligent search on hands and knees up above.

The pair then started working out from the cliff in small arcs, sweeping back and forth, searching for any small sign. There was nothing.

Now, on the second day, they were sweeping out in arcs moving away from the arrow. They were still having no luck, but Chris Colt was determined to unravel at least this part of the mystery.

It was late afternoon and Colt was several miles to the northwest of the base of the peak and below the summit of Poncha Pass, a small ten-thousand-footer running up from Poncha Springs and Salida and connecting them with the San Luis Valley. Man Killer was several miles to the southwest of the peak. Suddenly, Colt heard the distant report of a gun, and he turned to see Man Killer fire a second shot in the air. A few seconds later, Man Killer fired another series of two shots.

Three shots fired in successions of three

was a universal warning signal for emergency, but the two and two was a prearranged signal that one of them had found something. Colt imitated the whistle of a red-tailed hawk and War Bonnet, cropping grass nearby, trotted to him. The marshal took the bridle off the saddlehorn and slipped it over the big horse's head, taking extra care around the sensitive ears.

Colt grabbed the saddlehorn with his left hand and swung up, his right leg swinging over the back as he landed firmly in the saddle. He kicked War Bonnet with the insides of his calves and the mount took off at a canter while Colt reached for the stirrups with each foot.

Ten minutes later, Colt slid to a stop in front of Man Killer and led War Bonnet by the reins as he walked forward and knelt down.

He looked at the ground and saw a faint impression of a very large foot. It was their Bigfoot—whatever it, or he, was.

Man Killer said, "Great Scout, if you had not taught me to trail, after first learning from the mighty Chief Joseph, I never would have learned to find this trail."

Colt looked carefully as Man Killer pointed back toward the direction of the backtrail. Colt stood and watched and could barely make out a path that came across the high meadow grasses. He walked back and saw where the person had carefully moved the grasses back into position, and by getting on his knees, he found what Man Killer had. The killer had straightened the tall weeds back into position behind him as he moved along, even wrapping some with adjoining weeds to make them stand up. After discovering a few tracks, however, an experienced tracker like Colt or Man Killer could actually look back and see a faint backtrail, unless the area was heavily forested. They stuck another arrow into the ground at the track Man Killer had found and carefully worked their way along the backtrail. The task took the rest of the day. That night they made camp nearby and resumed their search in the morning.

The first tracks they found had been covered over, but they found two footprints; at that point, it appeared that the creature had fallen to his knees and covered the knee impressions over.

They searched all morning but could find no other starting point except for this, which was several hundred yards out from the base of the cliff. Colt could not decipher this—and that was what always made him so dangerous on someone's trail.

Chris slowly climbed up in the saddle, saying, "C'mon, partner, he has covered the trail too well here. Let's go back to the arrow and follow the trail out."

Man Killer nodded and jumped up into the cavalry McLellan saddle on his mount, Hawk. The two men rode side by side at a mile-eating fast trot until they reached the arrow. Dismounting, they followed the covered-over footprints that led west across the San Luis valley. The trail led closer and closer to the main trail running along the valley floor, leading south past the Great Sand Dunes and branching off west toward Saquache (Sawatch).

Both men thought the same thing as they came closer to the trail. This creature's trail was going to run into and join the main trail, where it would become lost in the maze of tracks going in every direction. An hour later, they got the answer they expected—the creature's trail did, in fact, end at the main trail.

There was a curiosity, however. Frustrated, Colt dismounted and removed the bridle from his horse's head so that War Bonnet could graze. Colt started gathering wood and tinder to build a fire and make lunch. Man Killer kept walking the trail out.

Colt said, "I'm making lunch. My belly

thinks my mouth ran off and left it cause no food's come its way since yesterday, I think. We're going to have to head back."

Man Killer said, "Go ahead, but I want to make sure of each track."

Colt started making coffee and food when he noticed Man Killer veering off the direction of travel and heading toward a pile of small boulders. Colt reattached the bridle on War Bonnet and rode over to him.

Hearing him trotting up behind him, Man Killer, now at the boulder pile, said over his shoulder, "Look at this, Colt. The feather of the mighty eagle."

Sure enough, stuck between two rocks was the white- and brown-tipped tail feather of a bald eagle. Colt rode forward slowly and stared at the feather as Man Killer prepared to pull it out from between the rocks. Colt saw that the base of the feather was wrapped with yellow cloth in two places to hold it on. He saw a leather loop coming out from under the yellow cloth; a piece of braided horsehair string ran through this and was tied to it and went between the two rocks. This was holding it to the rockpile. Man Killer grabbed the feather and Colt's eyes opened wide.

He kicked War Bonnet in the ribs and the big paint lunged forward and Colt dived straight at Man Killer just as he started to pull on the feather. There was a loud blast from the rockpile a millisecond after Colt's shoulder slammed into Man Killer's ribcage and the two fell to the side of the pile. As they flew sideways, Chris felt something tug at his pants leg.

The two men lay on the ground, Man Killer trying to get his air back and Colt breathing heavily. Man Killer gave his elder a puzzled look and Colt grinned and stood up, helping the Nez Perce to his feet.

Colt said, "What does the color yellow mean in most tribes, especially wrapped around the base of a feather?"

Man Killer said, "It stands for a new beginning."

Colt said, "Yeah, like the beginning of walking the spirit trail."

He moved several boulders from the pile and pulled a sawed-off ten-gauge shotgun from the pile's interior. The twin triggers had been wrapped with the other end of the braided horsehair twine, which was still attached to the eagle feather.

Over coffee, beans, and hardtack, Colt examined the horsehair string and the shotgun and said, "Well, now we know what kind of creature we're facing, Man Killer. The most ferocious there is."

Man Killer said, "Oh?"

Colt responded, "A man—a mighty big one, a mighty tough and smart one, a crazy one. But still a man."

Man Killer said, "I would rather face a sasquatch than a man such as this."

Colt took a sip of coffee and said, "Me, too, my brother. Me, too."

Colt started unbraiding the string while Man Killer watched with interest. It took a while, but soon Colt had one of the strands apart. He held it up and examined it carefully. It was cinnamon red. He studied it more carefully and got a questioning look on his face.

Man Killer said, "What is it?"

Colt said, "Just a second."

He whistled like a hawk and both horses ran over to him and Man Killer. Colt patted War Bonnet's shoulder and petted him, working his way back to the long black and white tail. He held the hair from the string up next to the long tail of the sixteen-hands-tall horse and compared the length. Colt whistled.

He sat back down and Man Killer said, "That is from a very tall horse."

"Maybe twenty hands tall," Colt said. You've been in the horse business. What kind of horse would be that tall?"

Man Killer said, "A draft horse."

Colt said, "Very good. What kind of draft horse?"

Man Killer said, "Could be one of several kinds, but all the Clydesdales I have seen have been chestnuts and have all had white stockings and blazes."

Colt said, "Very good, my friend. At least now we know that our killer is a man the size of a grizzly, and he is so heavy he has to ride a draft horse. It is probably a Clydesdale, but it definitely is a chestnut."

Man Killer said, "He is also a red man, or knows a lot about my people. He is either Indian, or maybe a scout, mountain man, or trader."

Colt said, "A man that size would have to be seen and spoken about. He is too large. I have not heard red or white men speak of such a man. Will Sawyer was that size and people heard and spoke about him near and far."

"Except when he became a fur trapper and lived in the mountains," Man Killer said with a grin.

Colt grinned, too.

He said, "So we want a mountain man who is bigger than any other man we'll probably ever see, who rides a large red draft horse."

Man Killer said, "And who is very, very smart."

Colt said, "And touched in the head."

The two men rode south for two miles, then made camp in a grove of trees. They would head home at daybreak and probably arrive after dark the next day.

Quite a few miners and settlers traveled both directions on the road through San Luis Valley. Two of these, one headed north and one headed south, came directly to the night location of the two lawmen. The first was a brave of the Ute tribe. He approached the camp while the two men smoked and talked, and he raised his hand in greeting.

Colt said, "Come—sit and have a smoke."

The warrior nodded and dismounted. Both trackers eyed him appraisingly. He stood about six feet tall and weighed around two hundred pounds, most of that muscle and sinew. A large scar ran down across his left pectoral muscle, starting a few inches above the nipple and running all the way down his bare torso to the breechcloth he wore along with leggings. His dress, hairstyle, and pony markings showed him to be Ute.

Colt handed him a cup of coffee and he accepted sugar from Man Killer. The two friends grinned at each other as they watched the newcomer scoop spoon after spoon of sugar into the coffee. Colt then offered and lit a cigarette for the Indian.

Finally, the Ute spoke. "I am Horse-That-Runs-Through-High-Waters. My band lives beyond Wolf Creek."

Chris said, "My young brother is Man Killer of the band of the mighty Joseph of the Nez Perce. I am called Wamble Uncha—One Eagle—by the Lakotah. My white-eyes name is Colt, Chris Colt."

"It is you I have come to seek out, but I was told you lived across these mountains."

Colt replied, "I do, but I am here hunting."

The brave took a long drag on his cigarette, blew the smoke toward the fire, and said, "Does the mighty Colt hunt a monster that kills like the mighty bear, but is smarter?"

Colt and Man Killer gave each other questioning looks, then Chris said, "Did your tribe have a killing like that?"

The Ute warrior replied, "A man and woman of my band were lying with each other along the river of the Animas. It came upon them and killed them and ate some of the woman, but first it put its seed into her and tore her."

Man Killer said, "And the man?"

The brave said, "He was in pieces like the camp dogs tear apart the entrails of the elk."

Chris said, "Have you eaten?"

The Ute said, "No, I must return to my people. I was told to seek out the mighty Colt, because this is not a bear or any animal we know. The band of Ouray said the mighty Colt would find this killer of our people."

Colt said, "My brother, he is a killer of the white-eyes, too. This is not an animal but a man, but he thinks and acts like an animal."

The warrior said, "But man is more dangerous than an animal. He can think."

Man Killer raised his hand and the men didn't speak. It was now full darkness and hoofbeats approached. The three men faded back into the shadows.

A voice called out of the darkness, "Hello the camp! I'm friendly."

Colt said, "Tex, is that you?"

Tex Westchester, the salty old top hand for the Coyote Run, dismounted at the fire and poured himself a cup of coffee as the three came out of the trees. Tex sipped the coffee and eyeballed the Ute. "Howdy, youngster."

The Ute nodded.

Colt said, "Tex, why are you here? Is something wrong?"

"I should say, Colt. I come ta fetch ya two home quick. Yer brother went on down to Westcliffe and got hisself shot up bad, real bad. He saved the life a thet Widder Rosenberg and the Klan was there. He smoked a bunch afore he went down, but I'm sorry ta tell ya, Christopher, they plugged him aplenty."

Colt jumped up and whistled for his horse. He grabbed his saddle and the others followed suit.

Man Killer looked at the Ute and said, "We will come to your village soon. We'll find you."

The brave said, "It is a good thing," and walked into the darkness.

Joshua Colt lay still and unmoving when Chris and Shirley Colt entered the Canon City hospital room and looked at him. Chris went to his bed and sat next to him. Shirley held his big hand.

Chris leaned over and spoke into Joshua's ear, "Big brother, this is Chris. Your name is Colt. I want you to fight your way back. Don't give up, Joshua. I promise you,

I'll get them all, every manjack one of them."

Shirley leaned over and kissed Joshua's forehead and whispered, "We love you, Joshua."

CHAPTER 4
Law Enforcing

The area's reported leader of the Ku Klux Klan at that time was a big man named Brent Abraham. He stood six foot three in his stockinged feet and had been a black-smith for a number of years, but now owned a small dry-goods store in Canon City.

It was a day that would be spoken about often when Chris Colt, fists clenched, stormed up the main street of the small town and entered the dry-goods store. It had been rumored, but not proven, that the outspoken Brent Abraham had been the Klan leader. Apparently, Chris Colt wasn't worried about evidentiary process. He was out to avenge his brother's attack.

Shirley watched from the whitewashed porch of the hospital as her husband marched down the street. At first she wanted to stop Chris, but she knew better.

Her words would do no good, and she wanted this done, anyway. Many prominent citizens of Fremont and Custer counties belonged to the secret organization, including several deputies and a county commissioner. Most of the citizens in Fremont County had been waiting to see if Chris Colt would brace Abraham; it seemed the whole town was watching the big marshal storm down the street and enter the store.

A local rancher and bully named Bob Charney was with Abraham in the store; it was well known that Charney, too, was deeply involved in the Klan.

Everyone watched with bated breath as Colt entered the store. At first, nothing happened. Then there were several loud screams as Brent Abraham crashed backward through the window and somersaulted across the board sidewalk and sprawled in the street. Next, Chris Colt ran out the door with the shorter, but much stockier and barrel-chested Charney across his back. Charney had his vicelike arms wrapped around Colt's throat and his legs wrapped around the lawman's waist.

Charney was screaming, "I'll kill ya, ya nigger-lovin' sumbitch!"

Colt spun around and ran backward, slamming Charney's spine against a support post for the porch roof. The air left the rancher in a rush and he released his grip. Colt spun and hit him flush on the jaw with a right cross.

By this time, Brent Abraham had risen. He tackled Chris, collapsing his legs from behind. Colt's head hit the edge of the board sidewalk and he suddenly felt panic as he saw stars flashing before his eyes. He shook his head and tried to scramble to his feet but his elbows wouldn't support his weight. A foot crashed into his face and his head snapped back, but the incident seemed to set off an alarm in his head.

Colt suddenly became alert. The cobwebs were gone, for he knew if he went out now, he would die under the feet of these two Klansmen who had tried to kill his brother. He jumped to his feet filled with a killing rage, grabbing Brent's right-hand lead and yanking the man forward as he grabbed his lapels. Chris pulled on the man as he struck forward with his own forehead, viciously head-butting the man in the face. Abraham's head snapped back, his nose bleeding profusely, but Chris Colt's forehead was torn open from the head-butt and his own nose and mouth were bleeding freely from the kick. He knew his nose was broken and several teeth were loose, but he didn't care right now.

Bob Charney had his wind back, and he waded into Colt, fists flying. Chris, now unconcerned about strategy or odds, stood toe to toe and slugged it out with both men at once. He took two blows for every one he delivered, but he was grinning now with the thrill of combat. He knew his punches were taking effect, and he wanted to punish these men severely.

One left rocked Charney back on his heels as Colt ignored the blows from Abraham and stepped into the shorter man, raining five punches in a run that sent the rancher over a hitching rack in a heap. He then turned and faced Brent Abraham and grinned through a totally bloody face. Shirley was now standing at the front of the crowd. A woman next to her fainted at the sight of blood on Colt's face.

Brent swung a hard right and hit Colt right on the cheekbone, and Chris didn't even attempt to block the hit. He just smiled even more and walked forward. The Klansman hit him with a left and Colt kept coming. Abraham tried another right, but Colt blocked this one and the left that followed, and then he swung a hard uppercut three times in a row into Brent's solar plexus. The third one actually lifted the big man two inches off the ground. Colt just held the man's right arm with his own left while he punched him. Then he held him up as he smashed three right crosses into the side of Abraham's face. By this time, Chris could no longer hold the man up because he was out cold on his feet. So Chris let go and hit him once more as he fell.

Shirley screamed, "Chris!"

Colt dived as a bullet from behind tore the shoulder of his shirt. He hit the ground in a somersault and drew while rolling, landing on his back and rolling to his left as he fanned his right-hand gun. The second bullet tore half the face off of Bob Charney and the third and fourth bullets took off the man's left shoulder. From his eyes, Chris shook the dirt that he received from Charney's second shot, which hit right next to Colt's face.

While the crowd stared in wonder, the totally worn-out Chris Colt walked over to the prone body of Brent Abraham and grabbed him by the collar, dragged him face down to the manure pile that had been shoveled out of the next-door livery stable, and stuck the Klan leader's face on the pile of manure. Colt then shoved down on the back of his head with his boot, burying Abraham's head in the freshly shoveled manure.

Then Shirley calmly walked up to Chris and put his right arm around her shoulder and walked down the street as if this had been an everyday occurrence. What nobody noticed was that she had also wrapped her other arm around his waist and was using all of her strength to hold him upright as he walked. People just stared as the two walked back to the hospital. Once inside a private room, Colt's legs gave out and he collapsed in a faint.

That night, Shirley checked them into the McClure House in Canon City, a popular hotel. They ate in the restaurant and Chris was able to manage some oyster stew, but his mouth was sore and swollen. Both of his eyes were almost swollen shut and his nose had been broken again. But none of that bothered him. He felt so much more fortunate than his half-brother.

The pair were joined by their attorney and his wife, Brandon and Elizabeth Rudd.

Brandon said, "Chris, I have a very rough case coming up on the railroad war and was wondering if I could come out to the Coyote Run next week and get some boxing lessons from you?"

The two women and Chris started to

laugh, but Colt moaned from the pain, which only served to egg on the young lawyer, who suggested, "Maybe you could teach me some of those famous face blocks you do."

All of them laughed even harder, and Chris moaned even more in pain.

Brandon said, "I was going to order scrambled brains and eggs, but I see you've already done that."

Chris now really moaned with pain as tears streaked down his cheeks, the more he moaned, the more he and the other three laughed.

Still laughing heartily, Brandon turned to his beautiful wife and said, "Darling, I would recommend duck, but don't ask Chris about it. He obviously doesn't know how to."

Everyone laughed even harder and Colt held his sore ribs and moaned even more, which even brought on laughter from several eavesdropping guests at tables nearby.

Brandon kept his puns and jokes going unmercifully all through dinner, but over an after-dinner brandy, he got serious.

"Chris," he said, "I must warn you as your legal counsel that that stunt you pulled today could cost you your ranch. You just cannot go beating people up because you suspect them. You are no longer a chief of scouts. You are a deputy U.S. marshal. You must abide by the law as you are technically an officer of the court, duly sworn to uphold justice. I want your word that you will hold your temper in check over this matter and pursue it as a lawman."

"I love my brother, Brandon. We take care of our own."

"Your word?"

Colt relented. "I give you my word that I will try to watch my temper as best I can."

Several minutes later, Chris picked up the tab and the couple bid each other adieu. Colt stood and turned, coming face to face with Allen Sarver, the Fremont County sheriff's deputy, a known Klan member. The man gave Colt a half-grin and Chris turned, his face beet red, and looked at Brandon apologetically. Brandon put his hands up and shook his head no, but it was too late.

Chris whispered to Brandon, "Sorry," and spun, hitting the deputy sheriff with a left hook that sent him flying backward onto a table that fell over and landed on top of him as he lay unmoving on the floor.

Colt headed toward the door and handed

McClure a hundred-dollar bill and said, "Sorry. That's for damages and our meals."

They headed up to their room, where Shirley helped Chris out of his clothes while he continued to moan in pain. She held a washcloth on his forehead and smiled at her rugged-looking husband.

She said, "There's no middle ground with you, is there, Christopher Columbus Colt? You have to go full out, no matter what the undertaking."

"Maybe you'd be happier if I was a milk maid or a dandy from back East. Is that your game, dear?"

She bent forward and kissed his forehead and smiled, "Not hardly, Chris. I married a man, the man, and I am totally happy with you the way you are, pretty nose and all."

He grinned and moaned with the pain again.

The next day, Shirley awakened with a start. She had slept more soundly than she had in ages, probably because Man Killer and Jennifer were watching the children and taking care of the ranch. Chris was gone from the room, but she figured that he was out back taking care of the natural order. She stretched and yawned and wondered how Joshua was doing this morning.

Suddenly, Shirley heard a commotion out on the street below, and she jumped out of bed and ran to the window. She shrieked as she saw her husband, a large crowd following, walking down the street, fists clenched. He entered the dry-goods store of Brent Abraham. Seconds later, Abraham crashed through the unbroken part of the window and rolled out into the street.

Chris came out the door and met Brent with an uppercut as he was getting to his feet. The man went straight up on his toes, then tipped over backward.

Shirley wanted to run down the street, but she knew that Colt would not have appreciated it. She watched as Chris lifted the man up by the collar and punched him in the ribs, then hit him on the temple. Abraham reeled and Colt shoved him headfirst into the manure pile again. Abraham scrambled with his arms to get out of the dung, and in the process, literally covered himself with the odorous mess.

Brent sat up and looked at the mess all over his body. Colt walked over to him and lit a cigarito, blowing the smoke skyward.

Without looking directly at Brent, Chris said, "Heard the weather's real nice down in New Mexico or in Arizona. See you tomorrow, Abraham."

Brent scowled as Colt walked away and the man yelled, "What do you mean by that?"

Colt turned around and said, "We're going to go through this every day that you're in this area. Bet you Rudd, Macon, or McClure would buy that store off of you if you're selling it cheap. Like I said, see you tomorrow, Brent."

Chris Colt turned his back to the man, further insulting him by challenging him to try a shot, and walked back up to the hotel. Shirley quickly lay back down in bed and feigned sleep.

Chris walked in a minute later and promptly gave his wife a kiss on the forehead.

Colt said, "Honey, I appreciate your acting job, but I saw you watching from the window."

Shirley turned and faced him and began chuckling. "I didn't want you to think I was interfering. I worry about you, but I know you know how to handle these type of situations, and I trust your judgement."

"Well, I let him know I'm coming back every day to give him a whipping, so he'll either leave or try to shoot me."

"Either way, you'll win," she said, smiling.

Colt grinned at her as he washed off his bloody knuckles.

After breakfast, they went to visit Joshua and both spoke into his ears, although he was still unmoving and unresponsive. After that, they went to the mineral hot springs down along the Arkansas River, across from the penitentiary. Chris decided to soak his sore body. What he didn't tell Shirley, although she'd already figured it out, was that he was going to stay another night in Canon City and return to Abraham's dry-goods store in the morning. Because of Brent's involvement with the KKK, Colt figured he wouldn't be smart enough to try to use the law to help him and, like everyone else, probably thought that the law couldn't help anyway. Chris Colt's brother was dying and the legendary gunfighter was killing mad. Who in their right mind would brace him?

Colt had figured right anyway, for Brent Abraham had decided he had enough of Canon City, Fremont County, and the whole state of Colorado. He was packing his bags and was doing a lot of thinking about the lush green grass and pretty vistas in Montana. By late afternoon, he had already made a sale of his business to Anson Rudd, who picked up the building, inventory, and everything for ten cents on the dollar. Anson was the uncle of Brandon Rudd and was one of the original pioneer settlers of Canon City.

After the Colts finished at the mineral hot baths, they rented a buggy and rode to Four Mile Creek for a picnic lunch under the trees.

When they rode back toward Canon City about midafternoon, they ran into a horseman on his way out of town. It was Brent Abraham. Colt just stared at him when he rode by and Abraham dropped his head in shame and kicked his horse into a fast trot. After he passed, Chris and Shirley, not speaking a word, exchanged knowing looks.

That night, when they returned to the hospital, there was no change in Joshua's condition and the doctor was concerned that Joshua would never recover. The pair sat next to Joshua's bed for about an hour, then Shirley accompanied Chris out to the back veranda so he could have a cigarette. When they returned to the room, Heidi Rosenberg had just finished kissing Joshua on the forehead. She smiled at them through a veil of tears as she prepared to leave the room. They accompanied her outside.

In front of the hospital was a rented

buggy and a trunk along with several va-
lises, packed and ready to go. It was obvious that Heidi was headed somewhere on a
long trip. A hired driver standing against
the buggy was puffing on a corncob pipe.
Heidi and the Colts sat down on wicker
chairs on the front porch of the hospital
after Chris got them each a cup of hot tea.

Heidi was crying and visibly shaken.

Shirley placed a comforting hand on her
shoulder and Heidi sniffed into a hanky,
steeling herself for the conversation that
was to follow.

"I want to tell you both something," she
said, "and I'd like to ask that you both let
me finish what I have to say. Please?"

Shirley answered for both saying, "Of
course."

Heidi went on, "I am very much in love
with Joshua, and I know he feels the same
about me. Regardless of what the doctor
says, I know, beyond any doubt, that he
will pull through and will survive all his
wounds. And when he awakens I shall be
gone."

Chris started to say something, but she
held up her hand and said, "I asked to be
allowed to finish what I have to say."

"Sorry," he said.

She continued. "Chris Colt, I know you

can trail anyone, anywhere, at any time, but I shall ask you to give me your word as a man of honor that you will not track me down when I leave."

Again, he started to interrupt, but she went on, "I have thought long and hard about this matter, and I prayed on it even harder. I have the courage to be married to Joshua, and you know what he did to save my life. The problem is society. It will not change overnight, and I love Joshua too much to allow him to be in the position of worrying about my safety and risking his own just to be married to me. It is too difficult a task to ask of anyone, and I do not want that kind of burden on myself, either, knowing I have put him into such a position."

She took a sip of tea and Chris interrupted. "Don't you think that is Joshua's decision?"

"Yes, and I know he would choose to marry me without giving it a second thought," she replied. "That is why I am leaving, and I want your word that you won't follow, for I will cover my trail well, and you are probably the only man I know, excepting Man Killer, maybe, who could unravel it. There is absolutely nothing either of you can say to change my mind. It is firmly set after much deliberation, so please, as friends, respect my decision and cooperate with me."

Shirley and Chris looked at each other and sighed.

Colt spoke, "We'll sure miss you, Heidi. You have my word."

Her eyes again welled up with tears.

Shirley added, "And my word, but what about your house, your store, all your trade goods?"

Heidi replied, "I have a good bit of insurance money from my late husband's estate. I am leaving the store, the house, and all the merchandise to Joshua. He can hire someone to run the store, sell it all, or do what he wishes with it."

Chris said, "But it's so much money."

Heidi laughed, "Oh, pshaw. How could I ever pay Joshua for what he gave me? My life. The money doesn't mean a whit to me, anyway. I want him to have it all. I learned from Joshua before that young Rudd represents your family, so I hired him to transfer the titles and deeds. Everything now belongs to Joshua."

Chris said, "Are you sure?"

"Totally. I'll be leaving shortly on the evening train and will transfer at a city I have selected and will go several different directions by train, switching at different cities, and traveling under assumed names. Shirley, I have a favor to ask of you."

Shirley said, "Anything."

Heidi said, "I want you to speak privately with Joshua, so he doesn't have to hide his feelings like he will around his brother. Tell him that I'll always love him with all of my heart, but I never want to see him again. I will start a new life, and he should do the same. If he tries to locate me and is successful, I will leave immediately and hide again. I mean that. I do not want him, or any children we may have had, to experience even a little bit of what has happened already."

Heidi stood and hugged both of them. Tears filled the women's eyes.

Shirley said, "Godspeed, Heidi. I'm not sure I agree with what you're doing, but I certainly respect you for it."

Chris hugged her and echoed his wife's words.

He then escorted her to the buggy and helped her up into the seat next to the driver.

Chris held his hand up and said, "Please wait a minute."

He disappeared inside the hospital and reappeared a few minutes later. Colt carried Joshua's ivory toothpick with the miniature eagle head carved into its head. He handed it to Heidi and pulled Joshua's well-used, well-cared-for walnut-handled Colt Peacemaker.

Chris explained, "This toothpick was sticking out of his teeth the first time I met him, and is probably his most prized possession. The gun has been with him for years and will always be there to protect you. I know he would want you to have them both."

Shirley asked, "How do we let you know about Joshua recovering?"

Heidi smiled and said, "You needn't contact me at all. I know for sure that he'll recover and be fine and strong like before. Don't let anyone convince you otherwise."

Heidi looked at the toothpick and the gun, clutched them both to her bosom, and smiling while choking back sobs, nodded bravely at the driver. They rode into the night without her looking back. If she had, she would have seen Chris holding Shirley gently while she sobbed against his chest.

The Klan called an emergency meeting, in light of the events of the recent days, changing their meeting site from Red Canyon, north of Canon City, to Temple Canyon, southwest of the town.

Allen Sarver, the deputy sheriff, sporting a black and swollen eye, left his house on the afternoon of the meeting, several days after Heidi Rosenberg's departure. He went out to his small barn and saddled the red roan half-mustang/half-quarter horse that had served him so well. He did not spot the two pairs of eyes watching him from the patch of trees next to his house.

Sarver placed his robe and hood carefully in his saddlebags, tightened the girth strap, and mounted up. He went at a slow trot out of Canon City and was followed by a white man on a black and white paint horse and an Indian on a large black Appaloosa, its white rump covered with black spots.

Colt and Man Killer left their horses in an intermittent drainage coming down off the canyon walls and pouring into Grape Creek. There was a small pinion-filled bowl with some grass where rains had collected, providing graze and water for the two mounts that had been trained to remain for hours where they were left. In Temple Canyon, a rock-walled canyon that surrounded Grape Creek, there was an amphitheater-like cave that was used by Indians sometimes for religious ceremonies and had been used for secret meetings by the Klan and other groups. Grape Creek ran down from Westcliffe, originating in the Sangre de Cristos, oddly enough, near the Coyote Run, and it poured into the Arkansas River at the east end of the canyon below the Royal Gorge and just above Canon City. Part of Temple Canyon widened out with numerous cedar- and pinion-covered rocky hills that were constantly being carved and reshaped with each new storm and every winter.

The two lawmen had carefully considered this terrain, figuring they may be making a quick getaway and hoping to avoid capture.

When the meeting started, the former scouts watched for several minutes. They had already made their plans, so on a hand signal from Colt, Man Killer moved into position. It took him about fifteen minutes.

Each stepped out from the two corners of the natural amphitheater, Man Killer with a standard Peacemaker in each hand, and Chris holding a Colt revolving shotgun.

Chris Colt explained earlier that as much as he disliked what had happened that this was America and people were allowed to believe as they wish, no matter how stupid their beliefs might be. He did, however, want to issue a strong message to the local Klan on the shooting of his older brother.

Colt got everyone's attention by blasting the middle of the big pinion fire with his revolving scattergun. Man Killer brought attention to himself, then, by splintering one of the hot brands with a .45 slug. All the hooded men raised their hands.

Chris Colt said, "All right, gents, left hands, starting over here. Shuck your guns one at a time, carefully and slowly, and nobody will die."

The local Klan had already tangled with Chris Colt and nobody was in the mood to play hero, or to act even slightly courageous. The men, one at a time, unbuckled their gunbelts and dropped them on the ground. Man Killer then kicked them all into a pile and returned to his post.

Colt said, "Okay, friends, now, I have a problem with people who like to talk rough but are so ashamed they have to hide their identity. So now I want you all to remove the hoods and robes."

There was some hesitation and grumbling, so Colt blasted the fire again, then fed two shells into the shotgun.

"This greener here is in a bitchy mood and would like to spit lead at something other than your bonfire. Take them off now," Colt said.

Everyone quickly removed their hoods and robes.

Colt and Man Killer carefully took in every man in the crowd. They had at least seen most of them, and they knew some, like Sarver, pretty well.

Chris Colt said, "I may be coming to pay some of you a more personal visit when my brother gets better and identifies who dry-gulched him, but for now, understand something: If my brother dies, each and every manjack of you will pay for his death in spades. Now I am speaking to you not as a lawman but a loyal brother. When we leave, you are to make a decision. I don't care—toss a coin, draw straws—but you are to go to one of your spreads tonight and get the family members and hands out, move the animals, and burn the place to the ground. If you don't do this thing, Man Killer and I will handle the fire setting around here, and you won't believe what will go up in flames in one week's time. Now, if you don't like it, you can try to dry-gulch us, together or alone, and see what happens. You can try shooting it out with us or burning us out. In fact, please try it. We're both in a killing mood. When you're watching the place burn down, just think what's going to happen if Joshua dies or you ever bother my family again. I can hunt any of you down one at a time. Now, Sarver, you are a lawman and belong to this bunch, so tomorrow you will resign your job. Understand?"

Sarver nodded, the color drained from his face.

Colt said, "All of you, turn around and keep your hands up."

The Klansmen turned around and waited apprehensively, but one of them finally peeked over his shoulder and Chris Colt and Man Killer had disappeared. They retrieved the guns and were strangely silent. Two hours later, Sarver tried to choke back tears as he stood by the others and watched his house and barn burn to the ground.

He wasn't crying from sadness but from anger. No—from rage. He had never had to take water like this before and had already heard enough kidding and teasing about his shiner from Colt. He was killing mad, too. He was mad enough to make a try at Colt or Man Killer. And if he took some bullets, so what?

Sarver resigned the next day.

But two days later, he got his chance to

make his play. Sarver was positioned behind an abandoned sod house not far from the hospital. He had carefully tied a well-rested black bay mare that had some legs under it. It had been acquired—stolen, actually—when he arrested a horse thief a few weeks earlier with few witnesses. Most people knew he rode a red roan, so the horse would not be suspect. Today Sarver wore a bandanna over his face in case he was spotted, and he had a carefully planned escape route ready in his mind. He should not be spotted after he put a .50 caliber bullet through Chris Colt's back. He figured it would only take one shot, and they could drive a wagon train through the hole.

Chris had left Shirley at the Coyote Run and had ridden the train down to Canon City. His horse was left with a rancher near Cotopaxi and would be picked up on the return home the next day. He'd been trying to visit Joshua three days a week, although the doctor still held out no hope.

Colt disembarked from the train and was picked up in a buggy sent by Brandon Rudd. When the buggy pulled up in front of the hospital, Sarver would take his shot. It would be simple with the Sharps, he concluded.

Colt saw the now-familiar front of the

hospital as he approached its whitewashed veranda. The driver took him at a trot down the driveway and the famous gunfighter had no idea that the iron sights of a Sharps .50 were now leveled on the middle of his back.

Sarver felt his heart pounding in his temples and in the veins running along the side of his neck. He felt his chest heaving in and out and stopped himself, wiping the sweat from his eyes. He was excited. This was too easy. Slowing his breathing, he took careful aim again, and his finger started to squeeze the trigger.

Click! The gun behind him made a loud metallic sound as it was cocked.

He gulped as he heard the voice of Man Killer say, "Be very easy for me to shoot a white man that wears a white sheet."

Allen Sarver dropped the Sharps as if it were a red-hot coal and he raised his hands above his head. Eyes bulging with fear, he turned to stare into the smiling eyes of a triumphant Man Killer, carefully pointing his Peacemaker at the crooked ex-lawman.

Keeping his eyes on Sarver, Man Killer yelled, "Colt!"

He heard the buggy turn and run toward them.

Chris Colt hopped down from the buggy,

looked at the Sharps on the ground, and understood what had happened. The look he gave Sarver made the former deputy sheriff feel chills running up and down his spine, and he blushed after experiencing an involuntary shiver.

Chris said, "Thanks, young brother."

He turned to the driver and said, "Thanks. I'll walk over to the hospital when I'm done here."

Facing Sarver, Colt said, "Go ahead. Pick up the Sharps."

Sarver shook and said, "No."

Colt said firmly, "Pick it up."

Carefully, gingerly, the frightened man picked up the Sharps. Chris Colt stood with his arms crossed, purposely taunting Sarver to make a play.

Colt said, "Now, cock the gun."

Sarver hesitated, then complied.

Chris now said, "Okay, use it now while I'm facing you or leave this state forever. Your choice. You have one minute to decide."

Sarver thought about it. All he really had to do was raise the rifle and pull the trigger. Then he looked over at Man Killer.

Allen said, "What about him?"

Colt said, "Kill me and Man Killer will let you go."

Sarver rubbed his trigger finger and

thumb together lightly. His lip twitched, and he really wanted to head for the nearest outhouse as soon as possible. He squeezed the rifle stock and thought to himself that nobody could be that fast with a gun. His was already cocked. Then he started remembering all the stories he had heard about Chris Colt, and all the deeds he had witnessed firsthand. Next, he pictured the faces of many of the men he had seen after they had been shot and killed. Another chill ran up and down his spine and he really wanted to go and relieve his bladder—he was worried that it would let go in his trousers.

Colt looked at his pocket watch and smiled at the deputy. Suddenly, Allen Sarver dropped the Sharps on the ground and spat.

He said, "The hell with you."

With that, he dropped his hands and walked quickly to the grove of trees where his horse was hidden; he mounted up and rode away at full gallop. Colt and Man Killer watched him ride out of sight up the road toward Pueblo.

Man Killer said, "Good thing he did not try to shoot you, Colt."

Chris said, "That's for sure. All he had to do was raise that rifle and squeeze one off.

Man, am I dumb. I can't believe I gave him such an opportunity."

Man Killer smiled and said, "He would have died."

Chris said, "I don't know."

Man Killer replied, "I do."

Walking toward the hospital, Colt said, "Hey, why were you here, anyway?"

Man Killer said, "To see Joshua. I care, too."

Colt said somberly, "Yeah, I know."

The two men walked slowly into the hospital, grim looks on their faces.

Seated by Joshua's bed, they looked down, wishing he would say or do something—flutter an eyelid, twitch, anything. But still he did not move.

The doctor walked up and placed his hand on the oversized shoulder of Chris Colt, saying, "I'm very sorry, Mr. Colt, but I'm afraid it's hopeless. He'll never awaken."

Chris Colt's hand shot out in anger and his jaw clenched tightly. Realizing he held the doctor up on his tiptoes, having grabbed the man's lapel with his right hand, Colt relaxed his grip and let the man go.

Calming himself a little, he said, "Doctor, his name is Colt. He isn't going to die. In fact, he will live and recover completely. Understand?"

The doctor cleared his throat and Man Killer said, "Look!"

The three looked at Joshua, who still lay with his eyes closed. But he had turned his fist sideways and his thumb stuck straight up in the air.

The doctor said, "Well, I'll be."

Chris went to his brother's side while Man Killer gave the doctor a sarcastic look and laughed at him.

Colt said, "Joshua, I know you can hear me. I had to wait until you got to this point, so I knew you'd make it. Man Killer and I have to go after the rest of the men who shot you now. Shirley will be visiting."

The thumb barely moved at first, then pointed up weakly again. Chris grabbed Joshua's hand, and he felt his brother squeeze back just a little.

Chris felt a twinge of guilt, so he said, "Joshua, I'll be here in mind and soul, brother, but I have to go out. I have a bad killer on the loose, too."

Joshua squeezed his hand a little more firmly. Chris realized now that blood was indeed thicker than water. He knew that he loved his older brother; the fact that Joshua was half white and half black was immaterial, and if Joshua didn't make it he'd never be the same. Having Joshua squeeze his hand and give him the thumbs up told Chris all he needed to know. Joshua had in him that rare quality that Chris had—a hard-headed attitude to never quit even when only the slightest hope remained. Colt didn't know if it was something in their blood or just the way they were raised, but they were survivors and winners. Chris knew Joshua would be okay now. It would take a lot of time—and he wasn't anxious to tell him about Heidi—but he would survive.

Chris Colt left the hospital with Man Killer at his side. The two men had a major challenge ahead of them. They would continue their search for an insane, cunning, gigantic, brutal killer. A man who was more monster than human, who had the same knowledge of woodlore and tracking as Chris Colt and Man Killer.

They arrived back at the Coyote Run that evening and Man Killer went on to his ranch and his wife, just beyond Westcliffe. They planned to leave first thing in the morning, foregoing the Klan members for now and searching instead for the mysterious killer.

Colt had gone to the telegraph office in

Canon City on the first day he visited his comatose brother, wiring lawmen all over the state and in New Mexico, Kansas, and Wyoming. He'd received several replies about strange killings and animal-type mutilations. But still Chris could not figure out how the man descended from the overhanging cliff and almost disappeared, how he could kill and maim like a large animal, and how he'd acquired such expertise in covering his trail. Chris Colt was faced with his biggest challenge ever.

That evening, Colt and Shirley talked and made love long into the night, falling asleep, as usual, in each other's arms. Shirley was the first to doze off as Chris lay deep in thought, looking down at the classic face and shiny auburn hair of his beautiful wife, and softly stroking her hair. Finally, he fell asleep.

It was some time later that he heard the noise. His eyes opened and he listened again. Moonlight came into Colt's house from somewhere, but Chris couldn't identify the source. The main thing he was aware of was the noise. His mind automatically catalogued numerous sounds that he heard during each night. If the sound was a normal one that he had heard before, his subconscious would register it as a safe one and he would remain in a deep sleep. But if the sound was a strange one, all his senses would come alert.

Such was the case now. Chris Colt's hand slid slowly to his left toward the guns hanging on the back of his elk-antler valet, near the bed. He figured out what he had already programmed himself to do in such a case—move his hand slowly toward the guns; when he could get no closer, he'd reach out and grab one, cock it, and be ready to shoot.

He head another slight sound, then a voice in the distance. It was Joshua's voice and it was very faint.

Joshua said, "Why are you leaving me in my deathbed, brother? Pa was never around for me and now you aren't, either. What's wrong, Chris? Aren't we really brothers? Have you been all talk?"

Chris shook his head to clear the cobwebs and tried to figure out where Joshua's voice was coming from. His eyes snapped around the room from one spot to the next, but he spotted nothing.

Colt whispered, "Joshua, I'm sorry. I have to go after a killer. You are my brother."

Chris slid his hand toward the gun. It was almost ready to close around the grip, and he felt a little safer, a little more secure. Two more inches and the gun would be in his hand.

Something big and hairy grabbed his wrist and a monstrous-looking half-man/half-grizzly stood up by his bed, grinning at him. It had blazing yellow eyes and large fangs, like a bear.

Colt's heart jumped into his throat and he sat up as quickly as he could, almost screaming. Shirley sat up next to him and put her arms around his big shoulders. His chest was heaving in and out and his heart pounded as if he had been in a foot race up the side of the Sangre de Cristos. He looked all around the room and realized he had been dreaming.

"Chris, you've been having a nightmare. Are you okay?" she asked.

"Sure, honey," he said, "I guess Joshua's on my mind. I feel guilty leaving before he's better. If anything happens to him . . ."

She interrupted, "He's a Colt, remember?"

Chris smiled, "I guess you're right. I'm being silly."

He didn't want to tell her about the monster haunting him in his sleep. Chris Colt was everybody's hero—how could he let the one person he wanted most to protect know that something was scaring him? Scaring the heck out of him. This killer he was going after was different than any other quarry he'd ever hunted.

Chris and Man Killer made camp at the base of Hayden Creek Pass the first night and grazed their horses on a grassy knoll with high mountain gramma grass fed and watered by the mineral-rich soil overrun from Hayden Creek. They sat around the fire after dark, smoking and drinking coffee.

The heads of War Bonnet and Hawk both suddenly came up and one of them whinnied lightly. That was all it took. The two men quickly melted into the shadows, guns drawn.

A rider shouted from outside the firelight, "Hallo the fahr! I'm a-ridin' up friendly-like and could use a coffee, ya'll."

Chris Colt yelled from the blackness of the night, "Keep your hands where we can watch 'em, stranger, and approach slow."

The man came forward and Chris Colt immediately recognized him as Rowdy Cobbs, a cowhand and member of the local Klan. Rowdy dismounted and walked up to the coffeepot while still holding his reins. He burned his fingertips on the pot then gingerly poured out a cup of coffee and gently sipped from it. Colt and Man Killer approached the fire. The three sat on logs.

Chris Colt took several sips of coffee and Man Killer followed suit. It was Rowdy Cobbs's call—they would wait for him to speak on his own.

After he finished half of the second cup, Rowdy spoke, "Mistah Colt, I been trailin' ya evah since ya'll left the valley."

Colt said, "Yes?"

Rowdy went on, "I heerd thet you was gonna hunt down and kill every man who was involved of the dry-gulchin' a yer brother."

Colt said, "Go on."

Rowdy said, "Well suh, I am ashamed ta say thet I was involved right in there amongst 'em all. I was a member of the Klan on accounta thet was how I was raised back ta home. But I'll tell ya somethin', suh. I don't care what color yore brother is, he went down a real man. I mean ta tell ya, they was everybody there a-shootin' at him, and he coulda ducked easy back into the store, but all he cared about was protectin' his woman. Now, I ain't no hero, but I ain't no no-account, neither. I don't hold none with how that was handled, but I won't die like a dandy. I'll die with my boots on. I come ta face up to ya suh, man to man. I know ya can outgun me, but I plan to try ta plug you first. If you'll jest give me a fair draw agin ya, suh, thet's all ah ask."

Chris sat there and gave a little whistle. He poured Rowdy another cup of coffee.

Finally, Chris spoke. "Mr. Cobbs, number one, I'm a lawman. I am not hunting down every man involved in that shooting to kill them. Number two, I believe in America with all my heart. I don't agree with a lot of things that a lot of people say or believe, but I'll fight to the death to defend anyone's right to say or think what they want. I respect you for the way you just handled yourself. You sound like you're a man who learned a lesson and who casts a good-sized shadow when you walk. If I remember, you have a wife and son. Correct?"

"Yes, suh," he said, "I do."

Colt continued, "Well, you ought to have a cigar with us and another cup of coffee before you ride home to them. They'll be worrying about you, won't they?"

Rowdy smiled and nodded as Colt handed him a cigarito and Man Killer refilled all the coffee cups.

CHAPTER 5
The Real Trail

The next morning was misty and Chris and Man Killer both had a strange feeling as they rode up above the mist and looked down below at the top of a cloud. They crossed over the Sangre de Cristos and dropped down into the San Luis Valley, spooking a large harem of elk in the process. They headed south down the valley road from Poncha Pass and stopped at the spot where they had found the eagle feather.

He had returned and left them another message that sent a chill up and down Chris Colt's spine.

There was a piece of brain-tanned leather rolled up and inserted into the rocks where the shotgun had been hidden. Before approaching the pile of rocks, however, Colt and Man Killer scoured all the possible areas where someone could be hiding with a rifle. Chris didn't believe, though, that the man they were after would ambush them like that. It just didn't seem to fit.

They carefully poked all around the piece of leather to check for any booby traps, but there were none.

Man Killer unrolled the buckskin and Colt looked over his shoulder. There was writing on the hide in charcoal.

It read: *"Qu'en un lieu, qu'en un jour, un seul fait accompli tienne jusqu'à la fin le théâtre rempli."*

Man Killer and Colt gave each other queer looks and shrugged their shoulders. The young Nez Perce rolled up the hide and tucked it into his saddlebags.

They mounted up and went on toward the southwest. Both men kicked their horses into a trot wanting to ride away from that scary pile of rocks as if it was haunted. After ten minutes, Man Killer finally said, "What are your thoughts, great scout?"

Colt said, "I'm scared, partner."

Man Killer laughed and gave Colt a sidelong glance.

The Nez Perce said, "You joke?"

Colt said, "No, friend, I'm as serious as a sky-pilot on the Sabbath."

Man Killer said, "I am scared, too."

Colt said, "I'd be worried if you weren't.

This man's a monster, and he's got a brain, too."

"He is playing with us, like we are little boys," Man Killer offered.

Colt replied, "Yes, he is, but at some point, we'll get tired of the game."

It was on the other side of Saguache and some hours later that the pair came upon a large herd of cattle being pushed across the big valley. The cattle were all Herefords in good condition. Colt guessed they probably hadn't been driven very far.

The two lawmen rode up to the point rider and stopped; all three brushed trail dust off their clothing.

The rider said, "Howdy, Marshal. You must be Colt from across the range?"

Chris said, "Yep, and this is my deputy, Man Killer."

The rider said, "The hell you say. I wouldn'ta guessed thet, pardner. Jest mebbe the fact thet everyone every week tells stories 'bout the great Chris Colt and the great Injun Man Killer and all the things you two have did. I'm right surprised ya ain't eight foot tall, each of ya."

Chris gave Man Killer an embarrassed grin and shifted in his saddle a little. One of the flankers rode up from the east and pulled the bandanna down from his mouth and nose. With a windburned face and lean frame, he had brown eyes set wide apart and between them a hawklike nose. His brown hair peeked down from under the headband of his sweat-stained Stetson, and his drooping moustache belied the accent that emerged from his lips.

Slapping the dust from his jeans, he said, "Sacre Bleu, Cord, why do you stop here?"

Colt said, "Mister, maybe you can help me. I take it you're from France?"

The man tipped his hat and said, *"Mais oui. Do you know Alsace or Lorraine? N'est-'ce pas?"*

" 'Fraid I don't," Colt said, "I'm from these parts but I have a note that is written in French, and I need it translated."

Cord, the point drover, chuckled and said, "Wal, Marshal Colt, ya know ya done come to the right party, ya know."

Chris said, "What do you mean?"

"Wal, ole François here, wal he was a per-fessor at the Sorebones," Cord replied, "Or what the hell is thet place called, Frenchy?"

François replied, "It was at the Sorbonne in Paris."

Colt looked at Man Killer and grinned, "I swear I have met Civil War generals, doctors, lawyers. If you wait long enough you will meet every kind of man in the world who has become a cowboy. I swear, one day I think I'll meet a cowboy who used to be president."

Cord added, "You mayn't a heerd a Applesauce or thet gal Lorain, but I bet ya have heerd a Sorebones or whatever."

Colt said, "Yes, I have, and I'm impressed."

He rode up to the French-born cowpuncher and offered a handshake.

Colt said, "Howdy, I'm Chris Colt, and this is my partner, Man Killer."

François bowed his head and said, "I am honored, messieurs. I have heard of you both. Beaucoup. My name ees François Belvoir."

Colt and Man Killer both shook with him and Chris then dismounted, digging the hide from the saddlebag. The others dismounted as the herd milled and fed on the lush, high-mountain gramma grasses. The four men spoke for a little while as several other riders rode up and joined the group. All present rolled and lit up cigarettes, speaking briefly about range conditions, new developments in the cattle industry, and the latest gossip. The big news was the upcoming Fourth of July celebration in Dodge City, Kansas. The cowboys were very enthused because there was going to be a

Mexican bullfight and then a horsestakes race, shooting matches, roping contests, and rodeo events. They were also excited because there was even going to be a baseball game and ten thousand dollars in cash prizes.

Finally, François got to the skin and smiled as he read it.

Colt said, "What does it say, François?"

The former educator said, "Eet ees a quote, Marshal Colt, from a French writer named Nicolas Boileau. Eet means, 'Let a single completed action, all in one place, all in one day, keep the theatre packed to the end of your play.' "

Again, Chris Colt felt a tingle run up and down his spine. A coldness ran through his body, and he knew he was afraid, genuinely afraid. Chris Colt had never before been confronted by an enemy like this.

That night, lying curled up in his bedroll, he awakened with a start and felt himself breathing heavily and sweating profusely. He lay there thinking back many years to his teenaged adventures. He had run away from home in Cuyahoga Falls, Ohio, a town near Akron, and joined the 171st regiment of the Ohio National Guard. He was assigned as a scout with Company G, after lying to everyone about his age.

Young Chris Colt proved himself to be the most courageous man in the unit, and he learned tracking very quickly. His best asset was figuring out what enemy soldiers were doing or planning by reading the signs and figuring out the entire story, including the tactics they were employing.

It was the summer of 1863, and his unit was fighting against members of the Tennessee Volunteers. The action took place in the Great Smoky Mountains along the border of Tennessee and North Carolina.

The very young Corporal Christopher Columbus Colt and his squad of five other young scouts had penetrated deep behind enemy lines. They didn't do this on purpose, but had been cut off after their initial penetration into enemy territory, so Colt asked each man if he was willing to go even deeper in order to find the total enemy strength in the area and the location of reserves, ammo packs, and so on.

That was a silly question, for the young Union soldiers would follow their courageous leader just about anywhere. He had demonstrated natural leadership traits on numerous occasions, had saved several of the squad members, and had helped several with personal problems. As a soldier, he asked no quarter and gave none in battle, and no one had ever seen him recoil from any situation, no matter how grave.

They had traveled up through a meadow filled with mountain laurel, seeking a better lookout view and hoping for a safe way back to Union lines. They had written several pages of detailed information about the Confederate forces and they needed to get it to their generals. Making the approach up the incline, Colt had no way of knowing that some of the Tennessee Volunteers had been placed on that mountaintop as an advance guard for a regiment moving into the area the next day. Because it was the highest vantage point around, their troop commander figured that any blue-bellies coming into that part of the mountains would try for the top, so they could also survey the whole area. That commander was right, and Chris Colt was wrong.

As usual, Chris rode point at the front of the rest of his men since he was approaching an unknown location. The fifty-six Johnny Rebs on the mountaintop heard the Union patrol coming long before they emerged from the trees, because there were rocks here and there on the slope poking up through the grasses and flowers, and the horses could not help but scrape shoes on them.

The commander had his men hold their fire as Chris rode up almost to the crest, then started circling just below it, not wanting to skyline himself or his men. When the entire patrol was in the midst of the killing zone, the ambush was sprung and Colt's patrol went down almost immediately in a hail of withering gunfire. Instead of running away, however, Chris Colt wheeled his horse and charged straight at the shooters, his head down low along the horse's neck.

He aimed his single-shot Springfield at the closest soldier and shot him through the heart. One bullet tore into his own left breast and exited the back, tearing a big hole in his shoulder muscle as it mushroomed out his back. Chris Colt weaved back and forth in the saddle and tears came into his eyes as he saw all his fallen friends with bullets riddling their bodies. Then he heard the cry of James Caliper, a sixteen-year-old private from Coshocton, in southeastern Ohio.

Colt immediately skidded his horse to a halt after charging past the ambushers, tearing right back at the Rebs as he saw the wounded James Caliper standing up by the body of his dead chestnut mare. The Confederate soldiers, in awe at this sight, stopped firing and stared as Colt jumped the makeshift log bulwark and reached out his good hand to his fallen comrade. Without slowing the horse, Colt leaned forward as James gripped his right forearm, and Colt grasped James's in the same manner. Colt let the force of his motion and speed swing James up behind him, and he raced toward the nearby trees. The twice-wounded Coshoctonite leaned his head against Colt's back and wrapped his arms tightly around his waist.

They charged into the trees as Colt heard the Rebs open up again with a fusillade of gunfire. He felt James flinch against his back once, twice, three times, then heard his comrade moaning in pain. James had taken three more bullets meant for Chris Colt into his body. The scout leader felt James's grip weaken around his waist, and he reached down and grabbed the young man's wrist with his good hand. Chris gritted his teeth as he tried to hold the reins with his left arm, although his own shoulder was gravely wounded.

Next, the horse flinched as he took a bullet through the flank, but the game steed ran on.

James Caliper whispered weakly into

Colt's ear, "I'm a goner, Chris. Save yourself."

Colt said, "Don't worry, James. We'll make it."

Just then, they started down a steep grade and ran straight into another Confederate patrol heading uphill. At first, they took the Rebs by surprise as they busted through, but then the shooting started. Suddenly James grabbed Chris Colt's right hand and pried the fingers off of his own wrist.

With a quiet, "So long, Chris," James Caliper threw himself off the fast-running horse and hit the ground rolling like a limp rag doll.

Chris Colt had tears running down his cheeks as he looked back at his dead comrade. He felt the horse start to falter, so he reached back into his saddlebags with one hand and pulled out the intelligence notes he and his men had written. He felt the horse flinch again as a bullet creased its rump and stung across Chris's right buttock as well. Colt stuffed the papers down the front of his tunic.

They were again hidden by a wall of trees, but the ridge now went steeply downhill. Colt pointed the horse's nose that way and leaned back as far as he could, his back hitting the horse's rump.

They came into another group of soldiers and more shots rang out as they approached a steep drop-off. Colt felt the horse take a hard hit and the gelding went up into the air, straightening his legs as blood spurted out of his nostrils.

The horse went limp in mid-jump and fell to the mountainside in a rolling mass, as Chris Colt flew out into space over his head. He saw a mass of branches coming at him, and he crossed his arms and hands over his face while he tucked his head and shoulders forward. He crashed through the branches and soared out over a cliff, spotting a small pond far below. He cycled his legs and waved his right arm for balance as he fell and fell.

Colt splashed into the cold water and felt himself plunging deeper and deeper. He kicked hard with both legs and slowly let air out as he went toward the surface. He broke the water's surface and gasped for air. No soldiers appeared above yet, so he kicked for the fern-covered hillside next to the pool and carefully crawled into the thick growth. Colt lay on his back among the ferns, panting heavily. Then he tore several fern leaves off their stems and plugged up the bullet hole in his shoulder.

He quickly pulled out a cartridge from his ammo pouch and pulled it apart with his teeth. He poured the gunpowder into both sides of the shoulder wound and gritted his teeth against the pain. He struck a match and lit the powder on front and back. The powder burned quickly and he could smell his skin burning and wanted to scream out in pain. But he had to block it out and hope that no soldiers had made it through the trees and brush to the cliff above yet. The thick fern growth filtered the black cloud of smoke somewhat, but it was still visible. Fortunately for Colt, though, nobody appeared.

He had to come up with an immediate plan, because he knew that Confederate soldiers would soon be searching every twig and bush, looking for him.

Luckily, he was still clearheaded; fainting or weakness from loss of blood hadn't affected him yet. The flaming gunpowder cauterized the wound, but for now, he would have to deal with a great deal of pain. But he was glad for that, for the pain helped to keep his head clear.

Chris looked back at the pond and saw the floating corpse of his dead mount, and thought also of his lost friends. He choked back a sob. He could not cry now or scream in pain. He had to survive. He came up with a plan.

Everyone would comb the mountainside looking for him, and they would definitely find him. Colt realized that the enemy commander was smart enough to hide his troops on the mountaintop, so he would be smart enough to send a blocking force quickly down the mountain while they made an orderly search of every shrub, tree, and depression all the way down.

So Colt's plan was simple yet daring. He would start climbing immediately, reasoning that the search would start at the pond. He could climb all the way back up the mountain and hide in the heavy cover near the command post—nobody would ever think he would be crazy enough to do that. It was too bold and too daring. It was also the only chance he had for survival.

Chris Colt started back up the mountain, trying to seek out every available route with deep or thick cover. He found a brush-choked ravine that ran alongside one of the steeper ridgelines, and he inched his way upward.

He was amazed at the number of soldiers dispatched to look for him. His condition only allowed him to crawl five or ten minutes at a time, but he'd have stopped, anyway, to avoid patrols moving down the mountain. The sounds of men coming down next to his thicket were many and varied, and Colt worried constantly about discovery and capture. He was feeling much weaker, and the higher he climbed the worse he felt.

He made it to the top after a two-hour climb. There, he found the thickest part of the crest to hide in—a dense laurel thicket. The hardwoods around the thicket were draped in poison ivy, but Chris Colt, who was not allergic to the triple-leafed plant, crawled right through, freezing in place several times as soldiers walked nearby.

Inside the thicket, Chris curled up in a ball and slept, listening to the sounds of the enemy soldiers walking all about him. Some time during the night, weary and very weak, he opened his eyes at the sound of thunder. Rain started falling, drops splashing in his eyes and soaking his uniform. But he felt distant from what was happening, and he drifted back to sleep, awakening hours later to a hot, dry late afternoon. Though he was still weak, he felt more normal than before, and realized that he must have been delirious. The storm had occurred during the night and he thought he remembered awakening several times during the day and night. His wounds ached horribly, and he was hungry and thirsty.

Colt risked sitting up and peering through the foliage. Only a squad had been left behind—the rest of the Confederates seemed to be gone. A gray-bearded old sergeant was in charge of the remaining squad; Colt admired the way the man moved and spoke to his men. They seemed to jump up to please him whenever he quietly bade them to do any chore.

Chris watched the men cook and eat dinner and he almost went crazy keeping himself from crawling out and stealing the food out of their hands and grabbing their canteens.

Just after dark, he decided he had to make a try for some food and water. He waited and watched carefully until the one man left at the cooking fire seemed to doze off. The others had apparently gone out on ambush patrols, or perhaps to their night sleeping positions back in the trees.

Colt crawled forward, carefully, slowly until he heard hoofsteps approaching. Just outside the light of the cooking fire, he had no where to turn or hide, so he froze in place and barely breathed. Someone behind him, in spurs, dismounted and walked toward him. He saw the shadow as the man passed within five feet of his fully exposed position and walked up to the coffeepot, pouring himself a cup. The other soldier at the fire slept on, sitting up, while this private drank his coffee and grinned. Colt could not believe he had not been spotted, but apparently he was just a shadow or a log in the man's peripheral vision.

He waited and held his breath again as the man poured out the last of his cup of coffee and returned to his horse, slowly riding off into the darkness. Colt made note of the horse, a magnificent buckskin gelding about sixteen hands tall who looked like he had bottom to him. Chris listened intently turning his head to see which way the rider rode.

Colt slid forward and made it to a canteen, which he looped over his shoulder. He grabbed an empty feedbag and filled it with biscuits and fried ham slices. Colt then dragged himself back into the thicket, stopping occasionally to try to wipe out the drag tracks he'd left. Satisfied with his quick and expedient efforts, he went quickly into his lair and ate like he had never eaten before. It was, to him, the best food he had ever tasted.

As he drank the last drops from his stolen canteen, Colt heard footsteps approaching from behind, and he froze as the steps got closer. They stopped right behind him, and he heard a low-voiced chuckle.

Young Colt rolled over slowly as the voice said, "Good idea. Nice and slow."

Chris looked up at the smiling face of the bearded old sergeant. The man stuck a cigar in his mouth and lit it, tossing another to the wounded Union scout. Chris nodded and smiled weakly, tucking the cigar into his tunic pocket.

The sergeant suddenly hollered, "Boys, I want y'all ta strike camp and saddle up! We've wasted enough tahm! We're movin' out!"

Another voice from near the fire yelled out, "Watcha doin' over thaer, Top? Ya need help?"

The sergeant yelled, "Naw, jest passin' mah water an havin' a smoke! Saddle up! Don't come this way nohow! This place is crawlin' with poison ivy!"

The sergeant looked down at the shocked capturee and said softly, "Young un. Been watchin' ya from the git-go, and yer jest too damned brave to go to a prisoner-of-war camp. Yer probably gonna go under anyhow, but ya need an even break, at least. Enjoy the cigar."

With that, he turned and went to his men, hearing Chris's voice behind him saying, "God bless you, sir."

As soon as the squad moved out, Chris Colt dragged himself to the dampened cooking fire and found there another filled canteen, a cigar, a bag of flour, and a side of bacon. He took a long drink, then leaned against a log and lit his cigar.

Chris Colt developed a real fondness for cigars that day and an understanding of the mutual respect that exists among men of honor and courage, even when they are enemies.

Tonight he lay in the Sangre de Cristos, eyes open, still rolled up in his bedroll. He quietly moved the blanket back and sat down by the dying embers of the fire and looked up at the clear Colorado night sky. He pulled out a cigar and lit it and, smiling, thought back to that night long ago.

Man Killer's voice penetrated the night, "You are restless, great scout, because we face a mighty enemy?"

Colt said, "Yeah, my brother. I think we're going to get bloody on this trail."

Man Killer said calmly, "You do not fear the blood. You fear the unknown?"

Colt replied, "Very much. Does that bother you?"

Man Killer rolled out of his bedroll and walked to the fire himself. He added a few sticks and blew on it, causing little flames to spring up. He accepted a cigar himself and the two sat smoking for a while.

Finally, Chris said, "You didn't answer."

Man Killer smiled, "The question was not worthy of an answer. You taught me that all men fear. Real men face that fear. You have always done that. That is why I follow you. Your question was stupid."

Colt chuckled at Man Killer's straightforward answer and his own silliness. The Nez Perce was right. Colt was scared but that meant nothing, for he would face the unknown, and his fear, and he would conquer them both. He thought of his brother and the fear Joshua must have felt when he was being riddled with bullets. The thing was, though, that Joshua had kept shooting. He was a Colt. Chris smiled.

Man Killer said, "You think of your brother and his courage?"

Colt nodded.

Man Killer said, "He is also your father's son."

Chris said, "That he is."

They finished their cigars and went back to their bedrolls. Chris finally fell asleep.

In the morning, they slept until the sun was already an hour in the sky. They ate a leisurely breakfast and saddled up. As soon as they started to ride southwest they noticed writing on a flat rock along the trail. They galloped over to it and dismounted. They read it and gave each other startled looks. A red sandstone rock lay at the base of the flat basaltic rock. Little flecks of red dust lay on the ground near the worn edge of the little stone that had been used as a writing instrument.

The message read:

Colt, Francis Bacon said, "I do not believe that any man fears to be dead, but only the stroke of death."

There was an eagle feather attached to a nearby bush; Man Killer checked it carefully before removing it. The two men looked thoughtfully at the plume, but their thoughts were not about birds of prey.

Without speaking a word, the two vaulted into their saddles and rode on. When they were a mile off, ten feet from the bush where the feather had been tied, the ground opened up and a huge hairy creature sat up, dirt spilling off the Indian blanket covering his massive body. He stared at the backs of the disappearing lawmen with a blank look, but in his mind he was finally feeling some excitement.

These two were mighty warriors and when he eventually ate their hearts, as he'd eaten the others, he would gain even more strength and power. For now, though, the challenge would make him start to feel more alive. Making a kill had become boring, but he felt himself becoming stronger with each heart he ate.

When he took the female ones he would feel some carnal excitement, especially when they screamed, but the kill was always too easy.

Eagle Bleu was a huge man, standing almost seven feet in height and weighing well over four hundred pounds. All those who had seen him were now dead—except for Joshua Colt and just a handful of others. But most of them had only had fleeting or distant glimpses.

His grandfather had been a fur trapper for the Hudson Bay Company and his father was a mountain man who attacked wagons going west over the Rockies, sacking the wagons, raping the women, and killing the witnesses. He filled his spacious hidden home with treasure from all the wagons he raided, stealing every item that could be carried.

Eagle Bleu's mother was a deaf-mute Chippewa woman who was simply a possession to be used at the whim of the father and, later, of the son.

A huge baby, Eagle had been born with the umbilical cord wrapped around his neck, cutting off oxygen to his brain and causing irreparable damage that was further aggravated by his father's continuous abuse. Eagle's pa decided that if he was stuck with a kid, the lad would learn to be tough and take care of himself from the start, and would bring in riches as soon as he was able to. When the giant of a boy reached his teenaged years, his father had his own mother teach him about sexuality. From then on, the woman was used for Eagle's personal gratification or for his father's, whenever either wished.

The boy was called Eagle from the beginning, and when he was old enough to understand, and the opportunity arose, he was shown why. His father and he were on a high alpine ridgeline scouting for victims when they came upon an eagle clutching a snowshoe hare in its powerful talons. Blood streamed down the animal's side and the eagle was just landing on the edge of its aerie. There were no eaglets at that time. The eagle tore the animal apart bit by bit and ate it, while Eagle's father pointed out how it would swoop down on its prey and take what it wanted, anytime it wanted. He also pointed out the power and sharpness of the talons and the beak, and how the eagle used them to tear its victim to pieces. That was the reason, he explained, that the boy was named Eagle.

When Eagle was around five years old his father handed him a crude spear and a sharp Bowie knife and told him that he would catch and kill his own food from then on. Any days that he didn't, he would go without food.

Once, when he was eight, the father caught Eagle's mother giving him food because the boy hadn't eaten since the previous day. The father beat the woman so unmercifully that she almost died and could hardly move around for weeks, though she was still expected to keep up with all her chores. Her injuries were so bad that she almost drowned while going into her home one day.

Their home was a giant cavern above timberline in the San Juan Mountain range of Colorado. The main entrance was an underwater cave in a glacial lake; there were two other entrances that required hard climbs in and out of large boulder fields. Most often it was easier to dive underwater and swim into the cave.

Oddly enough, the giant cavern was very well insulated, because the French-Canadian killer stacked the numerous books he had stolen over the years against the rock walls and created a wall of paper. When Eagle was not hunting food or helping his father raid wagon trains or miners' camps, he was reading. He taught himself to read, and then read everything he could get his hands on—classics, dime-store novels, the Bible, the Koran, magazines, newspapers. He could read and speak in both French and English and had a good working knowledge of several other languages by the time he was a man.

When the boy was in his mid-teens, his father, by now going crazy from alcohol abuse, began to indoctrinate him into cannibalism. The father told the giant teen that some Indians had learned to steal an enemy's soul and strength by eating his heart. When Eagle tried this on the next family they killed, he found it stimulating for him—but so far, he'd never had an experience that made him feel deep emotion.

Eagle, who had no conception of right and wrong, decided one day to kill both his parents and eat their hearts—he'd been bored, as usual, and had read everything in the walls of the home, and in the winter it was hard to get out of the alpine mansion. So he killed both of them with his Bowie and ate their hearts.

After that, the killer had given up stealing, for the years of looting and pillaging had already filled his mountain home with treasures. Now he just concentrated on killing his victims, using the strategies his father had taught him to make each attack look like it had been done by Indians. But eventually most of his killings appeared to have been done by wild animals, usually bears. In some cases, Eagle made it seem that animals had attacked, but sometimes the murders were so gruesome, that they appeared to be the maulings of a mighty beast.

Chris Colt was a new prey. He was different. Maybe he could provide some stimulation for the killer. Eagle had seen Colt sometimes in the mountains, always from a distance and he had once seen Man Killer. But he had read about both of them and sometimes heard of them when he was scouting new prey to kill.

Eagle had taken to killing more Indians than whites because many more of them seemed to have the warrior spirit, and their hearts would give him great strength. Chris Colt was a mighty warrior, though, and was spoken about in the lodges of many tribes and in white man's towns, too. If he could eat Colt's heart and Man Killer's too, he would be much stronger.

But he wanted them to at least challenge him before he took their hearts; they could make him feel the kill more strongly. He would challenge their minds and test their tracking skills.

And when he had terrified them and baited them enough, he would finally experience the small, exciting feeling of the terror he saw in the eyes of his prey before the kill.

He remembered one victim, who had been traveling for months with his family from the coast of Maine. Though his own eyes were filled with fear, he recognized the look in the eyes of Eagle Bleu. Some people had an evil look in their eyes, sometimes even a satanic look. But the man from Maine knew the look in the eyes of Eagle Bleu—he'd seen that same look many times in the eyes of sharks. It was a deep, vacant, emotionless look.

In the giant cavern, Eagle Bleu had stripped off his clothes and painted the talons of an eagle on his face in red war paint. He painted red stripes on his body and danced naked for hours, his body casting eerie shadows on the stacks of books all around the cave. He then went out into the San Luis Valley to give Colt clues and lead him to where he wanted the lawman to go. The kill would be made in the wilderness, in the mountains, but first there would be other kills, and more intimidation.

Eagle watched as the two scouts dropped out of sight, and he got out of the small hole he had buried himself in. He would cut them off when the time was right, but for now he would travel toward Wolf Creek Pass but wander a little west, to see the two on the other side of the pass.

Eagle lifted his Sharps .50 and took off at a mile-eating trot, as he done since childhood. He would run in a westerly direction for the six miles to the spot where his horse was left in the foothills. Then he would alternate between riding and jogging, leading the big draft horse toward the southwest. He didn't get off the gelding because he was concerned about the animal—he had run since childhood and preferred traveling that way. And it didn't take much to figure out that no horse would last very long with a rider of his size on its back.

Meanwhile, as they trotted across the southwestern end of the San Luis Valley, Chris Colt and Man Killer once again gave each other strange looks. Finally, Man Killer voiced what they both had been thinking, "Do you feel like we are being watched?"

Colt grinned, "You, too, huh? I felt it back there, but I don't since we left."

"Do you think he was hiding somewhere nearby?"

Colt replied, "Yes. You and I are warriors. You know that people like us feel those things. We both felt him watching."

Man Killer said, "So we go back?"

Colt said, "At a fast trot, young brother."

They wheeled their horses and kicked them into a fast trot. The two big steeds started back, eager to run because they were headed back toward home, and horses are always quicker when they are home-ward bound. Hawk and War Bonnet were no exceptions—as special as they both were, they were horses nonetheless.

Two hours later Eagle looked back from the mountain ridge and saw the two riders heading toward him at a hurried pace. His stare was blank, but he knew how to lose them both. His powerful legs carried him higher and higher toward the distant cliffs. He would lose them again and take care of them later. Eagle Bleu reached back and gave his pack a reassuring pat. Sweat poured down his body in rivulets, making streaks through the caked-on dirt and grime. The task didn't bother him, in the same way that going up a steep hillside to escape pursuit didn't bother a mule deer. It was just something that needed to be done.

Colt and Man Killer were both chilled when they found the shallow, gravelike hole that the big man had been lying in while they had looked at his sign just a few feet away. The horses pranced and whinnied nervously from the horrible stench at the hole as well—so powerful that even the two men could smell it. They took off at a fast trot again, easily following the huge tracks of the running man's giant moccasins. He was heading up into the La Garita mountain range at the western edge of the San Luis Valley.

The two men pushed their horses as high as they could and continued on foot after ground reining them at timberline. Again, they followed the tracks of Eagle Bleu up across the hard-crusted snow. This time he hadn't had time to cover his trail, but again, as before, the tracks came to a steep drop-away cliffside and ended, as if the predator had jumped off and committed suicide.

Man Killer scrambled back down the mountainside to the horses. He took a few gulps of water and retrieved Colt's powerful telescope, then went back up to their perch as fast as he could force his lungs and legs to move. The two men took turns looking straight down thousands of feet from the cliff, but they could not spot a body. After half an hour, they started looking out across the mountain range and finally Man Killer spotted something.

"Look! Look!" Man Killer exclaimed, "There he is!"

Colt looked and saw the giant of a man, running faster than Chris Colt figured he himself could run through the wilderness, especially for such a distance. He was dodging in and out of trees miles away. There was no way the two men could follow him. Chris and Man Killer would have to find a pass across the range and locate his tracks down below, delaying their search until the next day, at least.

When the two riders picked up Eagle Bleu's tracks the following mid-morning, there was still no sign of how he'd gotten down from the steep cliff. Just as he had done across the valley in the Sangre de Cristos, the man had once again made his way to the edge of the cliff and simply gone over. There was no sign of a rope having been employed—no telltale fibers of hemp caught between rocks, no scars on the cliffside where the rope would have rubbed. And, in any case, there were no rocks or trees where the rope could have been tied.

At the spot where they had picked up the tracks, the trail had been quickly and partially obliterated, but it soon just became a trail of a very large man running.

They found the place where he had to turn due south after a few miles, and finally back southeast to cross back over the same range. By mid-afternoon, they discovered why he had done all this backtracking. The lawmen found where the man's big horse had been picketed and proceeded to check the bushes and trees along the trail until they found bits of red hair, white mane, and white tail. With that evidence, and judging by the depth and size of the hoofprints and the length of stride, Chris and Man Killer concluded that their earlier guess had been correct—the horse was a very large blood bay draft horse, probably a Clydesdale.

Colt and Man Killer finally lost the trail in the rocks north of Wolf Creek, where the behemoth had taken great care to cover his trail. Colt and Man Killer rode out in large semicircles, leading their horses most of the time as they tried to pick up sign. But the huge man was an expert. He was, Chris concluded, every bit as good as them—if not better—at tracking and trailing. Their eyes were conditioned to spot the smallest details, to notice any little thing that was out of place. But this time there was nothing. Absolutely nothing.

CHAPTER 6
Escape

What they did not know was that Eagle Bleu had planned to cut them off after they crossed Wolf Creek Pass before they got to Pagosa Springs, but after their back-tracking and discovery he led them for miles in that direction, then covered his trail and suddenly cut back due east. He had ridden for miles and miles in a south-westerly direction and then had abruptly gone east. Who would suspect him of doing such a thing?

When he did cut back and cover his tracks, he was thorough. The man had been feeding himself in the rugged mountain wilderness since he was a toddler, and there was hardly a thing he could do in the woods that could be bested by Chris Colt or Man Killer.

But Colt and Man Killer were able to live rich, full lives, as Eagle Bleu could not.

They could each love a woman, marry, have children and love them. Each could have friends and laugh, or even get thrilled seeing a new foal jumping around his mother on spindly, springy, long legs. Each could get excited over landing a big fish, seeing a rainbow, or surviving a high mountain blizzard. Eagle Bleu, on the other hand, could not feel or be stimulated. He just knew killing and raping, tearing people apart and eating them.

Chris and Man Killer were tearing up the canyons, ridges, and hillocks north of Wolf Creek, while Eagle Bleu approached the chinked-log ranch house just a few miles west of LaVeta, Colorado, at the southern end of the San Luis Valley and the base of the incline leading up to LaVeta Pass.

As usual, he left his horse tied in a good hiding place several miles from the kill site, then ran on foot to a wooded hilltop over-looking the ranch and studied it for hours. There were two children playing outside, but he paid little attention to them. Their spirits were not mature enough to make their hearts worthwhile. They would be dispatched quickly just to get them out of the way.

Eagle Bleu watched as the father, a strapping big man in faded coveralls, worked hard until well after dark. The man labored with great care and precision as he worked the anvil placed near the big double barn doors, making a set of horseshoes for his matched pair of old Percherons. The man made a lot of extra money using that team to plow for other neighbors and to do other odd jobs that called for pulling power. Eagle could tell that the man had lots of sinew and muscle by the way he worked and handled the hammer. Eating his heart would provide much strength.

Eagle also watched the wife as she did laundry and hung it out on a line in the ranch yard. He liked the way she moved beneath the cotton dress, and he pictured her body with the dress removed. He pictured her lying beneath him, blood streaming from her face and abject terror in her eyes. She was a strong woman and would fight him hard. She too would provide him with strength.

Before killing these people, he would have to make them frightened. The big man would be hard to scare because he had been through much—Eagle could tell by watching him. He would need to frighten him the same way he had frightened the mighty Colt—by making him afraid of the unknown.

The moon shone directly down on the snowy peaks of the near-distant Sangre de Cristos; somewhere nearby a coyote yipped, then howled.

Lars and Inga Swenson slept soundly that night in their large feather bed. They had worked hard and saved a long time for that bed, but they needed a big bed to accommodate Lars. The trip out West from Minnesota had been long and arduous, and a Kiowa arrow through his right thigh, then an inadvertent kick to the left kneecap by a slipping ox, had caused the big man leg pains at night, especially if a storm or a cold front was setting in.

That had been ten years ago. Now the mines were behind him; the dreams of gold and silver had been replaced with an ordinary life. He now thought of years of hard work and strong ethics and raising a fine, proud family. He thought of the money he could save by selling beef to others but feeding his own family with venison and elk and antelope, which would only cost the price of an occasional bullet.

He now had two children, and he would see that they grew up with security and principle and pride. They would grow up in a free land and would do what they chose and go where they wished when they were grown. They would be a proud, strong young man and woman, the offspring of hard-working, grateful immigrants.

These things were always in the back of the mind of the large man, but he was unaware that the future was now gone for the two wonderful little children. Now, a pair of vacant eyes looked through the window at him and his sleeping wife. The eyes watched the rise and fall of Inga's breasts under her cotton nightgown, then switched to the open mouth of Lars as he snored loudly.

A rock suddenly crashed through the bedroom window and Lars instinctively threw himself across his wife's body. His eyes opened wide and he looked from left to right. Reality flooded into his mind and he tried to figure out where he was, what to do.

Inga, frightened, screamed out. Lars covered her mouth with a beefy hand and jumped out of bed, pulling his Henry off a rack near the bedroom door. Without speaking, he stepped over to his wife, who was now paralyzed with fear. He grabbed her wrist and pulled her onto the floor and shoved her under the bed. She got the idea and did not argue or resist.

She whispered, "The children!"

He said, "I know."

Lars slipped out of the bedroom door and went to the children's doorway, sliding back the wool blanket that served for a door. He saw the two still bodies and sighed with relief, unaware that the bodies would always be still. He did not notice that their window was open.

In the bedroom, Inga heard a deep, deep bass voice from the darkness just outside the window,

The voice said, "Hated."

Frightened out of her wits, she said meekly and quietly, "What?"

The deep voice said, "Thade."

She whimpered under the bed.

A hand grabbed her ankle, and she screamed in absolute horror. It was Lars. He pulled her out and held her in his arms, as he stared out the window.

She said, "It's not Indians," apparently ridding herself of her initial fear.

She went on, "He spoke from outside the window. It's a white man and his voice is so low, Lars. I have never heard anything like it."

"What did he say?"

"First he said 'hated,' then he said, 'thade,'" she answered. "It makes no sense."

Lars led her into the darkened area that combined living room, dining area, and kitchen. He grabbed his old Schofield .44 pistol and handed it to her as she sat at the table.

Lars said, "Stay here, woman."

He walked to the door, lantern in one hand and rifle in the other. He lit the lantern and walked out into the night.

Inga looked around the room nervously and broke out with perspiration. Her mind raced as she tried to picture what was going on outside. She had faced Indian attack, tornadoes, a confrontation with a group of drunken miners, and many blizzards. She'd even faced a grizzly trying to tear down their smokehouse. But nothing had ever prepared her for this.

Did she hear a noise?

Her ears strained to hear the slightest sound. She heard a mouse running across the cupboard. There was nothing from outside.

Boom! Crash!

A gun sounded right outside the house and there was the shatter of glass.

She screamed with fear.

Inga hysterically cried out, "Lars!"

There was complete silence.

The door crashed open and she screamed

again, swinging the pistol up and cocking it with both thumbs.

"No!" Lars screamed, "Don't shoot, Inga!"

Lars stood in front of her, a frightened look on his face. In one hand was his rifle and in the other was the lantern, with the glass and the wick shot away.

He ran over to her and set the rifle on the table. She stood up to be held but her knees buckled, and as she swayed he held her to his barrel-sized chest. Feeling his heart pounding rapidly scared her even more. She had never really seen Lars afraid of anything.

"What did he say?" he asked again.

She said, " 'Hated' first, then 'thade.' "

Suddenly, it hit her.

Inga's eyes opened wide and she said, "Lars, the noise. Why haven't the children awakened?"

She jumped up and started to run into the children's room, but Lars grabbed her and sat her down. He went into the room.

The door opened and the voice from the darkness said, "Dehat."

She stared at the door and couldn't breathe. The darkness outside was like a gaping black hole she looked into with terror within it. Out there was her carefully manicured flower garden and beyond that some well-tended crops. There was the swing where she and her husband had spent so many hours on Sunday afternoons, and the little mound of sand where the children had spent so much time playing. These things were all wonderful parts of her life, but now they were not visible. They were just part of the black hole she stared at.

Inga held her breath and the pistol and ran forward and slammed the door shut. Just before it closed, she thought she saw a pair of eyes staring at her and a chill ran up and down her spine. She wet herself.

Inga sat at the table.

She got out a piece of paper and pencil and lit a candle, deciding it was too late for caution.

She wrote down the word "Hated," then "Thade," then "Dehat."

Inga heard noises in the children's room and felt some relief. She pictured her big husband lifting the frightened children into his careful embrace.

She stared at the paper, and slowly wrote, "D-E-A-T-H."

The meaning of the word hit her, and she started whimpering. The footsteps coming up behind her were too heavy for her husband's. She smelled a stench she had not smelled since she and Lars had come upon the rotting corpse of one of their horses last summer. Inga just mumbled incoherently and started turning slowly.

He was dressed in furs and his head was bent over to keep from scraping on the ceiling. His hands came forward slowly and blood dripped off of them. She could not move or breathe as they grabbed the cotton gown at her shoulders and ripped it.

She tilted her head back as she stood in her nakedness, too numb to try to cover herself. Inga finally looked up to the eyes and the candlelight played on them. They were unfeeling, emotionless. Another chill run up and down her spine.

She knew her husband—her big, strong, strapping husband—lay dead in the other room, and her babies as well.

Her vomiting did not keep the big creature from slamming her down on her back. The smell was putrid and horrifying.

Miles away, Chris Colt and Man Killer arrived at the village where the Ute lovers had been killed. They were taken to a lodge and given food. In the morning, they could start interviewing witnesses.

After having one of his wives bring them a pot of antelope stew, the chief, Runs-In-The-Sun, said, "Tomorrow, Wamble Uncha, you can speak to the boy who saw a mighty bear with wings, and it flew from the mountain's top."

The two lawmen lay under their buffalo robes smoking cigaritos and thinking. It was hard to get to sleep but both finally drifted off.

It was the middle of the night when Chris Colt looked around. There had been a noise and Colt thought he saw a shadow in the corner of the cabin. His wife and children were behind him and he kept shooing them back. Little Brenna kept running toward the shadow and Chris got frustrated. He wanted her to listen and stay back, but she was so curious and fearless. He could not keep his eye on her and also on the shadow. It was so frustrating and frightening. The shadow moved forward, just as Brenna ran forward again, and Chris felt his breath catch and his heart skip a beat. He grabbed her and pulled her back as the big shadow came into the lantern light. It was a giant of a man dressed in furs.

Colt looked at the face and turned white. The man was Will Sawyer, over seven feet tall and over four hundred pounds.

Nervously, but trying to hide his fear, Chris said, "Will Sawyer, I killed you up in the Yellowstone years ago. I shot you and saw you fall in a boiling-hot mud pool."

Will Sawyer started laughing and said, "Why, are you scared of me, Colt?"

Chris gritted his teeth together and said, "No, I'm not afraid of anything."

Sawyer laughed again, aggravating Chris Colt. He asked, "Are you sure you are not afraid?"

Colt said, "Yes, I'm sure."

Sawyer said, "And you're not afraid of me?"

Colt said, "This doesn't make any sense. You are supposed to be dead."

Sawyer laughed even harder this time and said, "I am." He guffawed.

Chris's heart was pounding furiously now and he looked more closely at Sawyer's face. It was completely blank. The face was gone.

Colt screamed, "Who are you!?"

He opened his eyes and sat straight up, breathing heavily.

Man Killer lay covered up in his buffalo robe, unmoving, breathing softly.

Chris Colt was scared and needed to talk. Although it was ten feet across the tepee, Colt still managed to reach out and touch the Nez Perce on the shoulder.

Man Killer turned his head and smiled at

Colt, but his face looked different—It was the face of Will Sawyer. But then the face turned, in front of Colt's eyes, into that of a bear. Chris wanted to scream, but he couldn't.

The bear spoke with Man Killer's voice, "The killer is in your dreams, Great Scout."

Chris opened his eyes and looked at Man Killer, who was turned halfway toward him and sitting up under his robe. A little gray light showed up through the smokehole. It was almost daybreak.

Colt was perspiring and breathing heavily. He had just awakened from a horrible nightmare, he realized.

Colt said, "Did you say something?"

Man Killer smiled, "You also had a nightmare about this killer."

Colt said, "Also?"

Man Killer smiled. "It is good for me to understand you are human, too."

The two men got up and prepared to meet with the tribal leaders. They had some coffee, a smoke, and a swim.

They were then summoned and had a meal of jerked beef, corn, and tamales. They ate with several tribal leaders, including Horse-That-Runs-Through-High-Waters, and one young warrior who looked to be in his late teens. It was impolite to speak about business until after they had eaten and the host brought the topic up.

The tepee they were in smelled of food, sweat, and tobacco. It was full daylight now, but it seemed so dark in the lodge. It reminded Colt of being inside a catacomb, as the two smoked and heard about the gruesome attack on the two lovers. The man had been disemboweled and torn to shreds; his heart and liver were missing. The woman had been brutally raped and then torn into pieces.

As Colt listened to the details, a shiver ran up and down his spine, and he self-consciously glanced around at Man Killer and the others to see if anyone noticed his little convulsion. To his surprise, they apparently hadn't.

The chief introduced the teenaged warrior as Scars. The reason for his name was obvious—he had burn scars on his face and a fresher scar across his throat and left shoulder that seemed to have been made by a knife or spear, although an arrow could have gone across those areas as well, slicing through the flesh along its path.

Scars accepted Colt's offering of a cigarito, as did all the others.

The chief then said, "Scars, tell One Eagle of the bear who flew from the mountain."

Scars ceremoniously took a long drag on the cigar and blew the smoke in a circular motion toward the smokehole in the tepee ceiling. The young man knew that all the elders were giving him their undivided attention and his words must be right. And he wanted to milk his newfound celebrity status for all it was worth.

Colt and Man Killer both knew what was going on with the upcoming speech, so they prepared themselves for a long oration.

Scars said, "In the mountains of the red snow when the sun goes to sleep, I hunted for the wapiti. My father and his father before him were great hunters of the wapiti, and I am better."

In Indian culture, it was not only permissible to boast about yourself; it was encouraged. But lying or embellishing the story was strictly forbidden.

"It was in the moon when the snow leaves the mountains, and they cry like the little one. When their tears run down fast and make the rivers angry and fill their banks," Scars said.

He then stopped and took another long puff on his cigar, enjoying all the attention from so many important men.

He went on, "I saw many wapiti where

the mountain is steep, and I was below the mountain that looks like a teat."

Colt looked at Man Killer with understanding. He really didn't need to explain that the young man was speaking about the base of Nipple Mountain in the month of June.

After two more slow puffs, Scars went on, "I spotted a mighty herd bull. He had been up high on the mountain's shoulder. A younger bull came through the trees while I watched. He was looking for the old father bull."

Again, Scars stopped and motioned for coffee, then added several spoonsful of sugar. He drank it slowly, savoring the attention more than the taste.

Scars continued, "The young bull ran through the trees and looked everywhere while I watched from below. He found the old father bull and trotted up to him, holding his antlers high. I heard them speak."

Scars paused again to see how this last statement affected his listeners. Colt watched the others with amusement, as they seemed to be unaffected by the frequent stops.

Scars went on, "The young bull said to the old one, 'See that pretty cow with the red hair?' I looked down the mountain and saw many wapiti below. There was one cow with a red coat of fur. The old bull looked down at the herd, too. He said to the young bull, 'I see the pretty cow with the red hair.' "

It was time for another pregnant pause, so the young warrior took more puffs on the cigarito and Chris Colt wished he had never offered the tobacco. Man Killer, however, seemed unconcerned about the delays.

Scars spoke again. "The young bull then said, 'Why don't we run down the mountain and mount that pretty cow?' "

Scars took two more drags on the cigar, then continued, "But the old father bull said, 'Why don't we walk down the mountain and mount all the cows in the herd?' "

Scars now stopped and poured himself more coffee, while the tribal leaders grinned and nodded in assent. The young man strutted like a peacock, obviously quite proud of his little story, and several men made approving comments. Now it seemed that each man wanted to pour a cup of coffee, bringing Colt to regret his gifts of coffee and sugar as well. All he wanted was to hear the rest of the story and to find out about a bear flying off the mountain. Chris offered the lad another cigar, hoping it might prompt him to start talking again.

Scars blew several puffs toward the fire this time and admired the cigar, inspecting it from the side. He blew on the tip and it turned bright red. Scars stuck the other end in his mouth and took a big puff.

He continued, "What I tell you now might sound like a story, but it happened. It was the night I saw the bear with wings fly from that mountain that looks like a teat."

If there was one thing that Chris Colt knew, it was that very few Indians ever told lies. In some tribes, you might commit murder and maybe get away with it, but lying could cause you to be banished—it just wasn't done. The story this young warrior was about to tell might sound far fetched, but it would be the truth as the teller saw it.

Scars spoke, "It was after the sun went to bed over yonder. The sky was good, because the moon was wide awake. I was walking down with the elk I killed on that mountain, and I stopped because I carried much of his leg on my shoulder. I sat on a small rock and looked up at the sky. That is when I saw the bear."

He now paused for another puff of the new cigar, but this time Colt felt that the pause was not for effect, but because Scars was so overwhelmed by the memory.

The brave went on, "I looked up to the top of the mountain. It was on a high cliff, a very high cliff. There was something moving. It was a bear. I saw it stand up on its hind legs. Then it jumped off the cliff."

Colt couldn't help himself.

He said, "It jumped off the cliff?"

The brave ignored the white man and went on, "The bear had mighty wings above his head, and he flew down from the high mountaintop. I did not see him land, because he flew down between two places of many baby trees."

Chris looked over at Man Killer, and they both thought about the trail they found and the arrow they shot between the two groves of scrub oaks. Colt lit another cigar and studied the young warrior's words as he described the winged bear. Though Chris wanted to understand, it was a difficult story to grasp.

Colt's head snapped around, though, when Scars said, "I watched the bear hide his trail when he left the trees. He ran across the valley and his running was like that of a young dog soldier, not a big bear. The big bear did not run on his four legs. He ran on two like a man."

Colt and Man Killer exchanged interested glances again, then snapped to attention when Scars said, "Then the bear rode a horse which was hidden way out in the valley."

Colt said, "Scars, was this a Ute pony he rode?"

Scars smiled and replied, "No, it was a mighty horse. The horse he rode was a father and your horse is but a child."

Man Killed looked over at Chris again, then asked, "How did this mighty horse look?"

Scars motioned for another cigar and Colt offered it, then lit it for him. The young man again took two slow drags.

He finally replied, "This big pony was red, like that pot yonder. He wore white moccasins and leggings above them. These were white. His hair and tail, they, too, were white. His face had a big white blaze that ran all the way down to his mouth. And his mouth did not smile when the bear rode on his back, because the bear was so big."

Man Killer looked at Colt and said quietly, "Clydesdale."

Colt nodded.

The two lawmen rode out of the village the next day.

They rode as fast as possible toward Salida to the northeast. Several days later, they boarded an Atchison, Topeka, and

Santa Fe Railroad train and headed to Denver by way of Canon City. Colt got off the train briefly in Canon City and checked on his brother. His condition had improved slightly, but he was still not out of the woods. There had been no word from Heidi Rosenberg, but that hadn't surprised Colt. He and Man Killer sent telegrams to Westcliffe to be delivered to their wives, letting them know where they were headed. They went on to Pueblo, then headed north.

Colt looked out the window at the high prairie to the east and the nearby mountains to the west as they traveled northward toward Colorado Springs. He thought about the big war he was briefly involved in to get the railroad built through Canon City.

The founder of the Denver and Rio Grande Railroad was William J. Palmer, who lived in Colorado Springs, where Colt and Man Killer were now headed. In 1876, while Colt was still a chief of scouts with the army, Palmer decided that he wanted to run the Rio Grande Railroad down into New Mexico to try to pick up the lucrative freight business running up and down the Santa Fe Trail. Especially attractive was the possibility of government contracts to bring supplies into and out of Fort Union, the largest military supply post west of the Mississippi River.

The problem was that the general manager of the Santa Fe Railroad had the same idea as William J. Palmer, and a railroad war began. It heated up when the two railroads decided to try to run a spur to Leadville and get the rich mining trade coming in and out of the mountainous community that lay up the Arkansas River Valley from the Coyote Run Ranch, but it was at ten thousand feet elevation. The Colt's ranch, however, was at close to eight thousand feet elevation.

The drop from Leadville to Cotopaxi, which was close to the Coyote Run, was best illustrated by the Arkansas River and its dramatic changes. From Leadville down past Buena Vista and Salida, there were big drops, like Brown's Hole, and gentler slopes in the wider mountain valley areas. But below Salida, most of the trip the water took was through a narrow, steep-walled canyon with many sets of churning rapids. Although still traveling at great speed, the river finally settled down where it entered the prairie at Canon City.

The railroads jockeyed back and forth during the late seventies and early eighties trying to lay track through this hazardous canyon. Some places, like the Grand Canyon of the Arkansas, as it was called then, had walls three thousand feet high.

The trouble started when the clever William B. Strong sent his best surveyor up to Colorado in 1878, disguised as a sheepherder who tended a herd of sheep while surveying a new roadbed over Raton Pass and into southern Colorado.

Strong then sent a road crew to Raton, along with dozens of heavily armed guards. When Palmer's men showed up in the morning, they found a large road crew already at work. The Rio Grande men tried a couple of bluffs with lawmen from Trinidad and Raton, but the toughs of the Santa Fe were not going to be budged by that. There were a few fights and even some gunfire, but eventually William J. Palmer pulled his men out of Raton Pass.

In 1879 the silver boom came to Leadville. Freighter wagons were making a killing hauling ore out of the high mountain community and hauling supplies back in for the thousands of miners who arrived weekly. Both railroads realized how much money they could make and the war got heavier handed by the day. But the main reason for the war's escalation was the fact that miners were shipping more than a hundred thousand pounds of ore daily from the Leadville silver mines.

Railroad workers and hired guns were firing at one another from both sides of the Arkansas River near the mouth of the Grand Canyon of the Arkansas, Royal Gorge.

Palmer brought Chris Colt into the fray because the Santa Fe had hired numerous gunslingers; Palmer, on the other hand, used lawmen and militiamen to try to win the rail war.

Chris Colt, no longer chief of scouts for the U.S. Army, had become a deputy U.S. marshal settled on a ranch close to all the hostilities.

When Chris took over the case and talked to railroad workers, many of whom lived in Canon City, he learned that a new hired gun, operating out of the big roundhouse in Pueblo, was heading the Santa Fe gunfighters. Colt heard the story from enough people that he figured it may have some truth to it, so the next morning he saddled War Bonnet and started the forty-mile journey to Pueblo, where he took a room for the night.

The next day, he rode to the rail yards and climbed down out of the saddle. Standing outside the roundhouse, he yelled,

"Whoever is in charge of the railroad gun-fighters, step outside with your hands where I can see them."

He waited anxious moments and was about to holler a further challenge when he heard the door being opened. A man walked out into the sunlight wearing two guns tied low. He had a moustache and wore a derby hat; otherwise he was dressed in a dapper way. The man carried a cane knobbed and tipped in gold and looked familiar to Colt, but at that distance, in the unforgiving Colorado sun, it was hard to see anything.

The man started walking forward and Colt could soon see he was grinning. Colt recognized him as somebody he would not like to have a showdown with. Gunslingers who wanted to fight everyone with a rep, just to increase their own, mostly ended up in Boot Hill. But Colt first looked for a peaceful resolution to every problem, shooting only after trying every other strategy. For in a gunfight there were so many variables—a gunsight might hang a barrel up in a holster, two bullets in a row might misfire, any number of things could go wrong.

Colt said, "Bat Masterson! Been a long time! You got some cool spring water in there? I got some cigars! Let's have a smoke and parley!"

Bat Masterson, the famous lawman, replied, "Chris Colt, how ya doin', pardner? Ya know I was hired to do a job. I got to fight anyone that tries to keep me from doing it."

Colt yelled, "Bat, you're no fool, and I sure don't want to have to fight you, and I don't think you'd want to fight me either."

Bat yelled, "Of course not, Colt, but when I'm paid good, honest U.S. money, I ride for the brand."

Colt yelled, "You aren't a pilgrim, either, Bat. I am a deputy U.S. marshal. You fight me, you're fighting what you've worked for all these years!"

Bat yelled, "Colt, I didn't know you were wearing a badge now. Of course, I'll talk. Come on, coffee's on!"

With that, the ex-Dodge City lawman simply turned his back and walked in the door of the big brick building.

Colt went into the roundhouse and saw gunmen around the building, watching to insure that no additional fighters were following Colt to the makeshift headquarters.

Masterson handed Colt a coffee and accepted a cigar at the same time. The two started talking immediately.

Chris Colt said, "Bat, these two idiots running this mess have been listening to each others' telegrams and decoding them, because they both are sharing the same telegraph wire.

"You and I both know that two Santa Fe men were killed yesterday and two were wounded in Cucharas. They are on their way here to take on you and all the riflemen you have in here."

Bat Masterson replied, "Yeah, I know. We decoded their telegrams about it. We're ready."

Colt said, "I'll make you a deal. You leave without fighting them. No bloodshed. I'll get a hold of their major stockholders, by wire, and tell them how silly this all is. They should be able to make the Rio Grande and the Santa Fe settle this peacefully. After all, it's their money at stake."

Bat Masterson paced back and forth for a few minutes while he pondered Colt's proposal.

He blew a puff of smoke out and studied the cigarito.

"Good cigar," he said. Then, almost as an afterthought, he added, "Makes sense, Colt. I'll do it."

One of the riflemen, a personal assistant and bodyguard to William B. Strong, stepped forward and faced Masterson, saying, "You cain't do thet, Masterson! You was hired by Mr. Strong ta kick hell outta these Rio Grande boys."

Bat Masterson folded his arms across his chest and quietly said, "Tell Mr. Strong to come down here and fight them himself."

The rifleman took a quick step forward, carbine held menacingly across his chest. Bat started into a gunfighter's crouch, but Chris Colt's arm across the man's chest halted everything as all eyes turned to him.

Colt said, "Mister, I don't know what you know about Bat Masterson, but you don't want any part of him. What you were just about to do only has one word for it—suicide."

The rifleman gave Colt a queer look, then peered at Bat Masterson. Exasperated, he said, "Aw, the hell with ya! With the both of ya."

With that, he turned on his heel and stormed out of the building. Several other gunmen followed suit. Bat Masterson smiled at Colt and the two walked over to an old rolltop desk and chair. Bat pulled a pair of saddlebags off of a peg on the wall and started unloading items from desk drawers, including pouch after pouch of bullets. Grinning, he pulled a hip flask out and placed it in the saddlebags, smiled, and pulled it back out. He unscrewed the cap and drank a swig, then offered the flask to Colt.

Chris hesitated, then took a pull on the flask. He held the amber liquid in his mouth a few seconds, swished it around, then swallowed it quickly, tilting his head back. He shivered up and down his back and gave a little shake. He made a face as if he had been sucking on a lemon, then smiled.

Colt said, "Smooth-sipping whiskey."

Bat Masterson laughed and clapped Colt on the back. He replaced the flask in his saddlebags and tossed them over his shoulder.

Saying, "Well, I guess I'm finished here," he turned and headed for the door with Colt at his side.

The other gunmen followed them out. In the sunshine, Masterson stopped at his horse and shook with Colt.

"Chris, good to see you again," Bat said.

"You too, Bat."

Masterson went on, "I'm sure glad we didn't have to test each other."

Colt said, "Reasonable men never do. There's always talking things out."

Bat had a wistful look on his face, but he

smiled and nodded. He saddled up, mounted up, gave Colt a little wave, and rode away.

A short while later, the majority stockholders of both railroads ordered Strong and Palmer to reach a reasonable accord and gave them an outline for doing so. The Santa Fe got to run a line down into New Mexico along the Santa Fe Trail. The Rio Grande got to build and run the Leadville line. But the two railroads also leased each other's rails, ending the railroad problems for the most part.

Now Chris Colt looked out the window and smiled, thinking back to his little railroad adventure. He noticed that Man Killer had fallen asleep to the swaying of the car. Colt thought that would be a good idea too, and, pulling his hat over his eyes, dozed off himself.

Chris Colt's wife, Shirley, had made a sizable nest egg by owning, then selling, a successful restaurant in Bismarck, North Dakota Territory. Colt had also saved up a bit over the years and bought the original lands for the Coyote Run Ranch with his savings. Joshua Colt brought cattle and some good stock horses to the ranch, and Man Killer, who owned a small percentage of the ranch, also started breeding and selling Appaloosa horses from the original herd of Chief Joseph. And now Jennifer Banta's fortune was added to his own.

Both men were financially set for life, enabling them to do what they wished—to work for the law. Most of the time, they acted and lived like cowboys, but occasionally they would treat themselves to something special, as they did that day, when the train pulled into Denver.

The two men boarded their horses, then took a buggy and checked into the posh Windsor Hotel, which had been opened a few years earlier, in 1880, shortly before Colt got involved in the railroad dispute. Built by a silver magnate, H. A. W. Tabor, the Windsor had 176 marble mantlepieces and a taproom with three thousand silver dollars inlaid in the floor.

The two men cleaned up and drew attention as they went to the main dining room for dinner. This restaurant employed seventy well-dressed and well-trained waiters, and served items such as sweetbreads glazed with French peas and tenderloin of beef with mushrooms; or baked filet of trout, Madeira sauce, and Parisian potatoes; and English plum pudding with rum sauce, and Neapolitan ice cream.

Man Killer grinned as he read the upper part of the menu, which reminded guests of the way things had been in Denver in the "good old days." It read: "1859 GRUB Beans, Bacon, Hard Tack, Dried Apples, Taos Lightning." Man Killer showed it to Colt, and as the two men looked around the room, it was easy to see how much things had changed in a relatively short time.

In 1881, Horace Austin Warner Tabor also presented Denver with an opera house valued at three quarters of a million dollars. Man Killer, who soaked up knowledge like a sponge, convinced Chris to attend the opera with him that night. There, the two men were the object of curious glances.

The next morning, Man Killer took off for Elitch's Zoological Gardens, a seventeen-acre entertainment complex in the middle of Denver; it was the talk of the town. In the meantime, Chris Colt headed for the well-stocked public library, the sole reason for his trip to Denver.

Later that night, over dinner in the plush restaurant, Man Killer said, "Great Scout, did you find the answers to your questions in any books?"

Colt smiled and said, "Yes. A few years back, there was a new contraption featured at the World's Fair in Paris. It was invented by a Frenchman, and I think that's how our killer is getting off the high cliffs."

Man Killer said, "What is it?"

Colt said, "It is called a parachute. It's a big thing that looks kind of like an umbrella and you can fall through the air with it real slowly."

Man Killer said, "Like the thistle glides along with the breeze."

Colt said, "Yep."

Man Killer said, "Yes, that makes sense."

The men rode out the next morning for Parker. Colt wanted to investigate the mysterious mauling by the grizzly he had been wired about. When he heard about the supposed bear hiding in the outhouse and yanking the redheaded cowboy through the hole, he knew immediately it was their killer.

Man Killer found a number of individual hairs, and also some animal hairs, down inside the outhouse, and the two men studied them carefully. Several of the human hairs were very long and some were shorter and curlier. The two scouts knew immediately that it was a man with very long hair and an unkempt beard. This was no great surprise, as they had heard the description from Joshua and had seen the killer from a distance.

They did determine—and this was important—that the hairs were a reddish color, but not the same shade as Colt had seen in red or auburn-haired men or women, including Shirley. As they studied several strands of hair and examined the texture, they gave each other knowing looks.

Man Killer said what they both had been thinking, "He is half-white and half-Indian."

Colt said, "I was thinking the same thing, little brother. Indian hair is thicker, and I have seen this color of brownish-red before on half-blooded people."

They also studied the animal hairs and determined that a few were from a blonde phase, silvertip grizzly bear. Two hairs were from a marmot found above timberline, and three thick guard hairs and some downy hair were from a timberwolf. Indians collect downy hair from wolves to weave into cloth, while the thick outer guard hairs provide the wolves with insulation and waterproofing against the elements.

The conclusions they drew from all the evidence were obvious. This killer had to live up above timberline in the big mountains. Although there had been occasional killings around places like Parker, most of the recent reported maulings and gruesome murders were within close proximity to the

Sangre de Cristo and San Juan mountain ranges.

Colt studied the old traces of trail through the draw behind the Parker ranch and mused, "I figure he must have two hideouts—one up above timberline in the Sangre de Cristos and one in the San Juans."

Man Killer said, "Why would he come away from the mountains and all the way up here from down there?"

Chris sat down and lit up a cigar, handing one to Man Killer. The brave offered smoke up to all four compass points and started enjoying the tobacco.

Colt said, "I've been wondering about that, too."

The two men slept in the bunkhouse, after Colt had ridden into town and sent a telegram to the sheriff in Denver. The next morning, they left Parker and picked up the train later that day at Castle Rock.

CHAPTER 7
Back Home

They were in Canon City by that night. The two lawmen stayed at the mineral baths down near "Old Max" state penitentiary, after visiting Joshua in the hospital.

The next day, Chris Colt rode to the Western Union office, arriving just as a long telegram came in from the sheriff in Denver. Colt wired back his thanks and acknowledgment to the sheriff, and went outside to read the wire by the hitching rail.

Marshal Colt STOP The only major crime in the area those dates were as follows STOP saloon holdup STOP legal gunfight STOP theft of crate of books for public library STOP Sorry could not help more STOP Respectfully yours STOP Sheriff Colgan STOP

Chris and Man Killer soon headed up Grape Creek, deciding to head home cross-country. From the mineral baths, they had only to ride up the river a few minutes and they were at the mouth of Grape Creek. They forded the river just above the mouth of the watercourse and headed up the rocky gulches heading southwest toward Westcliffe.

Riding through the clear stream water at a narrow spot in the canyon, Man Killer asked, "Did you find out anything with your talking wire, Great Scout?"

Colt grinned, always amused when Man Killer switched back and forth between the poetic conversation of a Nez Perce brave and the discourse of a learned scholar.

Chris said, "Yep, I think I know why our killer went all the way to Denver."

Man Killer waited for the answer.

Colt said, "Books."

Man Killer repeated, "Books?"

Colt said, "Yes, there was a crate of books stolen that was headed to, or at, the public library."

Man Killer smiled softly and said, "Yes, I understand this."

Nothing more was said for several minutes, but Colt knew that Man Killer understood, for the Nez Perce warrior had been educating himself since his teenaged years, reading every spare moment and amazing Chris and Shirley Colt with his self-acquired knowledge.

When his love had been kidnapped and taken to Australia by her uncle, Man Killer got himself purposely shanghaied so that he could sail there to save her. The adventure itself was a learning experience, and on the long cruise back the couple was married by the ship's captain. Man Killer's education continued at the side of the former famous cavalry chief of scouts, and he learned more about the law when Colt became deputy U.S. marshal and Man Killer, although red, became his special deputy. But mostly, Man Killer had learned about the white man's world through books. He had gone to a Catholic missionary school at his home in the Wallowa Valley, near the borders of Idaho and Oregon, where he had learned to read. An inquisitive youngster, he had a thirst for knowledge that could not be slaked.

So when Man Killer said he understood why the predator had sought out books, he was drawing from his own experience.

At Reed Gulch in the Wet Mountain Valley, they split up, with Man Killer heading south to Jennifer and Colt heading north to the Coyote Run and his family.

Chris played with his children and made love to his wife all night long. The next morning, he told Man Killer to wait to hear from him, and he took the train to Canon City.

He went right to the hospital, where Joshua lay sleeping, looking helpless. Around noon, he awakened and a friendly nurse brought a tray of food. Though he could have used help, Joshua Colt insisted on feeding himself. The nurse brought Chris a cup of tea and a china pot of hot water, and he sat down and built a cigarette. Joshua reached out feebly for the makings, but Colt hesitated.

Joshua smiled and said weakly, "You my mother or my brother?"

Chris handed him the makings and the elder Colt rolled a cigarette, accepting a light from Chris. He blew a long stream of blue smoke toward the ceiling and smiled.

Joshua said, "Ah, it has been a long time. You know, little brother, men sharing a good cigar or cigarette is one of the few pleasures left to us."

It troubled Chris to see his normally strong and powerful sibling look so frail and speak in a whisper. He had lost a lot of weight.

Chris said, "What are you talking about?"

Joshua said, "Women. I'm talking about women. They are taking over, Chris. They don't want men to be the head of the household anymore. Look at these suffragists."

Joshua was so weak, but he was grinning and becoming very animated in his speech.

"They want to run a woman for president."

Colt said, "What?"

Joshua said, "Yeah, can you believe that? Belva Lockwood. The National Equal Rights Party wants to run her for president of the United States. On top of that, the woman is ugly as sin. I saw a tintype of her."

Chris was laughing by now.

He said, "Where did you get all this from?"

Joshua said, "Been reading magazines and newspapers and talking to the nurses. This Belva Lockwood is so ugly her father used to hook her up to the buggy by accident two of three times a week."

Chris started chuckling with renewed vigor.

Joshua took a long drag on his cigarette, stared at it, and blew smoke toward the window.

Just then, a nurse walked into the room carrying a bedpan in her hand. Joshua tried to hide the cigarette next to the bed, but the nurse saw it and became perturbed, storming over to Joshua, yanking the cigarette out of his hand, and tossing it out the window. Joshua acted like a little boy who had been caught stealing a piece of apple pie from the windowsill.

The nurse said, "Mr. Colt, what am I going to do with you? First, half the men in Fremont County punch bulletholes through you. We plug them up, then you try to rot yourself from the inside with smoke."

"Smoke!" Joshua said, "How is smoking going to hurt you?"

The nurse pursed her lips and cocked one eyebrow.

She said, "Mr. Colt, why don't you just stick your head in the cooking fire next time you're driving cattle. That's right, just stick your head in the fire and breathe in and out a few dozen times. That's basically what you're doing."

Chris laughed, "No, Ma'am, it's not the same thing. If a man sticks his head in the fire, someone might set a coffeepot on it."

"Pshaw," she replied, grinning and giving Chris a wave of her hand.

She set the bedpan down beside the bed on the nightstand and left the room, still smiling.

When she was gone, Joshua reached over to the nightstand and picked up Chris's papers and tobacco pouch. He quickly and deftly rolled another cigarette and lit up. After taking a puff, a serious look came on his face.

He said, "All right, brother. Now, I want to know what's up. Everyone has been so cheerful around me—too cheerful. You're the only one who will lay the cards out for me without palming one. Where is she and why hasn't she been here?"

Chris blew out and walked to the window, looking out at the nearby rock-, sand-, and pinion-covered foothills of the Front Range. His gaze lingered on a large ridgeline directly to his front, referred to by locals as the Hogback.

He dreaded this task more than anything he remembered doing.

Chris said, "Joshua, she left."

Joshua said quietly, "I've already figured that out, Chris. What happened?"

Chris sat down on the chair by his brother, looked at him and sighed.

"Joshua, she really loves you—" Chris started to say.

Joshua interrupted, "Sure, right."

Chris said, "Joshua, you took I don't know how many bullets in your body to save her life. She does not ever want that to happen to you again."

Tears started running down Joshua's cheeks, and Chris got choked up, too.

He continued, "She got on the train and left, Joshua, and made me promise not to try and track her down."

Joshua was crying when he said, "How could you let her do that, Chris?"

Chris said, "How could I stop her? She's a strong woman. She was determined to leave, no matter what. I could see that, so I gave her my word. I'm sorry."

Joshua looked up at the ceiling, tears streaking down both cheeks.

Chris said, "She left you her house and business. The deed is in Brandon Rudd's office."

Joshua said, "I don't want that. I want her. You have to find her, Chris."

Chris said, "I can't."

Joshua got angry, "Why not? You can trail anybody. How long has she been gone?"

Chris replied, "Weeks, but that's not the point. I can't because I gave her my word."

As frustrated and angry as he was, Joshua understood. His brother had given his word to Heidi, and no matter what, he would not break it—which upset Joshua even more and made him feel helpless. If only, he thought, he could just find Heidi and speak with her, he could convince her to return and marry him.

But though he accepted the fact that the woman he loved was gone and would never return, he was curious.

"Chris, you said she's been gone for weeks. I was still unconscious then. What if I had died?"

Chris smiled softly and replied, "Joshua, she had absolutely no doubt in her mind that you would recover fully. Big brother, I want you to understand something. This woman loved you completely. That's why she left and was very determined to never return. Society would cause you both too much trouble. She did not want you to have to spend the rest of your life defending her, or yourself."

Joshua said, "I don't care about that."

Chris said, "She knew that, but she did care. You've got to let her go, Josh."

Joshua stared out the window, tears welling up in his eyes again. Neither man spoke for a full five minutes.

Joshua finally smiled and said, "How's Shirley been?"

Colt breathed a sigh of relief. He knew his brother had accepted his fate.

Chris said, "She's fine. She's bringing you

down some of her pies tomorrow and bear sign."

Joshua managed a smile.

Chris said, "You know what a lot of the Plains tribes do?"

"What?"

Chris said, "Well, you know that the Sioux, Cheyenne, Arapaho, Crow—all the Plains tribes are very family oriented. Well, in fact, all tribes that I know of are very family oriented."

Joshua whispered, "Sure, I know that."

Chris continued, "Well, they really love their children a heck of a lot, but it's very important for the boys to be trained right."

"What about the gals?" Joshua inquired.

Chris said, "Sure, it's important for them, but even more so for the boys. The reason for that is that the men and boys do almost all the fighting. Now, sometimes the girls and women end up fighting if the village is attacked and the men are already out in a battle, but most often, the men and boys do all the fighting. Because of that, they get killed a lot more often and at a lot younger age than the womenfolk do."

"Makes sense," Joshua said.

Colt went on, "That's why Indians so often turn tail and run away if the tide of a battle turns against them, or if they are confronted with a superior force. A lot of cavalry commanders figure they're cowards, but that's the last thing they are. They're just trying to preserve the male population of their tribe."

"Yeah."

Chris continued, "That was Custer's undoing. Anyway, because the preservation of the clan, the band, the tribe, the nation is so critically important to them, the training of the young boys has to be effective and tough, so you know what the fathers do with their sons?"

"What?" Joshua asked.

Colt said, "They turn them over to their brothers to raise, completely and totally."

"They do?" Joshua asked.

Chris went on, "Yep. They figure if they raise their sons themselves, they might be too soft on them. If they have a brother who is a good warrior, they actually send their sons to be raised by him and his wife until they're full grown. That way, the uncle will always be tough on the boy because he doesn't have the same emotional attachment."

Joshua smiled and said, "So they love someone so much that they let them go, so their life can be better and longer. That what you're trying to tell me, little brother?"

Chris smiled and looked out the window.

Joshua said, "So have you caught the killer yet?"

"No. He's the best I've ever been against."

Joshua said, "Scared?"

Chris said, "You bet."

Joshua replied, "Good; that will keep you alert and alive."

Chris said, "I hope so. Joshua, this man is a beast and a giant, but what makes matters worse is that he's a genius. He also is a mountain man and knows as much as I do about tracking and the wilderness."

Joshua said, "I thought he was an animal."

Colt said, "He is."

Joshua said, "Well, little brother, then you're going to have to be the hunter that tracks him down."

"Don't remind me," Chris said.

Though Joshua laughed, it still hurt Chris to see his brother's puffy eyes and weakened condition.

Joshua broke the pregnant silence by saying, "There's doctors and nurses to take care of me. You better get after that killer."

Chris smiled and headed for the door. He paused there, hand on the knob.

"Joshua," he said, "You really had a close

one, and now this man I'm going after . . . Well, if anything happens, I just want—"

Joshua raised his hand and interrupted, "Shut up and get going. I know. You and I never need to say those things."

Chris grinned and said, "I just want you to know, I couldn't have asked for a better brother."

Joshua blushed and said, "I know. Me too. Now, get out of here. Do your job."

Colt went out the door, and Joshua turned his head, directing his gaze out the window. On the white sheet, by his pillow, a large tear drop fell and created a small wet circle.

Chris headed back home and sent word for Man Killer to meet him the next morning at daybreak.

That night, Shirley Colt nearly panicked. She had never seen Chris Colt spend so much time cleaning his weapons and checking his ammunition. He pulled out his giant Bowie knife and spent a full hour keening the already scalpel-sharp edge. He went over his Cheyenne bow and quiver of arrows, carefully checking them and removing any cedar arrows that didn't have perfectly straight shafts. He even sharpened the chipped flint arrowheads as best he could, as well as those few that were steel tipped.

While he cleaned his Winchester carbine, Shirley walked up behind him and kneaded his bulky shoulder muscles, which were as knotted and taut as an anchor rope.

"What's wrong, darling?" she asked.

"Nothing, Shirl," he replied. "Not a thing."

Nothing in his demeanor or in the tone of his voice betrayed nervousness or anxiety, but Shirley was still troubled—in fact, since Chris was keeping his worries to himself, she became even more concerned. In the past, if he was working on a puzzling case or going after a killer of some repute, he always confided in her. This time, though, he had been unusually quiet. All Shirley knew was that the man was a murderer, and that he was somehow connected to that grizzly that had killed Joshua's horse.

The next morning, Chris Colt was up before first light, surprised to find that his wife was awake and a full breakfast was waiting for Man Killer and him.

"Thank you, Shirl," Man Killer said, "I left Jennifer in bed asleep."

Chris gave her a nice kiss and said, "Honey, you've never gotten up and cooked like this before when we were leaving. Thanks. This is great."

Shirley wrapped her arms around him and said, "Just want you to remember what you have waiting for you at home so you will be anxious to get back here."

Man Killer swallowed a mouthful of eggs and fried potatoes, saying, "I am anxious to come back already, and we have not yet left."

"Me too!" Colt said laughing.

Shirley, puzzled, could not figure out what was happening with Chris until it finally dawned on her—and she realized that the thought had been in the back of her mind all along, probably prompting her to get up early and prepare a special breakfast. This time, for some reason, Chris was so frightened that he did not want to tell her and cause her to worry.

Halfway through the meal Shirley nonchalantly asked, "Is this killer you're going after as bad as the ones you've been after before, Man Killer?"

Man Killer said, "He is much worse. He is big like the grizzly, knows the mountains and the woods like Chris Colt, quotes literature, and is mean like the wolverine."

Shirley looked nonplussed by this information; she was also certain Chris was studying every inch of her face for reaction.

She took a sip of coffee, "Well, maybe

you'll get hurt on this case, but you will kill him or bring him to justice. This coffee tastes good today, if I do say so myself."

Twenty minutes later, Chris gave Shirley a long kiss, climbed into his saddle, and rode alongside his friend toward the big range. Shirley waved, broom in her hand, and started sweeping the porch. Chris felt much more relieved.

He looked down at his big timberwolf, Kuli, who appeared out of nowhere and joined them. Kuli had been sleeping in the big pile of bedding straw in the new barn Joshua and Man Killer had built. This time, Colt decided, the big wolf would accompany them. He would give alarm well before they ran into the giant murderer. Or at least Chris Colt *hoped* the wolf could warn them. Wolves were very shy animals, but Chris couldn't help but believe that Kuli would attack anyone or anything that attacked Man Killer or him.

As soon as the two disappeared over the rise, Shirley dropped the broom, ran into the house, and ran to her bedroom, throwing herself across the big four-poster feather bed. Seconds later, she turned at the sound of Brenna's voice. "Mommy, why are you crying?"

Brenna crawled into bed with Shirley and

the woman held her daughter tightly. A few minutes later, Joseph climbed into bed on the other side and the two children snuggled up to their mother.

An hour later, Chris and Man Killer stopped to let their horses have a blow. They were at the main trail that ran along the face of the Sangre de Cristos. It ran north and south along the big range, varying from nine thousand to eleven thousand feet in elevation. Some referred to it as the Rainbow Trail.

Man Killer said, "What is our plan?"

Colt scratched Kuli behind the ears, chuckled, and said, "To try and keep our hides from getting ripped into a million pieces."

Man Killer laughed as Colt gathered up the reins to his big paint and vaulted up into the saddle. Man Killer followed suit.

Colt said, "Let's head south. Remember the cabin old Beaver had up above timberline in the Crestones? I want to check it out."

Man Killer remembered it very well. Beaver Banta was the very old uncle of Man Killer's wife, Jennifer. A hermit, the old fellow was a mountain man who used to live with the wolf Kuli. He had befriended Man Killer after the young brave had killed both a grizzly and a big tom cougar at the same time. Prior to that, the secretive oldster had become acquainted with Joshua and Chris Colt on separate occasions. A former hunting, trapping, and guiding partner of Kit Carson, the old man was in incredible shape and walked everywhere accompanied by the wolf. Though Beaver had been murdered, Man Killer had introduced his killers to justice—frontier justice.

The cabin they were seeking was in a high mountain bowl, well above timberline and teeming with bighorn sheep and large mule deer and elk. About eleven months out of the year, the area was covered with snow. The little cabin itself, built with chinked logs that fit tightly together, was on the shore of a glacial lake filled with cutthroat and rainbow trout.

It took the entire day to make the ride almost to the cabin. The men decided to make camp in the heavy timber a couple thousand feet below the ridge that would lead them into the alpine valley.

Eagle Bleu watched with the telescope from his high mountain perch near the summit of Crestone Needles, some of the most dangerous peaks in the Sangre de Cristos.

The sociopath knew that the former scout

would come to Beaver's cabin first, and he was not surprised when Chris showed up down below it. And since it was a day's ride from the Coyote Run to the cabin, Eagle was not surprised when he saw the men go into the timber and not emerge. His lookout spot was at fourteen thousand feet, where breathing was difficult even for him, so he decided to drop down into the bowl and make camp near the cabin on the side of one of the ridges.

He had prepared the cabin well, and he hoped his trap would work. He had spent hours and hours making the boobytrap for Colt. Now the big man would climb down to a closer observation spot, lay down among a big jumble of boulders, and sleep.

Chris and Man Killer, well hidden in the dark timber, prepared a hot meal and turned in early, hardly talking with each other. Kuli had been acting nervous and excited, and they both felt bad, because they knew the wolf was remembering his old stomping grounds.

It was after midnight when Chris Colt saw a giant shadow standing over him, and he sat up, almost screaming.

The nightmare again.

Colt rolled over and looked at the embers of the dying fire. He looked at Kuli sleeping peacefully not ten feet away. Why was he so afraid? he wondered. He had to conquer this demon.

Daylight brought relief. The two men got ready and were in the saddle early. The horses were well rested and had eaten on the high mountain meadow grasses during the night, and even Kuli seemed eager to go.

They slowly approached the cabin a few hours later. Colt spotted a small herd of bighorns across the canyon and Man Killer drew on a big buck deer they surprised when they dropped down around a large rockface along the trail. Chris grinned as the young red lawman holstered his walnut-handled standard Colt .45 Peacemaker.

They went up to the cabin at a slow walk, carrying their carbines across their saddle bows. When they were about fifty yards out, Chris put his carbine back in his right-side scabbard, and pulled the Colt revolving twelve-gauge shotgun from the right one. Man Killer had not seen Chris do such a thing before, and his caution put a lump in Man Killer's throat.

They dismounted in front of the cabin and immediately started looking for tracks. They saw none, but the two ex-scouts were still cautious. They got down on their hands and knees when they were less than ten feet away and studied the ground carefully.

Finally, Man Killer said, "It is too clean. Someone has even cleaned away signs of rats, marmots, and birds that might have come near—and something would have."

Colt said, "You're absolutely right, partner. He's good, but maybe too good. Look at the window. The big shutter is up and the lock in the window is not latched. I think we'll be safer to climb through the window than try that front door."

Man Killer said, "You are right, Colt."

The two men stood and walked toward the window, and suddenly the ground gave way under them both. They fell and fell into the blackness of a deep drywell or vertical mine shaft, and when they hit bottom, they lost their wind. It took a minute or so to recover.

Finally, Colt lit a match and surveyed their situation. He saw all the shovel marks along the walls of the shaft, which was twenty feet deep. The ground was damp and the bottom of the shaft was covered with a foot of water. Chris also saw the marks at the lip of the shaft, where a rope had dug into the side of the ground. The camouflaged cover they had stepped on, still partially intact, had been made of interwoven aspen branches and covered with a layer of sod. It probably wouldn't have collapsed with the weight of just one of them, at least not until they had stood directly on the cover—a difficult thing to avoid.

To the left of the trap cover, Colt remembered, was a pile of stacked firewood; to the right was an old handmade bench that Beaver used to do his skinning on. What a fool he had been, Colt thought. When setting a trap for an animal, you use natural items to funnel him into it. The genius killer had done that with them, by simply restacking the firewood pile and moving the bench. Leaving the window unlatched was a touch only a mastermind would have thought of, because the two experts would have clearly seen the track cleaning and been too cautious to approach the door. Colt thought of all this and a chill ran up and down his spine.

"You okay?" Colt asked Man Killer.

"Yes, but we are dead anyway, Great Scout."

Chris said, "Please don't call me a name like that right now, partner. Call me great fool."

Man Killer said, "Why? I stepped on this

trap with you, and I am not a fool. You taught me that, so then you must not be one, too."

The simple logic and profundity of Man Killer's statement hit him like a blacksmith's hammer on an anvil.

He wasn't a fool. Chris Colt was a master at tracking, warfare, and gunfighting. He would no longer allow himself to be paralyzed by fear of some unknown killer. He was at the bottom of a twenty-foot trap, which was maybe six feet wide all the way up, but somehow he would survive and this killer would not. Colt knew for certain that this man would never end up behind bars or at the end of a rope. He would die at the hand of Chris Colt. Or vice versa.

Colt gave out the whistle of a red-tailed hawk, and seconds later, War Bonnet was trying to look down the mine shaft, snorting and prancing. Hawk was next to him, trying to see his master as well. Chris and Man Killer looked up and called to the nervous horses for several minutes.

Finally, Chris laughed and said, "I forgot. We love you both, but horses are stupid, so I guess figuring out how to get one of you to drop a lasso is a lost cause."

Man Killer started giggling at this remark and Colt laughed at himself for his silly statement. Pretty soon, faced with almost certain death, the two dropped down into sitting positions in the water and held their sides laughing.

They laughed for five full minutes, then Colt pulled out the makings. He offered them to Man Killer and rolled a cigarette for himself. Man Killer lit both.

Colt took a long drag and said, "Young brother, you know this is one of the few pleasures that men can share together without women wanting to butt in. Besides, since we're both going to be somebody's dinner tonight, we might as well offer them smoked meat."

Both men started laughing again and were soon roaring hysterically, tears streaking down their cheeks. When Eagle heard this laughter, he wondered why he had never done that. He thought about it as he approached the top of the hole. Maybe after he received much medicine by eating the heart of these two warriors, he would be able to laugh. He tried to think back over his years and could not remember ever laughing or seeing or hearing anything that would make him want to laugh.

Colt and Man Killer heard a noise and dropped their cigarettes in the water. They both drew their guns and waited for long tense moments.

Suddenly, they heard a growl from Kuli, a scuffle, and then a squealing sound. Colt gritted his teeth together as he pictured a big knife going into the ribcage of his beloved wolf.

Then, they finally heard the voice of the mysterious killer, "Why do you laugh?"

The voice itself was enough to send fear into almost any man. It was the deepest voice Colt had ever heard and seemed like it would be the voice a grizzly bear would have if it could speak. It had a very slight French accent.

Colt and Man Killer didn't speak but just waited for a head to appear and blot out part of the sky. First, they would make the head disappear and then deal with getting out of the hole.

The voice again, "Colt, there is a Chinese proverb which states that the greatest conqueror is he who overcomes the enemy without a blow."

Finally, Chris said, "Who are you?"

The voice came back, "I am Eagle Bleu. You do not know me. Nobody knows me. Those who have seen me have had their hearts eaten, like you two will."

Chris said, "My heart doesn't leave my body too easily."

Eagle said, "I know. Man Killer's doesn't either. That is why I will eat both of yours, for it will make my medicine that much stronger."

Colt said, "Sounds like your name should be buzzard and not eagle."

Man Killer tapped Chris in the dark, wanting to shut him up.

The smell from the giant man finally wafted down to them in the downdraft and it made them both want to retch. It was a horrible, putrid smell that reminded them both of carrion. It was a scent that neither man would soon forget.

Eagle said matter of factly, "You are such a worthy enemy. You say words to anger me, and hope I will make a mistake. But I do not get angry."

Man Killer did not want to speak and confirm his presence, or disrupt anything Colt might have planned to say.

Colt said, "Well, I might as well get the formalities out of the way. Eagle Bleu, you are under arrest for murder. Want to drop us a rope and throw down your weapons?"

Eagle flatly said, "That would not be intelligent. I will go find herbs and wild turnips to eat with your hearts. I always eat hearts right from the body, but you are mighty warriors, so I will prepare a feast for myself. When I return I will kill you both and eat you."

Eagle made his statement this way for two reasons. Number one, he was serious, and number two, he did not understand why Colt did not act afraid or nervous. He would go fetch special seasonings which he thought would give him more power when he ate the hearts of the warriors.

Maybe, he thought, he would not kill them first, but bring them up from the hole alive. First, he would shoot one or both of them until they would throw all of their weapons up out of the hole. But he would just wound them severely. Then he would lower the makeshift ladder and let them climb out one at a time and tie them up. After that, he would use one or both as a woman and steal more of their power. This would make Colt afraid, especially if he used Man Killer as a woman first. He had not had a woman or a girl for a few weeks, and he wanted to see and hear the fear. After that, he would kill the Nez Perce first, then Colt, and then cut out both their strong hearts.

Satisfied with his plan, the big man turned and headed up the trail that would take him over the lip of the bowl and drop down into the timber below. He wanted to hurry and return before the water in the ground so close to the lake would cave in the sides of the trap and drown and smother his prized trophies.

In the bottom of the pit, Chris and Man Killer started to feel around the walls again, hoping for some sort of handhold. They found nothing. Both men stopped, though, at the slight sound they heard above.

Colt whispered, "Listen!"

They strained their ears and looked up at the top of the hole—movement, a whining sound. Both men smiled. It was Kuli. He was alive, maybe hurt a little but alive.

Colt whispered, "Hi, Kuli, good boy."

Both men were relieved to see the wolf's ears prick up and his tongue hang out. His eyes were bright and alert. He couldn't be hurt too badly.

Chris said, "We have to move fast. Kuli wouldn't be lying there if Eagle was around. He must really be hunting herbs to cook with us."

Man Killer said, "Would Kuli be smart enough to get a rope from one of the horses?"

As soon as he asked the question he laughed at himself.

Colt said, "Sure, he'd be smart enough, but only if he wasn't a real wolf and just one those writers back east tell about in those dime Western novels."

Man Killer said, "I have read some of those books and they are good. I like it where one white man with a pistol kills so many Indians with rifles and bows. Until I read that, I did not know I was so stupid. What shall we do?"

Chris said, "I don't know. Think."

After a few minutes, Colt said, "I have an idea. It may not work, but let's try it. Turn around."

Man Killer turned, and so did Colt. Chris reached back and locked his arms inside of Man Killer's.

Colt said, "Okay, pull forward on my arms and I'll pull on yours so we are locked together."

They both did this, then Colt said, "Now, we push the backs of our shoulders together, and we walk up the sides of the hole with our feet."

Man Killer got excited.

"Will this work, Great One?"

As they struggled, Eagle Bleu gathered up the last of the herbs and an armful of wild turnips and started back up the mountain trail.

Meanwhile, Chris and Man Killer worked feverishly to walk up the sides of the twenty-foot-deep death trap. They made it almost halfway, Colt getting higher than Man Killer with his feet. But then they both toppled to the ground, with Man Killer spraining his ankle. Colt jerked off his kerchief and tightly bound Man Killer's ankle with a figure-eight wrap.

Man Killer said, "Hurry, we must try again."

This time, they were both careful to pace each other stepping up the wall. They moved one foot and then the other, each man holding his breath. They made it halfway up and every muscle in their bodies was straining from exertion.

Voice quaking, Colt said, "We make it to the top, we stick our feet out together and roll to my right and your left."

Man Killer said, "If we do not fall. My legs will not work anymore."

Chris said, "Yes, they will."

With renewed enthusiasm, both men pushed against each other's backs and kept climbing. Minutes later, they emerged at the top of the shaft and stuck their legs out a few inches beyond the lip. On Colt's signal, they quickly rolled across the top of the hole and lay there on solid ground, panting and shaking.

Chris jumped up and checked the loads in his guns and Man Killer followed suit. They shook hands and smiled at each other, then both men hugged Kuli, who wagged his tail and showed no signs of injury until he walked, when he favored his left hip. Man Killer gave the call of a red-tailed hawk and Chris felt all over the wolf's leg and hip.

Colt stood, saying, "I think he's just bruised or got a pulled muscle."

The two horses ran up from the area behind the cabin and the two men noticed them both looking off to their right, ears pricked forward and nostrils twitching. They looked, and saw Eagle Bleu standing on the lip of the bowl, an armload of wild turnips and roots in his big grasp. He dropped them as Colt grabbed for his carbine. Chris wheeled and tried a snap shot, quickly bringing the gun to his shoulder. It was a two hundred–yard shot and Eagle was already moving back up over the lip of the bowl as Colt's bullet sent up a puff of dust next to the monster.

The two lawmen swung onto their horses' backs and took off at a full gallop. This time, he would not have time to cover his trail. It would only take the time for two fast horses to cover two hundred yards—less than half a minute. He might still be in sight.

They topped the ridge with Kuli half-limping and half-running behind them. The man was nowhere in sight and they slid to a stop. Kuli did not. Nostrils going in and out, he passed them like they were standing still and headed straight downhill.

Colt said, "Come on."

The two men leaned back and plunged their horses straight down toward the trees below. Then they saw the path he took down the mountain. He crashed through grasses and brush, leaving a very obvious trail. No matter how fast he was, they both thought, he was still a man and would not outrun them this time. He was also running down into trees and would not be jumping off any cliffs with a parachute. Both men were excited now with the chase, although one misstep by either horse could mean the death of one or both men. The mountainside was so steep that the horses' rumps dragged as they went down the almost vertical face of the ridge.

Colt could not believe how fast the big man had gone down into the trees. Kuli was almost out of sight now and not limping at all, his adrenaline was pumping so hard. The trail was very clear now down through the trees, and Chris wondered if the trail wasn't just too clear. The thought crossed his mind that Eagle Bleu may have tripped himself and rolled part or all the way down the mountain.

No sooner had he thought this than he saw a large deadfall tree down in the trees and there was a large ball of fur piled up against them and Kuli was tearing into it right now. Apparently the fall had killed or knocked out the sociopath. And Kuli was showing that he did not care for people who injured him.

Seconds later, the two former scouts were able to slide their mounts to a stop on unsteady legs. Colt's heart sunk as he got off of War Bonnet. Kuli vigorously shook the big fur coat of Eagle Bleu, wrapped around a big boulder that would have taken two or three strong men to move. It apparently had been quickly picked up and tossed down the mountainside by the killer after wrapping his bulky coat around it. The rock was so large and heavy that it kept plowing its way through anything in its path until it came to rest against the blowdown.

Colt looked down at the coat and over at Man Killer. They both knew what happened. Eagle Bleu had gone uphill and sent the rock downhill.

Undaunted, he jumped back up on his horse. Colt spurred War Bonnet down and to the north along the mountainside.

He yelled over his shoulder, "Come on!"

Man Killer tried to figure out what the marshall was trying to do now, but knew Colt well enough to know that it would make sense. After a quarter mile, the Nez Perce caught up with his mentor, still weaving in and out of trees and jumping blowdowns. The big Appaloosa, Hawk, always did a little better when the two horses were up in the mountains, but nothing could outrun War Bonnet down on the flatlands.

Pulling up alongside Colt, Man Killer looked over but said nothing. He knew Colt would explain the method of his madness.

Colt explained, "I guarantee you that he is climbing up Crestone Needles right now, where he's got his parachute cached. He'll jump off the peak somewhere and glide down into the San Luis Valley, where I also guarantee you his big horse is corralled somewhere."

Man Killer said, "So, why do we ride north?"

Colt said, "The next major cut in the mountains is Medano Pass. We'll cross over and try to pick up his trail while it's fresh. Maybe we'll get lucky."

Man Killer hollered, "Maybe the wind will change while he is falling and blow him into the rocks."

Colt said, "I wish."

They soon slowed the horses to a steady trot and made it to the Medano cut in an hour. They headed back uphill, slowing the horses to a walk. Colt gave Man Killer a cigarito and had one himself.

Man Killer said, "I do not understand why Medano Pass is spelled M-E-D-A-N-O but is pronounced Mad-Now."

Chris grinned and said, "Don't ask me."

Man Killer said, "Why?"

Colt replied, "I'll get mad now if you ask."

Man Killer moaned.

Chris got serious and spurred his horse ahead at a trot, saying, "Come on. We have to keep a steady pace."

Hours later, as they came down the western side of the pass, they stopped at one vantage point overlooking the San Luis Valley and spotted a white object floating down from the fourteen-thousand-plus–foot Crestone Needles. Even under the parachute canopy and at a great distance, Eagle Bleu looked like a monster.

The horses had been stopped twice to

rest and were in great shape anyway, so Colt again mounted up, and Man Killer followed as they tried to head toward the area the parachute would be landing. They were very close to the Great Sand Dunes where Man Killer had almost been killed saving his future wife from some renegade Utes. Being so close to such a place made him nervous, but he shrugged the feeling off.

It was shortly before dark when they arrived at the place where Eagle Bleu's parachute landed in the foothills of the big range. Because the western slope of the Sangres was so steep, it wasn't long before the foothills gave way to the broad valley.

Within minutes, Bleu found a spot where the man stopped on a small hill and looked back toward the direction where they had came from. He observed them for a short period of time and took off for his horse at a fast jog. The big man knew he was being closely followed and made no effort to hide his trail.

They followed the tracks for over a mile and found where he made a quick attempt to brush them out with a pinion branch. But the attempt had been made way too quickly, and neither man had to leave his horse to spot the trail. Eagle had even purposely made clear tracks, leaving the trail

and heading into some thick scrub oaks,
but neither Colt nor Man Killer fell for this
trick, either. It was obvious to Colt that
Bleu was desperate right now, and that
didn't seem like him.

Colt reined his horse back a little and
said to Man Killer, "Let's slow down a little.
Let the horses walk. We could run right
into a trap."

Man Killer said, "This is smart."

They went another three miles before
they found where he had his horse in a
makeshift corral in the midst of a small
meadow in the scrub oak. A small creek ran
right through the meadow.

CHAPTER 8

Trap!

Shortly after the monster took off on his horse, Man Killer spotted something in the trail. It was just a small piece of cloth, but he slid his horse to a halt under a grove of cottonwood trees to inspect it. He was two feet away when the trap was sprung, and he winced in pain but did not scream.

Colt was twenty feet behind him when he slid to a stop and was now doing the same. All he could see was that Man Killer's left leg had gone through the ground, presumably into a hole maybe a foot deep. Man Killer held his leg and his face had turned almost pure white, but he would not cry out.

Chris got on his hands and knees, scrambling up to his partner as his eyes continued to scour the ground. He quickly brushed away the rest of the camouflage cover around the hole and saw immediately what Eagle Bleu had done. The hole was only large enough for one man's foot to go into it, and it was a hastily dug hole about a foot to a foot and a half deep. Deer antler tines, sharpened to a point—maybe ten of them—had been jammed into the ground with the points pointing downward at angles all the way around the hole. The reason for this was obvious: A person sticking his foot into the hole would try to yank it out right away and impale his leg all the way around with the antler stakes. This was exactly what had happened to Man Killer, who was now bleeding profusely. Colt had to act fast.

His Bowie knife came out in a flash, and he commanded, "Step back down into the bottom of the hole."

Man Killer complied, and Chris started furiously digging away at the edge of the hole, going around it and digging out the end of each antler tine. He lifted Man Killer's leg out of the hole and, as quickly as he could, yanked the sharpened stakes out of Man Killer's leg. Man Killer gritted his teeth and broke out in a heavy sweat, but did not yell or moan.

Blood streamed from the deep holes, and it was very obvious the tines had severely broken his leg as well. Chris wrapped his kerchief around the leg and bound it tightly but that did not stop the flow of blood from the back of Man Killer's calf. The blood spurted out at regular intervals, the sign of an arterial cut. Colt ran to his saddlebags and yanked out the clean towel his wife always kept packed there. Chris jacked out three .44 rounds from his Winchester carbine and tied them together with a leather thong he ripped from his shirt fringe. They now formed a triangle-shaped side by side. He placed them over the wound area where the artery was cut and wrapped the towel over them tightly. He tied it off as tightly as possible, hoping and praying the direct pressure from the bullets on the wound would stop the bleeding.

It did.

Colt was relieved, for he had seen men lose legs and arms because of unmanaged tourniquets so far from professional medical help. He had wanted to avoid using a tourniquet on his partner's leg.

Man Killer started to get a little more color back into his face.

Colt said, "Lay down."

Man Killer protested. "Thank you, Great Scout, but you must go on from here and chase him. I will take care of my leg now that you have the bleeding stopped. I will make it back to the Coyote Run. Go."

Chris said, "Be quiet and lay back."

The marshal and Man Killer had an unwritten code that they never discussed. Man Killer had learned much of what he knew from Christian missionaries, from the famous Chief Joseph himself, and, most of all, from Chris Colt. If there was an absolute emergency or critical life-or-death situation, Man Killer was to keep quiet and Chris Colt would give the commands. He was more knowledgeable and had much more experience, so Man Killer deferred to his mentor in those situations. When Man Killer looked into Chris's eyes, the look he saw and the tone of voice he heard confirmed Colt was totally in charge and arguing would be futile.

Man Killer lay back while Chris broke branches off the cottonwood overhead and quickly chopped the little branches and leaves off of each one.

He found a homespun shirt in his saddlebags, which he quickly cut into strips with his Bowie. He then fashioned a splint around Man Killer's lower leg, tying the strips of cloth around the outside of the four sticks he placed all around the leg for support.

Colt explained, "Your leg is badly broken and I need to fix it so it can't move."

Man Killer grinned and said, "I know that."

Next, Colt built a small fire and put a coffeepot on. He leaned Man Killer against the big cottonwood tree and gave him the makings. The lawman then ran into the trees.

He returned a half an hour later with some herbs that he pounded into a mush with a round rock on a flat rock. He then made a poultice and applied it to the open wounds after removing the bandages. The arterial bleeding was now nothing but scabs.

Chris started looking for long poles to make a travois and Man Killer spoke up, "No! Thank you for what you are doing, but this time I will argue. I rode a travois from the Sand Dunes before, but I could not do anything. I was almost dead. I will ride my horse."

This time, Man Killer had that look in his eye that he apparently got from Colt, so Chris just grinned and nodded, saddling both horses.

Colt said, "You are hurt bad. We can camp tonight or ride home. Your choice?"

Man Killer said, "Let's ride. You must get on his trail again."

They saddled up, with Man Killer taking

a full five minutes to get onto his horse's back. They headed back to Medano Pass, as the sun started to dip down over the San Luis Valley. As they started up the pass, Colt looked back out over the large valley and spotted a small dot headed toward Saguache. He pulled out his telescope from his saddlebags and looked.

"It's him," Colt said.

Man Killer said, "You will get him."

Chris turned in the saddle and squeezed with his thighs. War Bonnet walked forward.

Chris said over his shoulder, "Damned right."

It was almost daybreak when the two men reached Man Killer's ranch. Jennifer bit her lip and tears welled up in her eyes, but she steeled herself against the task at hand. She quickly kissed Man Killer, then looked at Chris, blinking away her tears.

"What do you want me to do, Chris?"

"Can you have a hand saddle me a fresh horse, so I can ride to Westcliffe and get the doctor?"

Man Killer raised his hand and said, "No, he's worn out. Send Carter."

Colt said, "No, I'm going myself. I want to make sure the doctor makes it here quickly."

Man Killer started to say something and Jennifer held up her hand. Now it was her turn to give one of those looks. Man Killer just had a sheepish one on his face.

While she summoned a hand from the bunkhouse to saddle a horse for Colt, he helped Man Killer out of his clothes and into bed.

When the doctor checked Man Killer's wounds, he said, "You did a very good job, Mr. Colt. The leg was badly broken in several places and the flesh was torn up by puncture wounds. If not for your treatment, he might have lost this leg. I believe that won't be the case, though. Mr. Man Killer, you've lost a good bit of blood, young man. Mr. Colt must have brought you home in a covered wagon with a feather bed, I'd say."

Jennifer bragged, "No, he rode his horse from San Luis Valley, riding over Medano Pass."

"Surely you jest," the doctor said.

Chris Colt said dryly, "No, Shirley is my wife, Doc. This is Jennifer."

The doctor turned and seriously said, "Why, I know this is Jennifer, sir."

He paused and finally got the joke and chuckled, while Man Killer and Jennifer both moaned.

The doctor said, "I understand, Mr. Colt,

you devil, you. Say, I'm going past your ranch. I understand you have had no sleep in a long time. Why don't you tie your horse to the back of my wagon and you can sleep in the back."

Jennifer said, "That's a wonderful idea, Chris. We will take a mattress from the guest bedroom and put it in the buckboard, and you can sleep all the way there in total comfort."

That sounded so inviting to Chris Colt, as his head was spinning. But after all, he was Chris Colt.

He said, "Thanks, Doc and you, too, Jennifer, but I have a murderer to go after, and I also don't want to have to say good-bye to my wife all over again."

He was not going to be argued with, so no one spoke.

Colt added, "But I will take you up on the feather bed, Jennifer. I really should get a few hours of sleep."

She showed him to a guest bedroom and Chris was asleep almost instantly after being assured they wouldn't let him sleep too long and that the hands would take good care of War Bonnet.

He opened his eyes and sat up suddenly. Colt reached for his right-hand gun, which wasn't there, and looked from left to right.

He realized where he was, and that it was almost dawn. His stomach felt like his throat had been slit, and his bladder ached.

Colt jumped up and dressed quickly. He tiptoed downstairs and left a thank-you note on the kitchen table. In less than ten minutes time, he rode a well-rested War Bonnet out of the big barn and headed for the big range looming directly to the west.

By noon, Colt was already riding across the floor of the San Luis Valley. He crossed at Music Pass instead of Medano, just in case Eagle Bleu had doubled back and was waiting to ambush him.

Chris had sent a letter to his wife by way of the doctor. But right now, there was just one thing on his mind—getting Eagle Bleu before the monster could kill and terrorize again.

All of a sudden, a thought dawned on him. Did Eagle Bleu really want to get at Colt, terrorizing him before killing him? Chris wondered what would be the best way to accomplish that.

Colt turned his horse and headed back toward Music Pass—he had to get to his family fast. Eagle Bleu would not go after Joshua because he was in Canon City, and Colt was certain that the killer did not like to be around any people.

At the ranch, Chris had old Tex Westchester, who was a hardened veteran of Indian battles, rustler battles, outlaw battles, and battles in general, as well as Tex's sidekick—big, strong Muley Hawkins. If Muley grabbed anything in a bearhug—anything whatsoever—his arms would encompass it, and it would get hurt. Both men had worked for Joshua Colt and, coming with him to the Coyote Run, had been through thick and thin with the Colts. Chris, however, had a wife who had been kidnapped—not once, but twice—and he vowed she would never have to go through such an experience again. So he was not going to take any chances.

He pushed his big paint as hard as he dared, but Colt was conscientious about protecting his horse from overwork. He had accidentally killed a horse crossing the Tuscarawas River in southeastern Ohio on his way home from the Civil War. It broke the young Colt's heart, and he had been determined never to push a horse that hard again.

The predator had indeed doubled back. Though Eagle Bleu was a ruthless sociopath with no remorse for his wrongdoings, he was not stupid—he was a cunning genius who never stopped plotting or planning, always trying, futilely, for emotional stimulation. At least this cat-and-mouse game with Chris Colt provided some glimmer of feeling. The lawman's one Achilles heel, Eagle Bleu knew, was his beloved family, and that was exactly who the predator was going after. Perhaps he would kill one of Colt's children, or violate and kill his wife—that would make the ultimate kill more enjoyable.

Eagle had hated trapping the men and taking one of them out of the race, but he had decided it would make the scenario more enjoyable. He could come back later to kill and eat Man Killer.

Now his targets lay below at the Coyote Run Ranch, some miles below him and to the east. He stood on the edge of a ridge of Spread Eagle Peak and spread his arms, yawning. He was tired, but he could not sleep right now. The potential kill made him alert.

At that moment, Shirley Colt had the two trusted top hands of the Coyote Run in her kitchen serving them up steaks, potatoes, and iced beers. She sat down to talk with them while they ate.

"Boys," she said, "I need your help."

Tex said, "Ya jest go head an' name it, ma'am, an' we'll do it. Ya need a tornado roped? Need an elephant throwed and hog-tied? Mrs. Colt, anything ya want, me an big ole Muley here'll be happy ta do."

Shirley smiled, "Well, Tex, I'm afraid it could be worse than all that."

Tex stopped eating, fork halfway to his mouth. He knew that the very unflappable Shirley Colt was serious. Something was very wrong.

She explained, "The man Chris and Man Killer are hunting is very, very dangerous. He is ruthless and cunning, and I have a feeling he will probably try to come after Chris's family."

"What makes ya think that, Mrs. Colt?" Muley asked.

Shirley took a sip of coffee and said, "The way Man Killer spoke about him. The note that Chris sent about Man Killer didn't tell me exactly what happened, but what wasn't written, and what Chris did not tell me, actually has told me more than anything."

Tex Westchester drew his old and weathered, but well oiled and clean .44 Russian and set it down beside his plate.

"Ma'am, if he tries to tangle with this family," Tex said, "they'll be writin' his 'bituary come tomorry. Don't ya worry none, ma'am."

Muley added, "That's right, Mrs. Colt. He'll have to come through Tex and me to get to your family. Don't you worry none at all."

Shirley smiled and poured each man some more beer.

She said, "I appreciate your words, gentlemen, but I also am very concerned. I have never seen Chris so preoccupied about someone he's after. I'm afraid this man is no ordinary killer, and we cannot let our guard down one minute. I really believe he will come after the children or me to trick Chris."

"Wal," Tex drawled, "we got five hands temporary in the bunkhouse gettin' ready fer the roundup. We'll put two on watch et a time. Ef'n ya don't mind, ma'am, I aim ta stay in the house here with ya."

"That's fine, Tex," she said. "If something happens, I'd like one of you to take charge and the other to get the children out of here."

Tex said, "Good idee, ma'am. Muley, let's make sure the buckboard stays hitched to thet matched pair a bays. They can move when they has ta. We'll jest keep 'em hitched in thet lungin' stall in the barn and make sure they can reach water'n hay when they want."

"Okay, Tex," Muley said, "I'll take care of that. If the killer shows up, you handle a team better than me, so you take Mrs. Colt and the children and get out of here. I'll cover you along with the other hands. Okay, Tex?"

"Shore, Muley, thet'll work."

Shirley said, "Just one thing, gentlemen. If he shows up here, I will stay with you to fight, and Tex, you take the children to Westcliffe. Tomorrow, I'll take them anyway."

"Ma'am," Tex replied, "Ah'm right sorry, but ef'n he shows up Ah'm a-takin' you and the young 'uns outta here. On top a which, Ah'm a-gonna do thet tomorry anyhows, and there jest ain't no arguin' 'bout it."

"Tex—" she started to say angrily. But he interrupted.

"Mrs. Colt, Ah'm shore Mr. Colt will unnerstan ef'n Ah gotta hogtie ya and gag ya, ef'n ya argue," he said firmly, "on accounta Ah'd be savin' yore purty hide. An' even ef'n he don't, its still mah job, an' Ah aim ta do it. Now, ma'am. Ah wanna know where ya stand. Am Ah gonna have ta do it the hard way or the easy way?"

She sighed and said, "You have more experience than I in fighting, Tex. If it comes to that, you're in charge."

He nodded his head and set his jaw, looking out at the towering mountain range.

Shirley said, "It's too late to go today, but tomorrow I'll go to Man Killer and Jennifer's to look in on him and find out more about this killer."

Tex added, "And Ah'll be takin' ya' and the young 'uns, ma'am."

Shirley smiled demurely replying, "Of course, Tex."

She went to the stove and brought them seconds, and Tex used this as an opportunity to soothe things a little, saying, "Mrs. Colt, Ah never have tested sech good food in all mah born days. Ah swear ya kin cook up a devil."

"Yes, ma'am. Your food tastes better'n my ma's was," Muley added. "God rest her soul."

"Thanks, boys," Shirley said, grateful that Tex had added a positive change to the conversation.

The predator was anxious to strike again. His horse was corralled once again in the San Luis Valley at the base of a nameless steep-sided mountain just south of Spread Eagle. Eagle Bleu was now in the trees halfway down the mountain and closely watching the buildings of the Coyote Run.

There were five cowboys in the bunkhouse preparing dinner—he could tell by the smoke coming out of the chimney. The old one and the big one were in the main house eating with the wife of Chris Colt—Eagle determined that because of the time they arrived and the amount of smoke that came out of the chimney while she cooked. Then he saw her walk outside and remove something from her adobe dutch oven just outside the back door. Even at that great distance of several miles and a several thousand-foot difference in elevation, he could tell she was the one he wanted to make scream in fear and pain. The sun caught the red of her auburn hair and set flames burning in the heart of Eagle Bleu. He had read about her and Chris Colt.

This woman had been kidnapped and repeatedly raped by big Will Sawyer, whose size equalled his own. Then she was kidnapped by a band of Cheyenne and held hostage, but soon gained prominence and respect among the men and women of the band for her hard work and her courage. In both cases, Chris Colt came and rescued her. Surely this woman was the key to his possession of Colt's fighting spirit.

Eagle Bleu made his decision. Normally he just dispatched the children, but since these were the son and daughter of Chris

Colt, they would have some of his spirit, so he would eat their hearts as well. He would capture this Colt woman with the red hair and plant his seed in her several times before eating her heart, too. When Colt came to rescue her and avenge his children, he would present her body or part of it, then strike the mighty man down and have a feast.

He didn't even consider all the men around her and the children. To him, they were just hills to climb over while making a journey. He got some thrill in those small challenges—if one of the men gave him a good fight, he would eat his heart when it was over. If he had time to stay on the ranch awhile, he would go ahead and eat the hearts of all the men.

The little old one who was in the house was the ramrod and the big one with him was his number-two man. He could tell by the way the cowboys responded to them earlier, and by the fact that they ate with Colt's wife.

He tried to picture the woman without her clothes and a look of terror on her face. He wondered if she possessed the cunning of Colt and Man Killer. This was indeed a good hunt, his best so far. He did not get angry when the two men escaped his trap—

it just showed that they were good adversaries. The harder it was for him to achieve victory, the more strength their hearts would bring him.

Indian warriors tortured a captured brave from an enemy tribe or nation longer and more viciously the more they respected him; it increased their own medicine and paid a high compliment to the victim. Their respect was even greater if the victim refused to cry out in pain. This concept was behind the killer's beliefs about eating people's hearts.

Eagle Bleu would wait a few hours until it was full dark, then go down and start his stalks. First, he would take out the five from the bunkhouse, then the ramrod and his assistant. Then he would take the woman and kill the children and eat them in front of her and see how frightened she would get. Maybe, if she cried and screamed enough, maybe after he ate her heart, he might be able to cry or yell or laugh like other people did. Maybe then his spirit would become strong enough to allow him to feel.

He tested the wind with his nose to see if there were any strange smells to be concerned about. There weren't.

In the San Luis Valley, directly across the

mountain range from the Coyote Run Ranch, Chris Colt cautiously approached the big Clydesdale draft horse in the meadow to his front. Colt tested the wind with his nose, trying to identify the horrible, putrid smell of Eagle Bleu. He could not.

He cautiously approached the horse and found the giant's tracks, hours old. Colt relaxed his senses a little and looked around for a bridle and saddle. They were both oversized and looked unusual. Chris had a sinking feeling in the pit of his stomach.

Eagle Bleu looked down on the ranch, then closed his eyes and decided to take a nap while he waited for several hours.

Chris Colt was fighting panic while he led the big horse away from the corral. He had tied a large pine bough with his lariat, which he hooked up to Eagle's saddlehorn, dragging it behind the big horse. They headed north, as he would cross at the Sangres just beyond Spread Eagle. There wasn't really a pass there—the closest was at Hayden Pass—but he had to get over and down to the ranch as soon as possible. It still would take hours. First, though, he led the big horse off toward the south and Medano and Music Passes, which were easier to cross.

When he came to a spot where they had to cross a little ridgeline with scrub oaks all over it, Colt shortened the lariat and sent the big horse packing. The bough behind it caused the Clydesdale to want to bolt and run off, which was what Chris had planned on. If Eagle Bleu came back down—if he had only wanted to make Colt *think* he was headed for the Coyote Run—he would assume that Colt had headed toward the easier passes to cross over.

As it was, Colt would still spend hours getting back to his ranch. He cut back to the west away from the big range through the scrub oak, very carefully obliterating his trail, then turning back north. The scrub oaks should hide his trail well. When he looked back from the oak-dotted ridge, the big red horse was already two miles to the south and still moving at a steady trot, turning sideways while it kept a frightened eye on the branch that was following it.

Chris kept trying to fight panic while he pushed his horse on. He thanked God for the powerful paint because there was no quit to War Bonnet, and he was in such great shape. The problem was that they would have to climb up and cross at maybe twelve or thirteen thousand-some feet at a place where there really wasn't a pass for people and horses over the Sangre de Cristos.

Colt's attitude was simple, though. He had a family to protect and the shortest distance between two points was a straight line. War Bonnet always sensed when Colt's situation was urgent and when danger was at hand. If they could pick their way over the top without having to stop, go back, or search for new routes, it would take hours off the already-difficult trip.

They scrambled toward the top; halfway up, Chris jumped off the big horse and led the way up, switching back and forth across the face of the steep mountain. Chris picked deer and elk trails that crisscrossed the mountain and followed them through the thick trees. It was hard to imagine how majestic bull elk, with their giant racks, could fit through some of the thickets, but Chris had witnessed this amazing sight on a number of occasions. The bull would tilt his head back so the long main antler beams were back along his body; if necessary, he would twist them from side to side while he passed quickly through the various tangles of branches and saplings in the way.

Coming upon a boulder field, Colt continued leading his horse as they carefully picked their way from boulder to boulder, a long, tedious process in the rapidly approaching dark. From what Colt could see, though, this route could cut more time off the journey if he could make it up the boulder field without having to stop and turn back. Once above the boulder field, Colt figured he could make it winding in and out of trees and climbing several ridgelines, until he was at timberline. It would definitely be after dark by then, but there was a full moon at this time of the month and maybe they could at least see some above timberline. The snow up there reflected the moonlight and helped make it even easier to see.

Right now, though, Colt's real challenge was to make it across and up above the boulder field without breaking War Bonnet's legs or falling. After that, he would cross a large avalanche chute and traverse all the fallen trees in it and make it up to the top of a steep ridgeline and, he hoped, follow that ridge up above timberline.

Eagle Bleu, meanwhile, opened his eyes and looked at the Coyote Run. Darkness was approaching fast, but he could still make out the buildings at the ranch and could see the activity going on down there. Tex Westchester had one hand with him who was being placed in the hayloft of the barn.

Then Tex took another man with a rifle into the new house, which was west of the main house. This house was big, too—Eagle Bleu did not know that it was the whitewashed frame house of Joshua Colt.

The other three hands were all in the bunkhouse, so Eagle knew that they would probably be playing poker, and the big one and the old ramrod would remain in the big house with Colt's family. The big monster started down the side of the mountain at a slow jog. It would be full dark by the time he got to the meadows at the bottom.

It was shortly after dark when Tex made a round of the grounds and checked on the two sentries. He dropped in on the bunkhouse, where the men sat around the chuck table playing poker. One had a bottle of whiskey he had been pouring from and Tex, normally an easygoing, humorous man, walked over, picked up the bottle, and threw it at the far wall, where it made a loud crash. The cowboys stared in shock at the old hand.

Tex quietly explained. "That stuff has got more folks kilt then anything else." With that, he walked out the door of the bunkhouse, leaving the three men a little more serious in their demeanor.

Tex did not need to say anything else—he had survived many trials in his life and his horses had crunched a lot of gravel under their hooves. If he was that serious, they all knew that danger was imminent.

The sentry in the hayloft and the one in Joshua's house were both alert, much to Tex's satisfaction. When he went by the big bedding straw pile in the barn, though, he became more alert than ever, as Kuli sat up suddenly, nostrils testing the wind toward the mountains and ears pricked forward. The big injured wolf was still walking with a limp after the doctor had dropped him off when he delivered Colt's message.

Tex didn't know what had happened to the wolf, but he had a good guess. In any event, Tex decided that he would take the wolf in the house because he could provide the best early warning and he was in no shape to tangle with the killer. He could do more good directly with Shirley and the kids by providing a last line of defense. Chris Colt was determined not to put his family in danger again, and Tex decided that matter came before anything else. He would see to it that they would be moved away from the danger before it occurred.

"Come on, Kuli," he said as he left the barn,

The wolf jumped up, squealing with pain as he put weight on his hind leg. He limped along behind the old man and followed him to the big house, tail wagging despite the pain.

Kuli's instincts were on full alert. He picked up the scent of the human that had hurt him on the breeze coming down out of the mountains. Along with that, he could smell come fresh-cut alfalfa, the big harem of elk feeding on it, the decaying carcass of a lightning-struck black bear at the base of Spread Eagle Peak, the human smells around the ranch, and a skunk that had sprayed up on the mountain earlier. His instincts automatically categorized the various smells and let him know if they were bad or good. This one was very dangerous and it put him on full alert. He would protect his pack, although he was afraid of the humans he did not know, and he was normally very shy around them. He wagged his tail enthusiastically when he saw the old brave wolf leading him into the big house. He always liked that because he was around the alpha female of the pack and the pups would always pet him and scratch his ears. He also got lots of food in there.

Walking inside, Tex said, "Ma'am, Ah brought Kuli with me an' we'll put him in the wagon, ef'n ya got ta leave. He cain't do nobody no good right now tryin' to move aroun'."

Still wanting to pacify Tex because of her earlier remarks, she said, "Whatever you say, Tex."

She had analyzed the earlier conversation and her actions and realized that Tex was an old warrior who knew what he was doing—his longevity alone proved that. She did not have the expertise that he had in survival or winning battles, and she had no business trying to tell him what to do in an emergency situation like this one.

Tex said, "The sentries are on full alert an' Ah made shore the boys in the bunkhouse know this ain't no time ta act like pilgrims. Ah ain't gonna hide nuthin' from ya, neither, ma'am, cause Ah know ya don't respect thet. Kuli here is smellin' somethin' which he don't cotton to at all."

Shirley got a shiver and said, "What do you suggest, Tex?"

Tex replied, "Make sure you and the young uns has got yer travelin' clothes and yer own gun ready to go. If he gets more upset, Ah ain't waitin'. Ah'm a-gonna git ya'll outta here quick-like."

Shirley nodded and walked quickly to her room and grabbed a carpetbag, carrying it to the front door. She then pulled a Colt Navy .36 out of a hiding spot below the cupboard and tucked it into her waistband.

Jimmy Mueller was the youngest of the punchers and this was his first experience away from home. He was in his seventeenth summer and was from good stock. His father had a small ranch near Wetmore. His grandfather had been a prospector who settled in Hardscrabble, which no longer existed and never really did make anything anyway. He had come over from the old country, going straight out West and ending up in Colorado territory wanting to strike it rich.

Jimmy's father had seen all the heartache and pain and figured the real gold was in hard work and tilling the soil. So Jimmy had grown up learning to be responsible and to work hard, but he also had inherited his grandfather's wanderlust. He started rebelling against his parent's authority, and finally told them he had to go out and taste life. He signed on at the Coyote Run for the upcoming roundup and big drive and was fast becoming a good cowhand at the elbows of big Muley Hawkins and Tex

Westchester, who especially took a shine to him.

But his potential and his future ended abruptly when he walked from the bunkhouse to get a fresh bucket of drinking water for everyone. He'd taken about ten steps when some movement out of the corner of his eye caught his attention. He turned in time to see something that looked like a grizzly bear, and smelled horrible, looming over him. His eyes opened wide in horror, but it was too late as the giant war club smashed into his skull, caving in his forehead. He fell back and crashed through the lowest board in the corral with a loud crack.

In the house, Kuli sat up, ears pricked and nose twitching. He got the smell strongly now; the hair on his neck stood up and a low growl started in his chest. Tex grabbed the children out of bed and handed one to Muley and the other to Shirley.

He headed for the door and said, "Be ready ta go when Ah pull the wagon up, ma'am."

When Tex ran outside, he saw the hands assembled by the corral that ran up near the bunkhouse. He ran over and saw the body of the young puncher.

"Dammit," he growled. Then he said,

"Ah'm gittin' the family away from here. Muley's in charge. Do what he says. Right now, make sure yer guns is clean and loaded and keep yer long guns with ya an' cocked."

He ran to the barn, pistol drawn, and immediately got the team and wagon. Seconds later, he ran them out the big double doors and ran into the house. On the hill in the cottonwood trees, Eagle had water dripping off his beard from the cold Texas Creek. He watched as the punchers agonized over the body of their friend. Then he saw the old man enter the barn and emerge with the buckboard and team. He pulled up in front of the house and, seconds later, the Colt woman and children and the wolf emerged and got in the wagon with the old man. They all took off at a gallop. The big man ran to the other men at the bunkhouse.

Eagle had to kill these men quickly and find a big horse to ride after the wagon. He raised his big Sharps .50 buffalo gun and sighted at the head of the half-breed Comanche standing in the middle of the cowboys. He squeezed off the shot and half the man's head exploded. Everyone dropped to the ground, but Eagle started rolling to his right immediately after his shot. Bullets searched for him in the trees, but he was safely behind the trunk of a large cotton-wood.

He would not fire back. He would wait and be patient. Eventually, they would take a chance and try to maneuver forward to his hiding spot, thinking he had fled after firing. He would take another man then.

Five minutes after their searching fire began, Muley said to the other cowboy, "You cover me. I'm moving forward; you go past me. That shot came from the cotton-woods. We'll work our way up there."

Muley crouched down and dashed forward, drawing no fire. The other cowboy flashed past him but still drew no fire. Five minutes later, leap-frogging, they made it to the bank of Texas Creek and lay there covering and watching the blackness of the trees ahead. Muley bravely ran past the man and splashed through the creek up the bank and up the hill into the grove of trees from where the shot had come.

The other cowboy stared intently into the blackness ahead, but could see nothing. He listened for a sound from Muley but there was only the rushing of the water passing beneath. The cowboy strained his ears to hear any noise coming from where Muley had entered the trees. Suddenly, he got an overwhelming feeling of being watched; it made his spine feel an involuntary shiver. He gulped, then turned his head quickly, his eyes scanning all around behind him. There was nothing. He breathed a sigh of relief and turned his head back to look where Muley had gone.

With the speed of a lightning bolt, a hand shot up out of the water and grabbed him by the throat. He started to scream but the powerful giant hand choked off his windpipe. He felt himself being yanked into the cold rushing waters of Texas Creek.

He went underwater and grabbed for his six-shooter, but a vicelike grip crushed his hand against the handle. The hand around his windpipe squeezed so hard it forced his mouth open, and his eyes bugged out in sheer panic and horror. He died feeling the water rushing into his mouth and lungs.

Muley was left in the trees while Eagle crawled out of the water and made his way down to the barn. He stayed in the blackness of the shadow along the corral fence, and it took him all the way to the barn unseen.

The man in the barn had made a couple of shots, but for the most part couldn't see to shoot. He kept looking, though, and needed only to point and pull the trigger of his Henry repeater carbine. There was a noise down below, which he identified as a rat. Then he heard another slight noise and he suddenly smelled a scent that had to be the smell of rotting, decaying flesh. He listened and looked. There was a light on the far wall of the barn down below, coming from the moonlight low on the horizon. On the wall, the puncher saw the shadow of a huge man and he was holding something straight up—a pitchfork. Crash!

He felt the tines of the pitchfork crashing through his body at the same time he heard them crash through the floor of the loft and into his prone body. He tried to get up but was literally pinned to the floor from below. He felt a pain in his back and reached behind him. He felt the tine of a hayfork that was sticking up through the lower part of his lung. How could that be? he wondered. Then he looked down at the pool of blood forming below his mouth and running out and off his chin. He was tired of playing hide-and-seek. His brother was always afraid to even come near the haystack, because he had laid on a snake once. He decided he'd take a nap before ma called him to do chores. His eyes closed, as he felt himself getting sleepy; even the tummyache didn't keep him from wanting to sleep for a while. He closed his eyes and relaxed, and died.

Eagle Bleu slipped out the back of the barn and looked up at the rifle barrel sticking out of the bedroom window. Eagle raised his Sharps and pictured the body of the man crouched behind the window. The killer aimed his sights at a spot on the side of the house where he figured the shooter's chest would be. He squeezed off the shot, and the rifle dropped while Eagle heard the man's body fly backward and slam into the wall.

CHAPTER 9
Tex's Fight

Tex Westchester stopped the wagon in the Texas Creek Road, several miles from the house. They could still hear the sounds of sporadic gunfire.

Tex said, "Ma'am, this here's the Carter spread and the segundo's a friend a mine. Ah'm a-gonna git off here and git me a horse, an' head on back to the ranch. Them boys'll be needin' mah hep. Kin ya handle the team on inta Westcliffe?"

"Of course I can, Tex," she said, "but you be careful."

"Yes, ma'am," he said, handing her his Winchester.

He cocked it first then eased the hammer off.

Tex said, "Now, Mrs. Colt, ya got a round in the chamber. Jest pull thet hammer back with yer thumb and yer ready ta shoot. Don't stop fer nobody, but he is obvious back there, so there's no danger as long as ya move on ta Westcliffe and don't stop fer nobody."

Shirley smiled and touched his hand, saying, "Tex, I've shot a long gun a time or two, and I give you my word. I won't stop for anybody. But why don't you take the Winchester with you?"

He said, "No ma'am, Ah wouldn't feel right at'all. Ah cain't even consider thet. Now, you an' the young un's git."

She said, "Tex, please be careful."

He said, "Ma'am, you see all these lines all over this piece a leather," pointing at his face.

She smiled broadly and nodded.

He said, "Ah didn't git 'em by not bein' careful-like. Now git."

She slapped the reins to the horses' rumps and took off south toward Westcliffe. In the meantime, Tex yanked his saddle out of the back of the wagon; this had apparently been his plan all along. He took off down the little road to the ranch house with the saddle over his shoulder.

Cowboys would often go from ranch to ranch throughout their careers, and they would ride what was given them and use the saddles provided for them by whoever was paying them. Old-timers like Tex, how-

ever, carried their saddles with them wher-
ever they went. Many, also like Tex, also
would take their own horse when they
joined a new spread.

When Tex came to the Coyote Run he had
a big buckskin gelding named Number 12.
He still rode the horse and wished it were
with him now, but he would borrow one
from old man Carter, ride cross country to
the Coyote Run, and help out Muley.

Less than five minutes after leaving Shirley Colt on the road, Tex Westchester was
in the saddle astride the back of a black
bay mare weighing better than half a ton,
and heading for the Coyote Run. Tex hadn't
heard any shots for several minutes; he
hoped and prayed that Muley had gotten
the murderer. Tex was worried for Muley
and the other punchers, but not for himself. He had the advantage of going into the
battle scene knowing the enemy was there
and already fighting. The others only knew
that he might come and were probably
taken off guard. A battle-scarred veteran of
many conflicts, with many years of knowledge about fighting in his head, he might
have been concerned for the others, but he
had a very strong survival instinct that
made him feel he'd die in a feather bed
some day in his sleep. He also figured that

day would come when he was a lot older—
and most people already considered Tex
very old.

Fifteen minutes of hard riding brought
him just outside the ranch yard. He dismounted in some trees to survey the situation. He saw several bodies lying just
outside the barn and there was a fire going.
A big, big man was sitting with his back to
Tex and was cooking something over the
fire. It had to be the killer. He was dressed
like a mountain man and was gigantic in
proportions.

Tex tried to figure out an effective plan
and wished he still had his rifle with him.
Muley was nowhere in sight. All of a sudden, Eagle Bleu stood up and Tex estimated
his height at close to seven feet. He walked
into the darkness of the barn and came out
seconds later, easily pulling the small
chuckwagon used for short cattle drives.

Tex almost gasped as he saw the big man
pull the back of the wagon up close to the
fire with Muley Hawkins, bloody and battered, tied spread-eagle, in the back,
gagged but trying to speak. The big man
stripped the gag away and asked Muley a
question, but Tex couldn't hear him.

He could sure hear Muley, though, as his
saddle partner said, "No, I ain't scared, but

you're going to be when Tex Westchester or Chris or Joshua Colt comes after you for killing me, you sidewinder."

The big man seemed to ignore him and took a frying pan out of the wagon. He chopped some potato or onion slices into the pan and set it on the fire. Tex was relieved. At least the big killer was going to fix him and Muley a meal, it looked like.

The big man stood again and walked over to Muley. He stared at Muley's face for several seconds, cocking his head from side to side, like a dog studying a music box. Then suddenly, he pulled out a giant Bowie knife and plunged it forward while the big cowboy let out a blood-curdling scream and Tex screamed at the same time. Eagle stayed in front of Muley for several more seconds.

He looked at Tex walking fast at him from the trees. Eagle turned and dropped the heart in the frying pan and turned back to face the irate cowboy. Tex's jaw was set, and he was ready to kill, and he choked back a sob at the same time. He could not stand seeing his friend's lifeless head drooping forward and hanging on his chest.

When Tex was twenty paces off, he halted and dropped into a gunfighter's crouch.

"That was mah compadre. Fill yore hand an' die, you cannibal sumbitch!" Tex fumed.

Tex drew and Eagle just stared at him. Tex fired and saw his bullet knock dust off Eagle's shirt front and the big man took one step back from the impact. Then Eagle came at Tex with the Bowie knife in his hand. Tex fired a second time, with the same result, then a third, fourth and fifth. Each time Eagle got knocked back a step but kept on.

Eagle had not faced many men like this. This old one would not shake or run.

Tex raised the gun up and said, "Fine. Let's see you bounce a bullet off'n yer forehead."

Eagle stopped dead in his tracks and raised his hands.

Tex said, "Ah don't believe in haunts and sech. When Ah see sumpin like ya jest pulled off, Ah know they's trick to it. So open up thet coat and shirt. What you got, a piece a iron under there?"

Eagle opened his fur coat and shirt and showed a leather vest hanging over his massive chest. Inside the buffalo hide was a large redwood board, concaved slightly to fit more snugly over Eagle's chest. It had several bullet holes in it and two of them had mushroomed pieces of soft lead showing.

Tex said, "Take that little Jim Bowie toothpick and cut the straps." With his blood-covered Bowie, Eagle reached up and sliced through the leather shoulder straps holding his body shield on. It dropped to the ground and as soon as it hit, Eagle Bleu threw the knife at Tex's face. Tex was anticipating that, though, and sidestepped the powerful blade, although it did cut the top of his ear as it passed by. Blood immediately started streaming down the side of his head, soaking the right side of his shirt.

As the knife swished by his head, Tex fired the pistol, aiming it right between the giant's eyes. Eagle Bleu was deceptively fast, though, and ducked to the side as he made his throw. The bullet nicked his right ear and blood started screaming down the side of his head, too.

The problem now was that Tex was out of bullets. Eagle licked the blood off his hand and started walking slowly toward Tex, who stood defiantly and spit toward the tall man.

Eagle said, "Your heart will taste good."

Tex said, "Go ta hell, buster!"

He spit at him again. This time, though, he hit the giant full in the face with the spittle. He grinned, knowing he had at least accomplished that. He would be dead in five seconds, he knew, but spitting in the giant's face had at least given Tex some satisfaction. Besides, he might only be five foot six or seven, but he still would go out with a fight. Tex drew his sheath knife and held it in front of him, ready to try to meet the challenge of the seven-footer in front of him.

Eagle was now just two steps away. He took one step, but stopped short when dirt kicked up in front of him. A second later, both men heard the report of a rifle, and they looked out at the mountain range. Thundering across the pasture was Chris Colt on War Bonnet, carbine in hand.

Eagle was without his big gun. It was behind him and Colt could make that shot. He was too big a target. He dashed forward and smashed an elbow into Tex's ear, taking a knife slash across his belly as he ran by. He felt the whip of a bullet through his furs as he ran to the big black bay mare. He jumped on the horse with bullets kicking up around him, and he tore off south down the valley.

Twenty seconds later, Chris Colt slid to a stop, bailed off his horse, and ran to Tex's side. Tex's left eye was swelling shut, but he was alive. Colt poured water on his face from his canteen and Tex opened his eyes sputtering and shaking his head from side to side. He sat up and tried to slug Colt, who caught his hand.

Tex said, "What the—? Oh."

He looked all around and recognition came back into his brain.

"Ah'm sorry, boss. Ah let 'im git away," Tex said.

Colt said, "Sorry? Man, he is the toughest I've ever been up against, Tex. Where's my family?"

Tex held up his hand saying, "They're alive and okay. Ah sent 'em packin' ta Westcliffe. Ah taken 'em partways down the road til the gunplay started, then Ah give Mrs. Colt mah rifle and sent her on her way. Ah bummed a horse from Old Man Carter and lit a shuck over here, but Ah was too late. He cut Muley's heart out jest like thet, whilst Muley was still alive. He's a beast, thet one. He got all the boys 'cept me. Ah shoulda been here, too, dammit ta hell an' back."

Colt said, "No, you shouldn't, Tex. You did just right, and I'm very glad you're alive. I need you now more than ever, Tex. Where did you send Shirley and the kids—to Man Killer's?"

"Naw," Tex said, "She'd have ta go beyond Westcliffe at night. Ah told her to go straight to the sheriff and ast him ta put her an the kids in a cell til mornin'. Ah figgered you'd show up soon, since that ole bugger was here. Thanks, boss, ya saved my worthless ole hide."

Colt said, "Did you get your knife in him?"

Tex said, "Naw, Ah sliced his belly, but it didn't go deep. Ah nicked his ear with a bullet, though, jest like mine."

Tex just wanted to keep talking and do everything he could to avoid thinking or looking at Muley's body.

Tex said, "Ah gotta go in and saddle Number 12, Chris. Ahm a-gonna hunt thet critter down and put 'im under."

Colt said, "No, let's go inside and get some coffee and talk. He won't be back tonight. I know him well enough by now."

"Where will he go?"

Chris looked up at Spread Eagle Peak.

He said, "Up there. He'll climb it tonight and jump off with the parachute. When he hits the bottom, he'll have a little walk ahead of him, though."

They went inside, and Tex told Colt about all the events of the evening, and Colt told him all about Eagle Bleu. They went outside and started loading the bodies in a wagon, after wrapping each in a sheet. Both men choked back tears but, in the way of the West, both hid their emotions.

They took turns watching that night with the wagon loaded with the dead bodies outside the back door. Chris Colt had no nightmares. He dreamt about shooting Eagle Bleu over and over again. No longer was the behemoth sociopath someone who would haunt Chris Colt's dreams and subconscious. No longer would he instill fear in Chris Colt, because he was no longer an unknown. He killed people and ate their hearts, trying to frighten and intimidate them first. It was as simple as that—he was loony.

Chris Colt knew this man was a genius and had as much knowledge as Colt in the wilderness, but he did not care. Eagle Bleu was going to pay for the death of Muley Hawkins, the wounding of Man Killer and Tex Westchester, the murder of Colt's temporary ranch hands, the killing of Joshua's horse, and the murder of countless others.

First thing in the morning, the two men took off for Westcliffe. War Bonnet was tied behind the wagon and Tex rode Number 12, using Colt's old McLellan saddle. Chris rode his fancy black saddle with teardrop stirrup covers, a wedding gift from his wife.

They made the town while it was still early morning, and Colt found his wife and children at the county jail. He thanked

Sheriff Schoolfield for his assistance and got them loaded in the wagon.

Colt went straightaway toward Pueblo, stopping in Silver Cliff at the Powell House to buy Tex and his family breakfast. For the children, it was an adventure. Colt then sent Tex to Man Killer's to apprise him of the happenings and check on his condition, then told him to go down to Canon City to look in on Joshua. Colt gave Tex direct orders to go to the McClure House and get a nice room, charging everything to the Colts. He was to remain there until Colt came for him or sent word. Tex tried to argue, but to no avail.

The Colts then headed down the mountain and across the prairie for Pueblo, making it by late afternoon and staying at a hotel for the night. The next morning at daybreak, he boarded his family on the southbound train, and they rode to Mora south of Raton Pass, in New Mexico. He checked Shirley and the kids into a hotel and sought out the sheriff.

Chris was walking down the street with his wife and children when he finally met the sheriff. As the lawman approached him, Chris noticed his resemblance to the man's two brothers, whom he'd met in the past.

Colt stuck out his hand and shook with

the sheriff, saying, "Sheriff, heard a lot about you. One of your brothers saved my bacon down here a few years back. Name's Chris Colt."

The man smiled and said, "Name's Sackett. I've heard lots about you, Marshal Colt—and all of it good."

Chris said, "This is my wife Shirley, my son Joseph, and my daughter Brenna."

Sackett doffed his hat to Shirley; Joseph stuck his hand out like a little man and shook with Sackett.

The tall, handsome sheriff said, "Got a real man growing up there, Marshal. Has a firm handshake and looks a man in the eye. What can I do for you, Marshal Colt?"

Chris said, "I have a really bad killer after my family and me. He's the toughest I've ever been up against, and you are the only close one I could think of where I know I could leave my family and know they'll stay alive."

Sackett stuck out his hand and said, "Mr. Colt, they'll be here waiting on you when you return."

Chris said, "Thanks," and the two shook hands.

Colt went on, "They're checked in at the Prairie House."

He took up his little girl and said, "Give

Daddy a big hug and kiss," and she complied.

He did the same with Joseph, but the little boy tried to push away and shake hands.

Colt grabbed him and said, "First we hug, then we shake."

They gave each other a big hug and Chris set him down. Then he pulled Shirley into his arms and kissed her long and hard. Brenna pulled on Joseph's trouser leg and giggled.

Colt stepped back and said, "I'll miss you. I love you very much, Mrs. Colt. Don't you worry—I'll be fine."

Shirley said cheerfully, "I know. I'm going to miss you, but we'll be here waiting."

Chris turned suddenly and headed for the railroad depot. A single tear ran down Shirley's cheek. She wiped it away, grabbed her kids by the hand, and followed after the sheriff.

Chris Colt boarded the train for Colorado and headed back north after a half hour's wait. He got into Pueblo in the late afternoon and stayed in a boardinghouse overnight.

The next morning, Colt rode War Bonnet to Canon City. He visited his brother that evening, then got himself a room at the

McClure House. He bought Tex dinner there, and they talked long into the evening.

Speaking with Tex reminded Chris once again of how strange things were in the West. He learned that Tex had been a brigadier general with the Confederacy during the Civil War and a professor of military history at a military school in Virginia. After the war, he'd returned to his native Texas to learn that his wife and three daughters had fallen victim to a cholera epidemic. He buried them on the family ranch and started drifting.

He wandered down into Mexico and hooked up with Texicaners on their way back up to the States after running a herd down with some questionable artwork on their hides. Just by coincidence, he had two gunfights in Mexico, which was very unusual for an already middle-aged man.

In the first gunfight, he had been in a small cantina drinking tequila with the other cowpunchers when a big moose of a man, obviously a gunfighter, came looking for trouble. He wore skin-tight leather pants and a pair of fancy cross-draw pearl-handled .44s in twin black holsters studded with silver conchos—the wear on the leather belt at the top of the holsters showed that the guns had been used over and over. His shirt and sombrero, too, were ornately decorated.

There was a bunch of tough-looking cowboys standing with Tex at the bar, but Tex stood out like a sore thumb. He was maybe five foot eight in tall riding heels and standing on a board or two, weighing maybe one hundred and forty-five pounds in all his clothes, soaking wet and holding a pound of butter. His hair was already gray at that time, so he looked like the easiest target.

The gunfighter swaggered over to Tex and bumped into him on purpose. He grabbed Tex by the lapels and angrily said, "Gringo, why you bump into me, huh?"

Tex kicked him hard in the kneecap, drew his pistol, and lashed it viciously across the bridge of the Mexican's nose, breaking it and sending blood everywhere. The shooter flew back against a table and chairs and grabbed his nose, his eyes watering. Tex holstered his gun and got in a crouch.

Tex snarled, "Ya know damned good an' well, ya bumped inta me yerself ta start a fight, so let's have at it, sonny boy. Pull iron and smoke it."

The gunfighter didn't expect such an aggressive response from what he thought was just a little old gringo. He was stuck now, and he licked his lips. Then he got angry that he was being scared by a little old man. His lips curled back in a snarl, and he dropped into the gunfighter's crouch and crossed his arms over his body, each hand hovering above the deadly .44s. His eyes flared, and Tex drew just as the man's hands closed down on the butts of the pistols. The Mexican grinned as he pulled his guns from the holsters. He knew he had the old man beat.

There was a loud boom in the room, and the Mexican wondered if one of his guns had gone off. Then he noticed a big red spot on his belly, and looked up at Tex in amazement. He saw flames stab out of the old man's gun again, and he actually saw the bullet as if it were traveling in slow motion. He saw it spin in the air right before it hit him right on the bridge of the nose and he flew backward against the room's center support post and slid down it in a sitting position. Blood drained out of the front and exit wounds in his head and torso. He was dead.

Tex's second gunfight came not far from the border of Texas. It was a very hot day, and Tex had left the rustlers because he just couldn't stomach making money off someone else's misfortune—he'd had enough of his own. Tex came to a tinaja that was sort of public domain, but there were two very dirty, ugly American men with low-slung holsters and carbines. When he approached the waterhole, one stepped forward, his hand hovering over his gun. The other smoked the longest cigar Tex had ever seen and drank from the dipper in the waterhole bucket. Tex could see what was coming and he was already angry as could be.

The man challenging him said, "Amigo, there's a charge to use this waterhole. It's gonna cost you a double eagle."

Tex lied, "Ah don't have it."

The challenger laughed and said, "Then die of thirst."

Tex said, "This ain't right. This hole is always used by everyone travelin' these parts an' its always been free."

The man grinned and said, "You kin always grab fer that hogleg, Grandpa."

Tex said, "Okay," drew and fired.

He fired again and again, while the extortionist stepped back, grabbing his chest with each bullet.

They buried him, too.

His partner sloped, as fast as his legs

could get him to his horse, and as fast as his horse could get him to the West.

Tex drank all the water he wanted.

He had been in some other shooting scrapes from time to time and had to fight Comanches on a number of occasions. He had a lot of respect for them, and they for him.

When Tex spoke about these things with Chris in response to Colt's questions about gunfights, Tex simply said, "Aw, Ah had me a little shootin' trouble in Mexico a time er two."

Changing the subject, finally, to matters at hand, Colt said, "Tex, I want you to leave tomorrow for Westcliffe and stay at Man Killer's ranch and help with chores there until I get Eagle Bleu."

Tex said, "What about the Coyote Run?"

Colt said, "I'll take care of the chores there. I don't want any other hands there."

Tex got angry. "Look Boss, Ah ride fer the brand. That critter kilt my ridin' partner. Ah ain't scared a him."

Colt smiled softly and interrupted, saying, "Tex, there isn't a man or woman who knows you that doesn't know that you're a man to ride the trails with. I don't want anybody else killed at the Coyote Run, and Eagle Bleu will want you now almost as much as he wants me. Hopefully, if you're at Man Killer's he won't spot you. He wants me more than anything, and he'll be keeping an eye on the ranch. Instead of me trailing him, I'll bring him to me."

Tex said, "What 'bout burnin' the ranch down?"

Colt said, "He won't do it. It wouldn't scare me or bother me that much. Buildings can be rebuilt. He knows I'd do it to get him if I had to."

"How d'ya know he knows 'twouldn't bother ya'?"

Colt replied, "He's a genius. He knows what I'm about. His goal is to scare people before he kills them. He eats their hearts."

"Damn," Tex said, "Ah was wondrin' what he was doin' with Muley, and all his fool talkin'. Why's he eat the heart?"

Colt said, "When I was at the Little Big Horn, one of the chiefs there was named Rain-In-The-Face. A few years earlier, he had gotten arrested by Tom Custer, George Armstrong Custer's brother, and he didn't like the way he was treated."

Tex interrupted, "Custer's brother?"

Colt said, "Yeah, he died with Custer. He was one of his company commanders, a captain. Won the Congressional Medal of Honor in the Civil War."

Tex cut in again, "Yeah, I do remember readin' 'bout it."

Colt went on. "Anyway, Rain-In-The-Face didn't like Tom Custer at all and swore that someday he would cut out Custer's heart and eat it. After the battle, I rode over the battleground and when I came to Tom Custer's body, his heart had been cut out of his chest."

Tex said, "Wait a minute. What do you mean you rode over the battlefield after the fight?"

Colt said, "It's not important."

Chris Colt ordered a couple of glasses of wine for the two while the old man looked at him in wonder. The stories that must be locked away in his brain that he'll never tell anyone, Tex thought.

Colt remembered that fateful day in Montana, when his friend Crazy Horse had him overpowered and tied so he would not get involved in the fight and try to save Custer and his men. Shirley was being held in the big encampment as a prisoner at the same time. After the fight, Crazy Horse released Chris Colt and the two rode together over the battlefield. It broke the scout's heart. He was also warned by Sitting Bull that he could never tell anyone that he was in the Indian's encampment during the battle, because people might accuse him of running out on Custer.

Now, knowing about the way Eagle treated his victims, the old man was concerned about Chris Colt for the first time. Eagle was like a monster. Tex said, "Wal, ef'n ya let me stay at the ranch with ya, we'd have a lot easier time takin' the old bugger."

Colt said, "I appreciate it, Tex, but I want to be able to move around and not worry about anybody else."

Tex said, "Well, what the hell am Ah, some young un to be babysat?"

Chris realized that his attitude was insulting Tex.

He tried to figure out how to get his way gracefully, saying, "Tex, Man Killer is laid up and really needs help on his spread."

Tex started laughing and said, "Hell's bells, Man Killer and his wife are millionaires. He kin hire the whole durned U.S. Cavalry to come in and work his ranch fer him."

Colt laughed, considering Man Killer's and Jennifer Banta's millions. And though Man Killer was a Nez Perce Indian who still wore long hair and native dress and chose to put his life in danger all the time riding with Colt as a deputy, he was one of the richest men in the West. But it wasn't often that Colt or any of Man Killer's friends thought of him in that way—he was so down to earth and real.

Tex said, "Boss, this loony bird is lahk a grizzly, an' tougher'n hundred-year-old leather. How ya gonna bring him in by yourself?"

Colt said, "Well, Tex, I plan on doing it because it's my job, and I'm sick of him getting away with murder. I just don't want any more people close to me getting hurt or killed."

Tex said, "Wal, what the hay. Do ya think Ah'm jest an ole pilgrim what needs a rockin' chair and a big live hero ta keep me alive?"

Colt felt ashamed, and he said as much.

"Tex, I'm sorry. I have the utmost respect for you, and I'd be proud to have you side me in this fight."

Tex nodded and threw his shoulders back, standing up.

He said, "Good. We best git some sleep and git an early start in the morning."

Chris smiled and rose, grabbing the check.

He shook with Tex, saying, "Actually Tex, I feel more relieved having you with me on this."

Tex said, "You will be when it comes time to clean out stalls and do some of the other chores around the ranch, too. By the way, where did ya put yer wife and kiddies?"

Colt said, "I don't want anybody to know."

Tex said, "Good thinkin', cause ya know this ole boy is smart enough to figger out how ta git anybody ta talk, and goin after yer family would be the best way ta git ta you."

Colt said, "Exactly. See you here in the dining room for breakfast at daybreak."

The next day, they headed for the Coyote Run shortly after daybreak. Colt bought them freight passage on a train headed to Leadville, so they loaded on with their horses and rode a boxcar to Cotopaxi, where they would off-load. When they got to the Five Points area, partway to Texas Creek, the train slid to a screeching halt.

Chris and Tex opened the boxcar door and dropped the ramp. They rode their horses down the ramp and took off toward the front of the freight at a gallop. Sure enough, when they rounded a big bend in the Arkansas River canyon and saw the locomotive, they saw two masked men holding guns on the engine crew. It was the McCoy brothers from Cotopaxi, known in

Fremont County for some train and stage robberies, as well as some fancy artwork on their cattle from time to time.

Tex made a snap shot and the two surprised men ran down the bank on their mounts and forded the late-summer river. A month earlier, they would have drowned; now they took off up the far bank and headed up into Five Points Gulch while Tex and Colt's bullets chased after them.

Chris rode up to the engineer, holstering his pistol.

The engineer wiped his forehead with a red kerchief and said, "Thanks, Marshal Colt. If it weren't for you two, we would have been goners."

Chris said, "I doubt that you had much to worry about. That was probably Tom and Streeter McCoy. They're a couple of local celebrities that have enjoyed the interior of the hoosegow from time to time."

The engineer said, "Are you going after them, Marshal?"

Colt said, "Nope, I'm a federal deputy, but I'll tell the sheriff about this. I'm after a bad killer right now. First we need to get those ties off the tracks for you."

Colt and Tex rode forward and started lassoing the ends of the big railroad ties piled up on the railroad tracks in front of the engine. They dragged them off and left them on the banks of the churning river. A half hour later, the train started chugging back up the grade and was soon letting Chris and Tex off at Cotopaxi. From there it was an hour's ride to the Coyote Run.

The first night at the Coyote Run was difficult for Chris Colt. His wife and children were gone. His brother was gone. Muley Hawkins and the other hands were dead. Although Colt usually had success working on his own, it was a comfort, now, to have Tex there.

Chris invited Tex to stay in the big house, but he declined, insisting that it made more sense for him to remain in the bunkhouse. That way, the two of them could better keep watch on all the ranch buildings and possibly get Eagle Bleu in a crossfire if push came to shove.

But Tex had a selfish reason for staying in the bunkhouse. Though he wasn't consciously aware of it, he wanted to pack away Muley's personal belongings. Tex had not grieved yet for his best friend, but badly needed to.

Alone in the bunkhouse, Tex started going through Muley's things. He found a single .44 round with an *X* cut into its nose. It had been one of his own .44s, as Tex always cut a notch in the nose of them so they would mushroom immediately on impact. He thought back to the time that he gave Muley that bullet and tears flooded into his eyes.

After the death of his wife and daughters, Tex Westchester had given up. He couldn't quite bring himself to crossing over the law, or more importantly, his own code of honor, but he didn't care. He was in a deep depression, and his drinking made things worse.

Tex awakened one morning with a splitting headache, the world spinning around him as he lay on a bedroll. The embers of a campfire were nearby and a large cowboy was sitting on a log breaking firewood over his knee. The camp was located right on the shore of a large pond in a grove of cottonwood trees.

Tex's head hurt so bad that he closed his eyes and suddenly felt a pair of hands grab hold of him and lift him easily off of the ground. Muley tossed him out into the water and Tex got a mouthful of it when he hit. He went under and struggled for the surface, sputtering and choking.

Tex finally yelled, "What did you do thet fer, partner?"

Muley said, "I figured you needed it, old-timer."

Neither man had ever seen the other before.

Tex hollered, "Why?"

Muley said, "I'll tell you when you climb out."

Tex climbed out of the water and dried off with a clean shirt from his bedroll. He sat down and Muley put a pot of coffee on to boil on the fire he just built.

Tex looked at the big man strangely. He was probably younger than he looked, the old man figured, and had an honest and innocent look.

The oldster finally said, "All right, ya said you'd tell me why ya tossed me in when Ah climbed out, so what's the story?"

Muley asked, "Do you remember last night?"

Tex thought for a minute and said, "Ah 'member ridin' inta El Paso."

Muley laughed, "El Paso is miles from here."

Tex said, "How many?"

Muley replied, "Over a hundred, anyway."

Tex whistled, then said, "Wal, that's the last thing Ah kin reckon."

Muley said, "When I rode up last night, you had a bottle in one hand and your six-shooter in the other. You was staggering like a broken rose trellis in the wind, and you was crying like a two-year-old. Then, you stuck the gun up to the side of your head and cocked it. I hollered 'No!' and you pulled the trigger, but you were so drunk you missed."

Tex looked up at the man with his eyes open wide in horror and shock. "The hell you say. That didn't happen."

Muley's face got red and he said, "Mister, I am about the easiest-to-get-along-with puncher in Texas, but if a person calls me a liar, it's only gonna happen once."

Tex said, "Aw, Ah didn't mean you was a liar, pard. Ah jest can't believe Ah would stoop so low or feel so sorry fer myself thet Ah'd do sech a thing. It's no wonder mah ear is ringin' like a church bell, but how could Ah a-missed mah head?"

Muley said, "When I yelled 'No!' I scared you and made you jump a mite. The gun went off and the bullet went right past your forehead and clipped the bark on that cottonwood yonder. See the scar, high up there?"

Tex looked where Muley was pointing and saw an ugly slash where the .44 round had chipped the bark after going past his forehead.

Tex said, "Mister, ya saved mah life. Mah drinkin' days is over. Ah ain't never gonna let mahself ride down sech a trail as thet again. Ah'm shore beholdin' to ya."

The two men started riding together, looking for trail jobs; a week later Tex gave Muley that bullet and said, "If you ever see me acting so full of self pity again, shoot me with it right in the britches." Apparently, Muley had kept the bullet all these years and the sight of it, and the memory, reminded Tex of everything Muley Hawkins was about. Clutching the bullet in his hand, Tex fell across the bunk and cried himself to sleep.

The next morning, Tex and Chris hayed and grained horses, milked the milk cow, and gathered eggs; Tex even started a big pot of stew for later. They cleaned out the stables and put down fresh bedding for an expensive mare and her newborn foal.

After that, they went into the house and Colt opened the big package he had carried from Canon City. Tex had been curious about it but didn't ask. The long oilskin-covered cylindrical container contained a large telescope. He set it up at the kitchen window, overlooking the Sangre de Cristo range directly west, toward Spread Eagle Mountain.

Looking through the glass, Colt said, "I

want one of us looking through this all the time, glassing the slopes."

Tex said, "Shore, boss, but when he taken off last week, he run thet way. Ya don't suppose he would be on the east side of the Wet Mountain Valley?"

Colt replied, "Nope, he wouldn't. First of all, he owns a big red Clydesdale horse, one of the biggest mounts I've ever seen, and he corrals him in the San Luis Valley. He escapes on him and always heads west across the big valley. I figure he must have his hideout somewhere on that side of the valley, probably up in the San Juans."

Tex bit off a plug of tobacco and started chewing, offering a plug to Colt. The lawman declined. Tex chewed a minute while Colt looked through the telescope.

Finally, Tex said, "Excuse me, boss, but ain't you most likely the best tracker in the West?"

Colt said modestly, "Well, I doubt that very much, but I have a little experience tracking."

Tex chuckled. "Yeah, shore. Ah think everyone Ah ever heerd of considers you the best. Wal, anyhow, since yer sech a good tracker, why in the hell don'tcha jest find his big red horse when he corrals him in the San Luis Valley and foller him home?"

Colt pulled away from the telescope and looked at Tex. He started chuckling, then laughing.

Finally Colt said, "The very best tracker there is, huh? Well, Tex, if I'm so smart, why didn't I ever think of doing just that?"

Trying to cover for Colt then, Tex said, "Wal, you know horses. He'd probably jest go find him some good grass an water or some other horses and mix in with 'em."

Colt said, "That's true, but if this man lives above timberline, like I am positive he does, he probably feeds his horse really good with grain. Now is a grain-fed horse going to stay long with horses in a pasture?"

Tex said, "Wal, horses is herd animals, but Ah s'pose thet he would try ta git home as quick as possible ef'n he was bein' fed real good."

Colt said, "Tex, I saw that horse, and he was fed really good feed. His coat was slick and shiny and healthy looking. He had plenty of meat and muscle on his bones, too. Wasn't sunken in the rump at all—his rump muscles were real rounded."

Tex said, "Mebbe Ah could stay here as bait, an' you could wait over there fer him ta show up."

CHAPTER 10
Colt's Plan

Colt stopped suddenly with the telescope, as if he had spotted something. He stared through the long tube for several seconds and smiled.

Tex couldn't wait any longer and said, "See 'im?"

Colt said, "Yep. Look."

He stepped away from the glass and let Tex look through.

Colt said, "See the bright shine between the two ridges at the base of that avalanche chute?"

Tex said, "How kin Ah miss it? It's blindin' me when Ah look through the glass."

Colt said, "That's his binoculars and the sun is coming up in the east just right so you can see it clearly."

Tex said, "Man, you know how many miles away thet is from us?"

Colt said, "Sun shining off a rifle barrel

has saved many a life out here, including mine. That sun is reflecting straight off his lens glasses. Now we can get him."

Tex said, "Ya wanna injun up on 'im and catch 'im in a crossfire?"

Colt said, "Absolutely not. He's too good. He'd be miles away before we even got there. I have an idea, and I think it will work."

Tex said, "What's thet?"

Colt said, "You are going to dress like me and ride War Bonnet up to the base of the mountain, so you're out of sight in the trees."

Tex said, "Thanks a lot. Ah've always wanted ta be a target. What're you gonna do?"

Colt said, "Go swimming."

Tex scratched his head.

Eagle watched the pair all through the morning. They did chores and spent time in the big house. Then Colt came out and continued splitting firewood. The old man was either napping or standing watch. Eagle then figured it out. The old man had been awake all night standing guard while Colt slept; now Colt was doing chores while the old man was sleeping. But it would do them no good, Eagle thought. In fact, it would make his challenge easier. There would only be one pair of eyes watching him at a time.

It was just after noon when Chris Colt slipped out of the water downstream in Texas Creek. He was five miles above the Arkansas River and just below where the land started to drop dramatically for six miles. He was out of sight of Spread Eagle Peak and he took up the lead line of the big red dun gelding he was leading. He was one of the better "using" horses on the ranch; he had real bottom and stay to him.

Colt tightened the cinch while the horse enjoyed the cool of the water running down his forelegs. The roan and white leopard Appaloosa behind him was one of Man Killer's best stallions and could outdo just about any horse in the mountains, except for Hawk. Colt slipped the bridle out of the saddlebags and put it on the red dun horse's head, flipping the reins back over the saddlehorn.

Colt attached the lead line to the halter on the Appaloosa. Then he tied it to the tail of the red dun. He mounted up and rode straightaway toward the big range. He was several miles north of the killer now and could not be seen, for he was below the drop of the land. Another half hour of hard trotting had him at the base of the ridges leading up Wulsten Baldy Mountain. He found a major elk trail where they bedded in the black timber and would head up high to escape danger or just look for better graze. Colt knew the trail. It was steep and rough, but it went up and over the big range between Wulsten Baldy and Nipple Mountain. He had to hurry and get up and over before Tex made his planned moves.

Chris made it over the top a few hours later and started down the San Luis Valley side. At the top, he had switched horses, saddling the Appy. He hurried down the steeper side of the range, making much better time because he was now heading downhill.

An hour and a half later, Chris Colt was treated to one of the best breaks he could have had. Before, when Eagle hid his horse, he had corralled it south of Spread Eagle, but he now had made a hidden corral in the scrub oaks north of Spread Eagle. A glacial stream flowed down out of the peaks and across the valley floor near Poncha Pass. Eagle had followed its banks from the peaks and located another meadow between stands of scrub oak and made the corral there, quickly attaching two strands of wire to trees with smaller pieces of barbed wire. Often, as many as five strands of barbed wire—even with close fence posts—were still not enough to keep cattle in. But two strands could easily keep a horse in.

Colt did not ride close to the corral but kept his horses back in the scrub oaks. He dismounted and slipped off his boots, pulling his soft-soled moccasins out of his saddlebags. Colt went forward very carefully, stepping on little rocks with his toes and the balls of his feet and avoiding contact with dirt or grass.

When he made it to the edge of the corral, he broke it close to one of the trees and pulled the top strand toward the inside of the corral. Again being very careful where he stepped, Colt used the index and middle finger of his right hand to make a series of V-shaped tracks that made it look like a large mule deer had run into the wire and broke it while trotting across the meadow.

Another idea occurred to him. He carefully made his way back to his horse, pulled some deer hairs out of the quiver full of arrows in his bedroll, and carefully returned to the scene he was creating. He stuck the hairs in the wire near the break. Checking to insure that he had left no tracks, he went around the outside of the corral and threw rocks at the big red horse, who took off out of the corral at a gallop and headed across the San Luis Valley.

Colt made it back to his horses and saddled up. He stayed a couple of miles to the north of the big horse and paralleled him as he trotted across the giant valley in a southwesterly direction, just as Colt had intended. But several miles later, when the horse started grazing, Colt pulled out his carbine and fired twice, kicking up dust behind the big horse's heels.

The Clydesdale took off at a canter and never slowed below a fast trot for a long while. Colt had to repeat the procedure once more, but after they were miles away from the mountains and getting into the foothills near Saguache, he finally let the animal walk more and cool down some. By then, dusk was approaching.

Eagle Bleu was shocked when he saw Chris Colt down below go into the barn and emerge several minutes later on his big paint. He rode directly toward him and Eagle Bleu started figuring out how to bait the trap to lure Colt. It was getting close to dusk. Colt rode up near the base of the mountain and stopped suddenly. He was still several miles away and thousands of feet below. Eagle couldn't understand when he saw Colt pull what looked like a buffalo gun with a sight on it and lay it along the back of his saddle, while the paint stood sideways. It looked through his binoculars that the lawman was aiming up in his direction.

Eagle saw smoke and flame belch out of the barrel and some seconds later, he heard the crack of a bullet as it passed overhead. Then he heard a very faint whump sound from the rifle's report.

Colt must have seen him. Maybe he had strong binoculars or even a telescope at his ranch. Maybe he had strong binoculars right now. Eagle Bleu wasn't alarmed, but he was alive because he was so intelligent. In a cat-and-mouse game like this, he left nothing to chance. Years before he had studied wild animals. If a deer or elk or even a powerful bear or lion was alarmed, it fled and got away from the potential danger. Sometimes a bear might fight, but only when it was forced—the fight-or-flight instinct almost always promoted flight. The hunter always wanted to hunt on its own terms, not the prey's. Man would look at a mountain and think it would be difficult to climb to get away, but animals would just go if that was the best direction of escape. Eagle Bleu did the same thing.

By the time he got down to the makeshift

corral, it was hours after dark. The blood bay was gone, and he found the deer hair and tracks using match light. Eagle was not suspicious.

Meanwhile, Colt studied the large meadow. It was full of deer and elk, along with the big Clydesdale. Tying the horses well back in the trees, he again slipped on the moccasins and carefully skirted the meadow, which, though high in the San Juan Mountains, was well below timberline. Chris looked all over for trails and finally found a small corral with high rails back in the pine trees. Next to it was a water trough with a wooden chute carrying water into it from a small spring pouring out of some rocks. Inside the corral was a feed bucket; a small shed was hidden among the rocks. The corral entrance was clever—the poles, going up seven feet high, twisted and turned in several directions and the horse had apparently been led through the mini-maze, so he knew how to get in the corral to eat grain. His numerous tracks in and out showed that, but the deer and the elk that shared his graze couldn't do the same.

Chris looked carefully and finally found a few faint trails going up the ridge. He returned to the horses and led them up until he cut the main trail again. Up higher the faint trails came together into one. He found a small bowl a short distance south; leaving the horses there, he returned to the trail. Guided by moonlight through the thin growth of trees on the ridgeline, Colt didn't have to light matches in order to follow the trail.

He climbed until he knew it was past midnight. Finally, well above timberline, the trail petered out along the shores of a high glacial lake. Totally puzzled, he headed back down to the horses. It was just a few hours before dawn when he turned and headed toward the bowl where he had left them. Just seconds after leaving the trail, he heard a noise behind him and turned quickly to see Eagle Bleu wearily walking up the trail. He must have stolen a horse or wagon, Colt thought, to have arrived so quickly.

He waited a few minutes and tried to visualize the moonlit trail. He remembered a few dips, so he waited so he wouldn't be seen and took off after the killer, hoping to be able to see the giant when he went down in the dips. It worked. Five minutes later, he saw Eagle in front of him as he was just walking up out of the first dip in the trail. Colt maintained a very careful distance and followed the big man until he spotted him in the last dip in the trail. The behemoth walked up the path and over the lip of the alpine meadow toward the glacial lake.

Colt rushed forward, a little less careful about being spotted but wanting to solve the mystery of the trail ending. He held up his carbine and eared the hammer back as he went up over the lip of the trail. He saw before him the lake and an empty little high mountain valley. Colt watched for several minutes without seeing a thing. There wasn't even a cliff close enough for Eagle to have jumped off.

Still puzzled, lighting matches, Chris went forward on the trail, to check the brand-new footprints, which went up to the lake and stopped. There was no boat in sight and here, above timberline, there were no trees for Eagle to have disappeared behind. Chris was worried that Eagle Bleu may have had a secret hole somewhere around the lake where he was hiding now. He backed away and headed back down the trail.

Instead of getting the horses, he went down below to the corral, where he found a pair of large quarter horses; one of them had dried blood on its back, and it wasn't from the horse. Eagle had apparently killed or wounded the owner and stolen both horses, which had unfamiliar brands on their rumps.

Chris climbed back up the trail and returned to the horses. He had covered his trail well and this was out of the way and out of sight. Eagle Bleu had been careless about his backtrail near this hideout, so Chris reasoned he could camp near the horses without fear of discovery. He was dead tired, and it was only about two hours until daybreak. He crawled into his bedroll and fell asleep instantly.

Just after daybreak a presence awakened Chris Colt. He was up immediately, gun in hand. Holstering his pistol, he grabbed his rifle and sneaked toward the trail, where he found Eagle Bleu's fresh tracks going downhill. Carefully, cautiously, Colt followed the tracks down to the meadow to find that the big Clydesdale and the other two horses were gone. Colt found tracks headed in a southerly direction toward the Wolf Creek Pass area—Eagle was probably leading the horses far away and would then cover his trail.

Colt went back up the hill as quickly as he could. He was sweating profusely and out of breath when he arrived at the lake, where he stopped and drank from the canteen that he had picked up from his hidden campsite. The air was so thin up there that the least exertion left him panting for breath—resting briefly and catching his wind, he went on to the lake and carefully inspected the shoreline.

He noticed something. Where the trail ended at the edge of the lake, there was a scarred rock underwater where someone's foot had slipped and scraped green moss off the top. A few feet further on was another worn, mossy rock. Then, in four feet of the crystal-clear water, was a large footprint on the bottom of the lake.

Colt backed up carefully and left the water, running around the treeless bowl and finally finding a clump of bushes to hide his rifle. He knelt down and stopped suddenly. Under the bushes was a long oilskin-wrapped package. Colt untied the leather thongs around both ends and opened the oilskin to find a Sharps buffalo gun, a Spencer repeater, and a holstered Colt Russian .44, along with a supply of ammunition.

Chris rewrapped the package and replaced it, carefully getting away from the bushes without leaving sign. He finally found a pile of rocks at the edge of the bowl where he could hide his own rifle.

Colt returned to the spot at the edge of

the lake where he had found the sign underwater and entered the chilly basin. He followed the tracks and dog-paddled in a straight line when the water got too deep. He had now concluded that Eagle must swim across the lake for some reason instead of going around it, perhaps because booby traps or pits were hidden around the far shoreline. The south side of the lake had nothing but steep high cliffside.

Halfway across, the water suddenly got warm, then cold again. Puzzled, Chris got out of the water. He could find no trail anywhere, and he kept thinking about the warm spot. Reentering the lake, he swam halfway across and stopped at the warm spot. He treaded water for half a minute and dived under. Just ten feet down, at the bottom, was a black cave entrance with warm water coming out of it. Colt swam up to the surface.

He gasped for air and treaded water again. Colt looked at the cliffside and realized that was the direction the cave entrance seemed to turn. Eagle Bleu must swim underwater through that cave, he thought.

The cave was dark and black and scary, but Chris Colt was a determined man. He took a deep breath and whale-rolled in the water. Without hesitation, he plunged straight down into the black abyss and followed it as it turned toward the cliffs. He swam about ten feet beyond the edge of the lake and he was certain his lungs would burst. Suddenly, though, the cave turned upward and he could see light. Colt started exhaling and had no air left when his head finally broke the surface. Gasping, he gulped in big mouthfuls of air.

Colt's mouth dropped open as he looked around. He pulled himself out of the water and found himself in a giant cavern furnished with the trappings of raided wagon trains and insulated with stacks of captured books.

In the corner where the stove was located, the rocks were black from years of cooking fires. Chris saw a split between the rocks about one hundred feet up, and he could see sunlight and blue sky from the smoke hole.

Chris Colt looked at all the bounty that had been stolen from all the raided wagons, and he was amazed. There were candelabras and thousands of dollars in pieces of silver and silverware. Photographs, paintings, tintypes, and keepsakes galore adorned the walls of the cavern, all hung on walls made out of stacked books. There was a large four-poster oak feather bed, a fancy mahogany hand-carved dining room set, leather chairs and sofa, and a roll-top desk. Colt found a big entrance to the cavern that did not go under water, and he walked out into the sunlight to find he was on a narrow ledge near the top of one of Colorado's high peaks. There was a hand-dug and hand-carved switchback trail going down the cliff face to a long ridge below. The lake and valley were on the other side. Colt could see the entire San Luis Valley and the Sangre de Cristo range off to the east.

Apparently, Eagle Bleu used the underwater entrance to keep from leaving a trail to the main entrance.

Colt explored the giant cave and looked at the writings that Eagle Bleu had in his roll-top desk. Enthralled, he read:

"He (Dr. Johnson) gets at the substance of a book directly; he tears out the heart of it." Mary Knowles

After that, Eagle Bleu had written:

Like Johnson dissecting books, I must do with mankind. When I tear out the heart of man, I have stolen his show, but when I eat it, I have strengthened my own. When my heart is strong enough, I shall at long last feel. I will laugh and cry like those I have seen. If I can make enough fear emanate from those who supply the needs of my spirit, right before the moment of offering, the heart shall enter my being with the strongest emotions intact.

Chris Colt tapped his teeth with the paper and looked off toward the large cavern entrance.

At that moment, he did not realize he had made one of the biggest mistakes of his career as a lawman, gunfighter, and scout. He had attributed moral, rational, common-sense thinking to Eagle Bleu. When Eagle Bleu had left with the two horses, he sought out deep, thick woods, where he would simply kill them and cover his backtrail.

He only rode several miles, leading the two horses, then dismounting, reached up and slit their throats. As they both lay kicking and thrashing in their final death throes, he stood there watching them with great interest, cocking his head from side to side, until both stopped moving. He moved to the head of one of the horses and sat down, watching the lifeless eyes with great curiosity as they slowly took on a milky appearance.

Back at the cave, Colt picked up another piece of paper, torn from a book of Shakespeare. Using a piece of charcoal, Eagle had circled one line. *"O! the blood more stirs To rouse a lion than to start a hare."* Below that, Eagle had handwritten: *"Christopher C. Colt."*

Colt felt a shiver run up and down his spine, and suddenly he smelled that horrible rank smell. He spun, drawing his right-hand gun, but a fist the size of a ham smashed into his face and sent him flying backward through the air. He felt hands yanking his guns from their holsters and he wondered what was happening. Then he suddenly realized he had been knocked unconscious. Colt shook his head, trying to get his mind working right again. His jaw was broken, and he couldn't move it.

It finally hit Chris Colt; he was in the house of Eagle Bleu and the man had sneaked in and attacked him. To lie on the floor was to die. Colt reached for both guns, but they were gone from their holsters— Eagle had tossed them into the pool.

The behemoth, soaking wet, had swum in and surprised Chris from behind. Colt clenched his aching jaw together and swallowed a big mouthful of blood.

Eagle lunged at the deputy and Colt dropped to the floor, diving off to one side. He caught the big man's shinbone with his left foot and kicked behind his knee with the other. Eagle Bleu flew forward and crashed into the edge of the big table, breaking a leg and knocking it against the stove.

Chris's head was still spinning, but he knew he had to maintain his faculties or he would be dead. Eagle did not get angry—he never did—he just kept trying harder.

He picked up a chair and smashed the hand-carved mahogany piece over Colt's head and upraised arms. Colt felt a bone in his hand break and a lump form on his forehead, but he could not let that deter him or slow him down. Eagle ran at him but Colt rolled out of the way, jumped up, and back-pedaled to safety.

Eagle pulled his big Bowie knife out and Colt reached down the back of his white buckskin war shirt and drew his own Bowie. Colt flipped the knife up and caught it by the blade, throwing it with all of his might. He couldn't believe the man's speed as Eagle twisted to the side. But the blade still buried itself to the hilt in the man's watermelon-sized right shoulder.

Eagle Bleu didn't flinch or make a face. He just reached up and pulled the knife out with his left hand. Now, holding a big Bowie in each hand, he came forward like a wind-mill or a tornado, swinging and chopping at Colt with each knife. Chris held his hands up defensively and tried to back away, but he knew he was in big trouble.

Things got worse. Colt felt the back of his legs hit a stool, and he fell on his back. Eagle dived forward and slashed Chris's left hip as he rolled away. Colt sprang to his feet and looked around for something to help him.

Eagle tore his big wolfskin coat off and threw it down. Blood oozed down his mas-sive arm, which looked even bigger and more powerful without the coat on. He came forward, slashing and chopping again, and backed Chris around the room. Colt had nowhere to go.

Eagle took a massive swing at Colt's neck and Chris ducked it and dived for the pool. He went down and his eyes searched franti-cally for one of his guns. He spotted one, wrapping his hand around the familiar grip. He kicked for the surface and immediately ducked when his knife was thrown at his head. He pointed his gun at the center of Eagle's head and quickly squeezed the trigger. Click! The cartridges were wet. He cocked it and fired again as Eagle rushed forward. Click! Eagle raised the knife and Colt fired again—still the chamber was empty. He fanned the gun in desperation and the sixth bullet fired.

It tore into the big man's already-wounded shoulder, but it didn't make him drop the knife or even express pain. It did turn him slightly, though, causing the knife to pass by Colt's face. Chris grabbed the killer's knife hand with both of his and yanked with all his might.

Eagle fell into the pool, and Chris quickly pulled himself out, feeling the break in his hand but using it anyway. His adrenalin was pumping and he was in the thick of battle. Eagle's size and strength didn't bother him, for he was a warrior who didn't believe he could be beaten. He wanted to defeat this man for all of his friends, for all the innocent people he had killed.

There was a splash and a giant hand grabbed him by the leg and tried to pull him back into the water. Colt struggled as the hand pulled, and Chris finally lifted his other leg and kicked it. Eagle let go and Chris did a backward somersault. But at the same time, the big man almost flew out of the water and onto Colt.

It was as if someone had dropped a dying buffalo on top of Colt. Eagle's hands closed around Colt's throat and Chris panicked. He had never been gripped so tightly and he couldn't breathe or swallow. Chris's right fist shot up and punched the behemoth in the bullet and knife wound, but that had no effect.

He felt himself going out as the blood in his carotid arteries stopped on its way to the brain. Colt had one quick chance, and he jabbed forward, poking the big man in both eyes with the points of his first two fingers. Eagle grabbed his eyes, and Colt squeezed Eagle's left leg against his own side, using his right arm. He quickly twisted to the right and pushed up with his left arm. The big man flew off sideways.

Chris scrambled to his feet and looked around.

Eagle Bleu got up and faced him. "The eagle tears his prey apart with his talons and his beak. He shreds its miserable flesh."

Colt said, "My name is Wamble Uncha. It is Lakotah for One Eagle. I am the One Eagle around here. I am like the real eagle, which only kills when it must, and it kills quickly and effectively. You are under arrest, Eagle Bleu. I assume you do not want to lay down your knife and give up peacefully?"

Eagle was inching forward, while Chris kept backing around the room, searching desperately for something to help him.

Eagle said, "You are a worthy enemy. I will soon eat your heart and be much stronger. Then I will take your wife and eat her, then I will dash your children's heads upon the rocks."

Chris Colt stared at Eagle and said, "You aren't gonna do nothing but die, Big Man."

Eagle rushed forward, his knife held in front with its blade up. Colt backed into a table, blocking his retreat, and his hand closed around the base of a silver candelabra. Colt swung it in front of him and smashed Eagle's knife hand with it.

Two or three fingers broke and the big man dropped the knife. Chris Colt's family had been directly threatened again, so now it was his turn to move his arms windmill-style as he backed Eagle up, swinging the big candelabra left and right. He saw an opening and jumped up and forward, striking the giant in the face with the silver holder.

Blood spurted out of Eagle's nose; his left

eye swelled shut and blood ran from the corner. Colt kept after him and the big man held up his arms defensively to ward off the blows. He backed all the way out the entrance of the cavern as Chris Colt beat him unmercifully.

With his one good arm, Eagle finally caught the candelabra on one of Colt's downswings. He yanked and Chris fell forward at his feet. He kicked Colt in the chest, breaking two ribs. Chris remained on all fours in front of Eagle, trying to breathe. The big man raised the candle holder high overhead. Colt couldn't roll either way. He knew it was over; he would die right here is his beloved high lonesome, where the eagles fly.

He waited for the blow, thinking about Shirley and the kids. Boom! The candelabra fell on the back of Chris's head, while Eagle Bleu flew out sideways into space, his heart and part of his left lung blown all over the cliffside. Colt rolled over and looked down the switchback trail at Tex Westchester, who was holding a smoking buffalo gun. The two men heard Eagle's body bounce off the rocks far below.

Tex said, "Guess that was one eagle what couldn't fly. That was fer Muley. He was mah friend."

Chris gave Tex a puzzled look.

Tex explained, "You shore ain't the only expert tracker around here. Ya ain't gonna git lost in no snowstorm with thet spotted horse a yourn still alive. He brung me right to ya almost."

Colt rolled over and looked down at the massive body, then at the candelabra, an English family heirloom crafted to resemble the foot and talons of an eagle.

Chris pointed at it and started laughing. He held his ribcage and laughed until tears came into his eyes. Tex joined in.

Chris Colt sat on his favorite rocking chair on his back porch. His shirt was off and he was being warmed by the afternoon sun. There was a tight bandage around his ribcage and a crutch at his side. His finger was in a splint.

Next to him sat Man Killer, crutch at his side and leg bandaged up. On the other side was Joshua Colt, pale and thin but much healthier than before, though he still wore several bandages. And on the far end of the porch sat old Tex. All four men were smoking cigars and looking out at the towering mountains.

Shirley Colt walked outside carrying a tray with coffee; Brenna walked behind her carrying a hot apple pie. Joseph sat down by his dad on a keg of nails, putting his feet up on the porch rail as the men often did. He was sporting a black eye from a ten-year-old in Westcliffe who—until recently—had been a bully.

Shirley set the tray down and looked at the men.

"The Colt men," she said. "The men of the Coyote Run. Do you suppose any of you could ever get into a fight and not get half-killed yourselves?"

They each grinned and kept staring up at the mountain range.

She grinned, too, and said, "And don't you ever tire of looking at those mountains that have almost killed each of you?"

Chris stood and kissed her, eyes twinkling, and replied, "No, ma'am. That's God's country. It's the land of the eagle."

Be sure to read every novel
in Don Bendell's **Colt Family Saga**

Justis Colt

When Texas Ranger Justis Colt is ambushed by a gang of murderers, a mysterious stranger called Tora enters the fray to save Colt's life. But the Comancheros, a motley crew of outlaws and cutthroats, demand revenge and kill Tora's wife and two sons.

Vengeance, however, becomes a double-edged sword covered with blood as Colt and the man called Tora face the great challenge of hunting down every Comanchero involved in the killing of Tora's family. While Justis Colt knows how to walk on the right side of the law, he also knows how to use his guns to bark out the final reckoning of justice in an untamed land. . . .

Coyote Run

On one side stood the legendary Chief of Scouts, Chris Colt, with his hair-trigger-tempered half brother, Joshua, and the proud young Indian brave, Man Killer. On the other side was a mining company that would do anything and kill anyone to take over Coyote Run, the ranch that the Colts had carved out of the Sangre de Cristo Mountains with their sweat and their blood. Their battle would flame amid the thunder of a cattle drive, the tumult of a dramatic courtroom trial, the howling of a lynch mob, and a struggle for an entire town. And as the savagery mounted, the stakes rose higher and higher, and every weapon from gun and knife to a brave lawyer's eloquent tongue and the strength and spirit of two beautiful women came into powerful play.

Warrior

Chris Colt, Chief of Scouts, sought peace on his ranch in the Colorado high country, but he was drawn back into the violence of a West that made him strap on his guns again. For Man Killer, the young Nez Perce warrior whose life Chris Colt had saved and shaped, is riding into battle against Apache raiders led by Geronimo himself. Joining them is Justis Colt, Chris's cousin, a tall and tough ex-Texas Ranger committed to help save Man Killer's beloved Jennifer from a crooked relative and two infamous outlaws on a bloody crime spree.

Horse Soldiers

In the embattled Oregon territory, Christopher Columbus Colt was a wanted man. General O. O. "One-Armed" Howard, commanding the U.S. cavalry, wanted this legendary scout to guide his forces in his campaign to break the power and take the lands of the proud Nez Perce. The tactical genius Nez Perce Chief Joseph needed Colt as an ally in this last ditch face-off. Rich, ruthless Rufus Potter wanted Colt out of his greedy way and six feet under the rich Oregon soil. And only Colt could decide which side to fight on in the most stirring and savage struggle the frontier ever knew. . . .

Chief of Scouts

Christopher Columbus Colt, Chief of
Scouts and nephew of gun-maker Sam
Colt, was always the best man for the
job. His skill with weapons was legendary, his service to the Seventh Cavalry
invaluable. But as a friend to the La-
kota Sioux and Chief Crazy Horse,
Colt's loyalty to the Indians ran dan-
gerously high. At Little Big Horn, by
the side of General George Custer, Colt
faced the hardest choice of his life:
fight for a tyrant against overwhelming
odds or side with the warriors who
planned a killing field that would live
forever in infamy. Rich with the pas-
sion and adventure of real history, this
is the roaring saga of frontier military
life and of a hero who had to work
above the law to uphold justice.

Colt

Christopher Columbus Colt, legendary chief of cavalry scouts, was in for the biggest fight of his life. Forced to lead an all-black U.S. cavalry unit on a suicide mission into the very heart of the explosive Apache Wars, Colt would have to overcome million-to-one odds—and his own prejudices—to come out of this one alive. And even if the chief of scouts could conquer his own doubts, he would still have to reckon with two names that struck fear into the hearts of every frontier man: Victorio and Geronimo, renegade Apache chiefs who led their warriors on a bloody trail that any scout could follow—but few dared.

WHISPERS OF THE RIVER
BY TOM HRON

They came from an Old West no longer wild and free—lured by tales of a fabulous gold strike in Alaska. They found a land of majestic beauty, but one more brutal than hell. Some found wealth beyond their wildest dreams, but most suffered death and despair. With this rush of brawling, lusting, striving humanity, walked Eli Bonnet, a legendary lawman who dealt out justice with his gun ... and Hannah Twigg, a woman who dared death for love and everything for freedom. A magnificent saga filled with all the pain and glory of the Yukon's golden days....

from **SIGNET**

FALCONER'S LAW
BY JASON MANNING

The year is 1837. The fur harvest that bred a generation of dauntless, daring mountain men is growing smaller. The only way for them to survive is the way westward, across the cruelest desert in the West, over the savage mountains, through hostile Indian territory, to a California of wealth, women, wine, and ruthless Mexican authorities.

Only one man can meet that brutal challenge—His name is Hugh Falconer—and his law is that of survival....

from **SIGNET**

Prices slightly higher in Canada.   (0-451-18645-1—$5.50)
